DEVIL'S ANGEL

JULIE CAPULET

Three powerful families. Three arranged marriages. And one mysterious stranger with a secret who changes everything.

Cassidy

They say family is everything. Mine abandoned me long ago. They say true love is a myth. Mine showed up as a beautiful devil who almost killed me.

I fought back.

Our bodies and our hearts knew, even if our realities would never allow it.

Knox

I'm one of five heirs to the Ramsey fortune and a hundred acres of tropical paradise on the island of Kauai, Hawaii. I'm also the chosen one—a detail that's about to destroy my life. My marriage will be arranged, to secure the alliance between families.

But when a chance encounter with a mysterious stranger literally slays me, she changes everything.

This is more than obsessive lust. It's the kind of fated love worth dying for. And it's a risk I'm willing to take. Because settling for a future without her is no longer something I'm willing to do …

Devil's Angel is the explosive first book in the epic Paradise series, full of steamy love, dark secrets and forbidden temptations, set in the paradise of Hawaii. It's a standalone enemies-to-lovers romance with an HEA and no cliffhangers.

Paradise Series, Book 1

Julie Capulet LLC

DEVIL'S ANGEL
Copyright © 2022, 2025 by Julie Capulet

DEVIL'S ANGEL is a work of fiction. The characters and events portrayed in this book are fictitious. Any resemblance to actual persons, living or dead, events, or locales is entirely coincidental.

Some of the places described in this book are real locations on the Hawaiian islands of Oahu and Kauai. Some have been reimagined.

I first started writing because there were a lot of stories rolling around in my head that wanted out. They often feel like daydreams and they sometimes lead me down roads I'm not expecting. This book is one of those. I could hardly keep up with it as I was typing, and that is the most fun a writer can have. Knox and Cassidy's story definitely has a mind of its own.

This book is an enemies-to-lovers arranged marriage romance with a twist, full of steam, adventure, lust, love and lots of action. I hope you have as much fun reading it as I had writing it.

xoxo,
Julie

RAMSEY	FITZPATRICK	KING
REMINGTON	SILAS	ENZO
BLAISE	MALACHI	RAVEN
KNOX	TATUM	STONE
WOLF	PERRI	JAGGER
ECHO	VIVI	AURORA

DEVIL'S ANGEL

1

KNOX

THROUGH THE SCOPE of my .300 Winchester Magnum, I take aim. My finger rests lightly on the trigger. I scan along the line of the craggy hill, scouting for signs.

This weapon could comfortably hit a target up to 1500 yards away. Which is a long fucking way. I don't really expect them to make a move on a clear sunny day in eighty degree heat, but you never know. They'll strike when we're least expecting it.

My family owns almost a hundred square miles of tropical paradise in Kauai, Hawaii. Our great great great grandfather, whose name was Nathaniel Ramsey, had to make a quick getaway from post-gold rush San Francisco because a bounty had been placed on his head, so the story goes. So he, along with three other men in the same boat, sailed to Hawaii in the early 1900s and settled here. Over time, the four of them bought as much land as they could get their hands on.

The other three travelers settled in Oahu. One of them lost all his money—its own story—and the other two families now own half of Honolulu.

But it was Kauai that lured Nathaniel.

Now, four generations later, most of my extended family lives in a small town that, somewhere along the way, was named Paradise. There are around a hundred or so houses, a main street and every state-of-the-art amenity you could ever want. A fortified wall surrounds most of the property. Cliffs provide a natural barrier along the northeastern ridge.

It's me, my two brothers and my two sisters who are the direct line. I guess you could call the five of us the royalty of this place. Which I wouldn't mind except for one glaring detail that's about to ruin my life.

We all got sent away to school in California, to experience life off the island. To get an education, play football, make friends with the wider world and so on. Some people thrive on that shit and end up staying longer, but for me it might as well have been a four-year prison sentence. I came back with a new appreciation for ocean views and uninterrupted solitude.

Kauai often gets called a nirvana and to me that's exactly what it is. My blood and bones are made of this place, or at least that's how it feels.

My hair is too long, windblown and bleached from the sun. My eyes are the exact same color as the water, my skin deeply tanned, gritty with salt and sand.

My gaze follows the horizon line, searching for movement.

Something catches my eye.

I zoom in but it's just the waving fronds of a palm tree.

I scan further and it's clear. No threats as far as the eye can see.

Taking one last look, I click the safety on and strap the rifle over my head and across my bare chest. I hardly ever wear a shirt. My life is one long, hot summer of hunting, fishing and overseeing the workings of our ranch. I'm built as fuck from all the physical activity, along with the non-stop training we do.

I'm tempted to strip down, grab my speargun and dive into the clear blue water. But my phone pings in my pocket.

I'm late. And the others are getting impatient.

I lock up my speargun, which is still propped against the railing from last night's dive, and a few of my other weapons. With the help of a couple of our builders, who happen to be my cousins, I built this house myself, here in the sheltered, hidden bay behind the rugged green hills of my family's land. It's my retreat and my favorite place on earth.

The house is rustic, with a huge deck that extends over the water. The top floor is a bedroom loft, the ground floor an open living area with a wall of glass doors that slide all the way open.

Here, I can be alone. It's the one place I can almost

forget that my future is already cast in stone. It's a future I didn't choose and one I don't want. But it was never going to be my choice. Which is fucked up, but there it is.

My phone buzzes again.

I ignore it, for now.

I know what they want from me and I'm prepared to give it. But not easily. Not fucking happily. If they want me to commit to ruining my life then they can chill the fuck out.

We have a meeting.

My doom needs to be discussed. Again.

My time is running out.

2

───────

KNOX

I PULL on an old t-shirt that fits a lot more tightly than it used to and I make my way up the hill along the track. Through the farmland and the grazing cattle. Along the wall where the orchards and gardens stretch out across the rolling landscape that overlooks the turquoise ocean. The avocado grove and the rows of banana trees. The coffee plantations and the acres of vegetable gardens.

We don't *have* to be self-sufficient, of course we don't. But we prefer to grow, build and make most of what we need. Ramseys have always lived like pioneers. When you're running wild on this much rich, volcanic soil and have available all the pristine, untouched ocean fishing you can handle, you might as well put your skills and resources to good use.

It's what we do. Hunt. Fish. Train. Make sure the ranch is as productive and profitable as it can be. Expand our holdings wherever we can. Monitor and grow our investments. Keep our ear to the ground when it comes to everything that's taking place on the islands of Hawai'i and most of all this one.

For the average tourist, the islands are a safe, idyllic getaway. For us, they're as much a battleground as they are a haven. An old, entrenched alliance between our family and three others, broken by some and bonded by others, rules our lives. The bad blood runs in deep, twisted rivers.

So we're armed to the teeth and as wired as it's possible to be. We own every caliber rifle and every cutting-edge gadget known to humankind. Remy insists it's for our own protection and I agree. I happen to be a lot less enthusiastic about living my life online than some of my siblings and cousins but it's easy enough to tune out from that side of it.

I carry my phone in case they need me but I prefer to be untraceable, untouchable and unknowable in every other way.

I walk toward the stone homestead that sits on the hill. It's our headquarters and it overlooks the estate and its views. The stonework of the front gate is part of the original cottage built by Nathaniel Ramsey himself. Each generation has built their own additions as the family grew and it's now a modern four-story castle with a dizzying array of architectural styles.

There are seven updated apartments, a huge living room we call the lodge, conference rooms, three kitchens, a movie theater and the great hall, which holds several hundred people and opens out onto the palatial deck and the pools.

One of the apartments on the top floor is mine but I hardly ever use it. I prefer my beach house, or the cabin I built at the edge of the mango grove with a view down to the western ocean and the best sunsets on the island.

Seeing the estate in all its glory now brings the familiar spear of pent-up rage I feel whenever I think about leaving.

Which is only a matter of time.

3

―――――

KNOX

I WALK PAST THE GYM, a low, large building made from obsidian, wood and glass, which holds our main training arena and our armory. All of us practice mixed martial arts. We need to be not only armed but also lethal in any fight. If you're a blackbelt in karate, you've mastered the key moves in wrestling and you can also throw a well-practiced left hook, it might give you the edge when you need it most.

Target practice is a given. All five of us are as well-trained as Marine snipers.

Great great great grandpa set us all up for life. He also left behind a violent legacy that makes all of the above a necessity.

"Look who finally showed up." My brother Wolf is standing in the archery lane with our cousin Nero. The two of them have similar interests: namely, owning and mastering every kind of weapon ever made. My younger brother spends most of his time fighting, designing weapons and practicing their precision.

"Remington Nathaniel Ramsey III is getting on my nerves," I tell him.

Wolf laughs and takes aim. "You and me both. I told him I'd hunt you down if you weren't here within the next ten minutes."

"Check this out, Knox." Nero nods toward the heavy metal disc Wolf is holding. "It's called a Widowmaker."

Wolf tosses the disc at a target, where its razor-sharp teeth sink deep into the leather bullseye.

"I can see why."

Nero is a metalworker and makes the inventions Wolf designs. The two of them are equally dedicated. Or obsessed, depending how you want to look at it. Wolf wears a leather holster belt and has at least ten different contraptions strapped to his body at all times, including—today—a hunting knife, a taser and a Glock 18.

Nero walks over to the target and retrieves the Widowmaker. "You want to try it, Knox?"

"Later." I've probably tested Remy's patience long enough.

"When's the wedding?" Nero asks off-handedly. His question is sympathetic but matter-of-fact. Everyone knows it's up to me to honor the alliance.

"Nothing's been decided yet." I hear the annoyance in my own voice. "Wolf, let's go."

As much as I'd like to run, we all know duty comes with a price.

KNOX

WOLF WALKS with me toward the homestead. He contemplates me more thoughtfully than he usually would. I'm only eleven months older than Wolf. We don't look that much alike, even though we're both around 6'3" and built. We've been told I look more like our father and Wolf has the look of our mother. Neither of us can remember them. At this point our memories are shaped mostly by other people's stories and a handful of old photographs.

Wolf's hair is a few shades darker than mine, his eyes a shade lighter. "So who's it going to be?" he asks. "Perri?"

"No. Not Perri."

"You're not into her?"

"No." I don't allow the small flash of hope in my own question. "Why? Are you?"

"Hell no," he laughs, but it's almost an apology.

My phone starts vibrating in my pocket as we walk through the gate and into the house.

Our older brother Remington is standing in front of the stone fireplace that takes up most of an entire wall and rarely gets used, pacing, holding his phone to his ear. He sees us walk in and ends the call. My phone stops ringing.

"Hey, Rem." I pat him on the back as I walk past him.

There's a pissed off scowl on his face. "Where have you been?" But there are layers to his mood. Fury, sure. But I can also feel his gratitude, and his regret. We both know he owes me one and it's a fucking doozy.

"Where have I *been*? Oh, you know. Hanging out. Doing my best to ignore the big, black, shark-infested tsunami barreling toward my immediate future."

If I didn't actually believe true love existed—which, irritatingly, I do—I probably wouldn't mind that my choices are five of the wealthiest heiresses in the world.

Their money is irrelevant to me.

Blaise is sitting behind the gigantic mahogany desk, some relic of one of our grandfathers that weighs a ton, now strewn with iPads, phones, papers and several desktop computers. My older sister acts as a sort of diplomat in our family, Remy's wingperson. She's also a computer whiz and our intelligence expert. It's because of her mad skills that we so often pre-empt any planned attacks against us.

The crime ring that targets us has been around as long as our families have been in Hawaii. The history of the feud began soon after Nathaniel Ramsey arrived, along with the three other men who also had plans to spend and grow the fortunes they'd made in California. Their names were Luther King, Ransom Fitzpatrick and Jed Archer.

For a few years, their business partnerships thrived.

But, according to folklore, Jed got greedy. In those days you staked your claim and you defended your holdings or you lost them to the next guy who came along and wanted it more. Jed Archer formed an underground crime ring. He tried to take the land from the three people he'd once called friends or allies—no one really knows the details of how it all went down. What we do know is that Nathaniel Ramsey shot Jed Archer in the heart with the Remington revolver he'd carried with him from his mining days. We still have it. The Archers lost their patriarch and, soon after the battle that followed, their fortune.

They've spent the last hundred years trying to get their revenge.

Some generations have been less violent than others. Ours doesn't happen to be one of them. Over the last five or six years, the bloodlust of the group has gained serious momentum. The followers and recruits of the Archer family call themselves Arrow, a reference to the Archer family name. They want land and they want violence. To them, the other three families are responsible for every injustice in their lives and they're hellbent on making sure we suffer for it.

Their ringleader's name is Axel Archer. He's one of the few Archers still left. Most of the original family were either killed off in the very early years or they chose to leave for the mainland instead of dedicating their lives to the legacy of a traitor who got shot because he betrayed his closest friends.

But Arrow's numbers aren't dwindling. They're growing. And Axel is more bloodthirsty than his father or grandfathers were. He's a twisted lunatic who's hungry for a fight and who has no limits.

In the past few years, the group has become seriously brutal and lawless. I don't even know if it's for revenge so much anymore, or because they want to hold a grudge against someone or something and it might as well be us because of who we are and what we own.

Axel recruits people off the streets—mainly the young and displaced who have something to offer in the way of brawn or recklessness or have nothing to lose. He and his gang train them, arm them, light the fuse of their rage, fan the flames with bribes and rewards, then point them in our direction and let them loose.

We've heard that Axel's goal is to marry into one of our families. He wants back in to the alliance.

It's the reason we guard our sisters especially carefully.

The Kings founded the first banks in Honolulu and they now own and run some of the most profitable businesses that power the economy of Oahu. The Fitzpatricks settled mainly along the beaches, building some of the first luxury resorts of Waikiki. Today, they own more hotels than any other family in Hawaii and their family compound in Waikiki is the most expensive in the United States.

And our ancestors settled on Kauai. Our holdings comprise around a sixth of the island. Our land is some of the most valuable real estate in the world.

"We've been avoiding this for too long, Knox," Remy starts. "It's time to make the arrangements."

5

———

KNOX

Echo, the youngest of the five of us, is sitting at one end of the long window seat, scrolling on her phone. Behind her, the expansive view of the peach orchard opens out over the town and the beach beyond it. My youngest sister is dark-haired and petite. Blaise is our hacker but it's Echo who has her finger on the pulsing beast of social media. She knows everything about everyone from Kauai, to Oahu, Los Angeles, New York, London, Tokyo and beyond who posts anything online—which is most of humanity. She's so tuned in to the psyche of the pop culture masses, it sometimes seems like she can predict the future.

Being the youngest, she's dodged a bullet. She's also the most empathetic person I know. She feels for us.

Wolf sprawls into one of the leather chairs. The metal of his weapons clangs as he sits.

No one else is around. It's just the five of us. Remy must have dismissed the rest of them.

Remy runs a hand through his hair. This whole deal weighs heavily on him. We're all aware it's because of him that my own marriage is being arranged. I don't hold it against him. I made the choice to allow him an out a long time ago, and for good reason.

Blaise's green eyes watch me. Her future is also at stake here. It's up to her and me to make the matches. And her choices are no better than mine.

"Let's go through your list, Knox," she says.

"I know who's on my list." Of course I do. This shit's been hanging over my head for a long time. Crunch time is closing in.

"Raven King," Blaise begins anyway.

"We're really doing this?" I take a seat on the leather couch, propping my feet up on a coffee table. "Fine." Might as well get comfortable.

"I heard Raven's IQ is somewhere around 130," Wolf says. "That's genius level."

"She's definitely a genius at being unhinged as fuck. I'll give her that much." Raven King is always making headlines for her theatrical and very-public meltdowns.

"What's she been up to this week, Echo?" Wolf holds his Glock in his hands, twirling it around his trigger finger. Echo doesn't even look up. We're used to it. He's never *not* handling something life-threatening.

Echo scrolls. "Last Saturday night Raven had to be talked off the railing of her thirty-seventh floor penthouse balcony dressed only in a fur coat and a diamond necklace worth six million dollars."

"Who wears fur coats in Hawaii?" Wolf laughs. He can joke about my doom because he's not the one staring down the barrel of marriage to a medicated drama queen who I really don't want to be the mother of my future children. "It would keep life interesting."

I glare at him. "If you like life *that* interesting maybe you should fucking marry her."

"How about Aurora?" Echo asks me, ignoring Wolf. "She's the quirkiest of the Kings."

"Quirky," smirks Wolf. "If quirky's code for she's slept with half of Hawaii, then yes, she's extremely quirky."

Echo coils an end strand of her hair around her finger. "She's a free spirit." She's trying to put an optimistic spin on things but I can feel the walls closing in.

"Tatum Fitzpatrick," Blaise continues. "She's a movie star. That's not horrible, right?"

"She's currently filming on location in Las Vegas and is dating one of her female co-stars," Echo tells us.

"Hot." Wolf grins at me. "Could be a fun wedding night."

"I'm glad one of us can find some hilarity in this hellscape of arranged marriages and life sentences," I mutter churlishly.

Blaise stays on task, ignoring Wolf. "Vivi Fitzpatrick. Her beauty is legendary."

"Is she even old enough?" Remy's leaning against the wall, all brooding 6'4" of him. My brother looks like he's been working out more than usual lately. He's buff as fuck. It almost makes me wonder if he's been bulking himself up specifically in case he and I need to fight it out over all this. Last time we fought I got him into a head-lock and it took a full week for his shiner to fade out. It was the first time I've ever beaten him in the ring and he wasn't happy about it. He's *still* not happy about it, judging by his scowl.

"She's nineteen," Echo says. "Almost twenty. She's painfully shy, seriously introverted and socially awkward. But one-on-one, she's nice. She has a wistful soul."

"A wistful soul," Wolf scoffs, like he can't think of anything worse.

The few times I've met Vivi Fitzpatrick, she seemed to be hiding in corners like a spooked deer in the headlights. She's thin and frail-looking. You get the feeling a random sea breeze might blow her away. "A wife that's terrified of me and everyone else is hardly a recipe for a match made in heaven."

"And then there's Perri." Blaise says the name carefully, like she's aware it'll get a reaction from me.

"Knox," Remy eases into his pitch. "Silas keeps calling me. It's getting tedious. He said he's been trying to get in touch with you but you never answer your phone. He said Perri wouldn't stop talking about the last time she saw you. She told him the two of you connected. He said she's ... requesting you."

6

____

KNOX

"It's not a bad option, Knox." Blaise is the smartest person I know, level-headed and the the most reasonable of all my siblings. But she has *this* equation all wrong.

"Perri Fitzpatrick and I did anything but 'connect.' We had a three minute conversation about her fucking Instagram following." My voice sounds gruff. Which isn't surprising, considering what they're asking me to do. It's not *their* fault, of course. But it's still the heaviest thing that will happen to me in my lifetime. "Which confirmed to me that I very definitely do *not* want to be shackled to Perri Fitzpatrick for the rest of fucking eternity."

Blaise chews on her lip. It's up to the two of us to honor our family's obligation to the ancient "rule," devised by Nathaniel Ramsey and his two allies, Luther King and Ransom Fitzpatrick. It's known as the Angel's Alliance and it requires a person from each of our three families to intermarry, one each generation. More often, we call it the Angel's Curse.

One of the five of us has to marry a King and one has to marry a Fitzpatrick. That's the rule.

Soon after Jed Archer betrayed the others, our forefathers came up with the idea that the three remaining families should remain linked. Inter-marrying would strengthen the bond, making strategic alliances and mergers of land and financial interests more likely. Our strength would be in our numbers and our family ties.

Even I can begrudgingly admit that we *do* have strength in numbers. When a thriving crime syndicate is doing it's best to get inside your walls, kidnap your sisters and steal whatever they can get their hands on, having alliances comes in handy. It gives us an edge.

But marriage isn't the only way to form alliances.

"It's time to get rid of the curse," I say. "It's superstitious and outdated. I say we ditch it." I'm not the first person who's suggested this over the past hundred years, of course, and I say it without expecting it to gain much traction. As much as I'd love to sway my brothers and sisters, they'll never budge when it comes to the alliance.

People *have* broken it.

Many of them.

And the histories of our families are riddled with the kind of tragedies you wouldn't wish on your worst enemies.

Bad shit tends to happen to the people who choose to ignore it.

Remy knows this better than anyone.

"No," he growls. "We are absolutely *not* breaking the curse."

7

KNOX

THERE ARE a lot of legends that surround the curse. One of them tells the story of how the great grandfathers were approached by a vision. The golden mirage of an angel who gave them an eerie warning: if the families break the bond, there will be dire consequences.

The bond must not be broken.

It's a mantra we all wish we didn't feel as deeply as we do.

Who knows what our ancestors were smoking, but that's how the rule became known as the Angel's Curse.

Which would be fucking laughable if it weren't for one thing. In Hawaii, there's a well-known legend. Most Hawaiians have heard of it and it's searchable on Google. Some people call her the White Lady, others call her the Goddess of Fire. She takes different forms and is said to roam from island to island. She's sometimes found hitch-hiking or dancing at the foot of volcanoes. Most often she's young, outrageously beautiful and has white or platinum blond hair. Sometimes she's glamorous, other times she looks disheveled, like she's been on a long journey. She'll disappear from the bed of a pick-up truck at a stop or a bend in the road. She sometimes asks for favors. She tests the kindness of strangers. If you don't treat her with respect, or *aloha,* the consequences tend to be catastrophic and heartbreaking.

It's this legend—told around bonfires, whispered by children, feared even by seasoned locals—that only fuels our own family's sense of duty and dread.

Still, people don't tend to enjoy being forced into arranged marriages, so the rule or curse—whatever you want to call it—has always caused a lot of friction. Every generation has had its own backlashes and fallouts.

And every single time the rule is broken, something terrible happens to the people who defy it. Brutal, bloody accidents no one sees coming.

Our parents broke it.

Our father fell in love with our mother, a Swedish tourist, and ignored his order to marry a King. Our parents were blissfully happy for six years. But then, only two months after Echo was born, they died in a fiery plane crash and had to be identified by the charred remains of their teeth.

We thought Remy might get off more easily. He married for love and we all allowed it. He met his wife Minka, a college student from Brazil, at a party. They both fell in love at first sight. As the oldest, it should have been him to honor the alliance. But the five of us decided that at least three of us should marry for love.

For better or for worse, all five of us are die hard romantics at heart. Maybe because we've been listening to the love story of our parents on repeat all our lives.

And since Remy found love, it made sense for him to go with it. The rest of us—and me in particular—willingly picked up the mantle, because the two of them and the way they satellited off each other was just such a beautiful thing to watch. We could *feel* how happy and besotted they were with each other. It reminded us of how we always imagined our parents must have felt.

At the time, I didn't overthink my own fate. I figured things would somehow work out. I genuinely thought Remy deserved his happily ever after. And because we *agreed* to it, we thought that might keep him safe from the curse's black cloud.

We were wrong.

His wife died in childbirth around a year and a half ago. He lost them both. His beautiful wife and their stillborn child, a tiny girl Remy named Jade. He'd had the best doctors flown in but even they couldn't save Remy's family.

We haven't seen Remington smile since that day. His grief has become the biggest thing about him. He bears it—barely—by training and working out like a maniac and at this point he's a cut, well-oiled machine of sorrow-fueled rage. We all hope that he'll eventually be able to move on from it, but no one's going to push him. We figure it'll happen when he's ready for it to happen.

I know he'd offer to marry again, now, to get one of us off the hook. But the alliance won't allow it. All the matches have to be first marriages.

So it's up to me and Blaise, unless Wolf or Echo volunteers.

Which is unlikely, considering the options.

"Perri wants you, Knox," Blaise says. "There must be something about her you like if you've already ... shared a moment." She pauses, implying the obvious.

"We didn't 'share a moment'," I snap.

Remy gives me a look. "She told Silas you had."

"Well, she's lying." I hardly ever go to Honolulu, and it was only the fifth or sixth time I've been to Seven Mile Beach, which is the Fitzpatrick's family compound. But a few months ago, one of my cousins was having a bachelor party that was nearby and there was an afterparty, so I went along. Perri was there. She followed me around. The Fitzpatrick women are known for their supposedly exotic beauty. And maybe they are beautiful, from afar. But the closer I got to Perri, the less beautiful she became.

The kind of beauty Perri Fitzpatrick basks in is a very groomed sort of beauty. It requires teams of stylists or whatever to achieve. She has YouTube channels and cosmetics lines. Her face is basically a walking advertisement for all the products she's constantly selling.

Beauty isn't just about the packaging. Real beauty sits under the surface layer. This was what ran through my mind when she started talking to me, and continues to hit me whenever I think of Perri Fitzpatrick. It was *that* part of her beauty that was missing.

I don't know if I've been in denial about my future. I don't think about it, except when I'm forced to. I let her talk to me that night because I knew she was on my goddamn "list."

What surprised me most about her, despite all the followers and the fame, was how fucking desperate she was. Maybe publicity can have that effect on a person. There's a flip side to the coin of adoration. The scrutiny and the unavoidable criticism. Maybe it takes its toll after a while. Her insecurity was the only thing she talked about.

It had been one of those perfect tropical nights when the moon hangs low and the water is as warm as the air. A band was playing and there was an open bar. I thought about it, sure I did. It's the only reason I go to Honolulu or the North Shore or Maui or the Big Island from time to time—because most of the people I see on a daily basis are my first, second or third cousins or are married to my first, second or third cousins. When I'm at home I live like a fucking monk but there are times when the animal in me craves a whole lot more.

But that night, I couldn't bring myself to go with it. Something about Perri Fitzpatrick was just ... off. I could read the misery she would imprint onto my life in her expressions and in the way she moved. My own doom was inked into her eyes. I could see there that she would cross every line to get what she wanted. She was needy and borderline insane.

At first I tried to give her the benefit of the doubt.

It would have been so easy, if we'd clicked right then and there.

We didn't.

I didn't, more specifically.

My reaction to her was almost violent. It bordered on repulsion. I wanted to get the fuck away from her. In hindsight I was a total asshole about it but I can't quite bring myself to regret that.

She cried and begged me. She pleaded. She wanted me to stay with her. Unbelievably, she invited me to move in with her. And she made a point of making sure we were seen together. Until I shook her off and disappeared into the night.

Looking back now, maybe it was her plan, to lure me into a trap. Exactly like the one I'm in now.

"So ... you didn't have a meeting of the minds?" drawls Wolf.

"No."

Blaise asks it carefully. "Do you think you could ... potentially ... *have* a meeting of the minds?"

"No." Even though Perri is sort of the obvious choice to everyone else, she'd be my last choice. I stand up, needing to move.

"She's hell-bent on making it happen, Knox," Remy says. "She asked Silas to arrange it. She told him the two of you are already 'bound.' She told him you were … her first. She said she might even be …"

"Be what?"

"Be tied to you … in a family way."

"I never even touched her. And even if I had, trust me, I wouldn't have been her first. I'm not marrying her." I'm pacing now, like a caged lion.

Remy seems uncomfortable with the entire topic. "She told Silas you've put her in a compromised position."

"She put herself into all kinds of compromised positions. Right around the time I left her to it."

Echo's still scrolling. "She spent last weekend at Cooper LaSalle's house in Puako." She holds up her phone, which shows a photo of Perri and Cooper together, with very few clothes on.

"Looks like she's already moved on," Wolf comments.

"Thank fuck." At this point my mood is beyond dark.

Remy's doesn't seem much better.

"It would be a marriage in name only, Knox," Blaise offers. She's feeling this as much as I am, but at least she won't have to leave. That's the other requirement of the rule: the men have to move to the women's family estates, to "become one with their families," according to the original document. "To be treated as royalty, with power and command equal to the decision-makers." Which means I'd have to move to Seven Mile Beach. Not something I'd ever choose to do, obviously. "It doesn't mean you can't … you know … have other conquests and interests."

Wolf grins, but I can tell he feels for me. "Yeah, Knox."

"If my misery is so entertaining to you, brother, maybe *you* should marry her."

"No way. Not her. She's the type that would make your life a living hell."

"Exactly," I mutter.

Is is really my destiny to live out the rest of my days in a living hell?

Please, I silently pray to my ancestors, the universe, the Goddess, or whoever might be listening. Even though I know it's all but useless.

Show me the way. Let me find true love.

8

KNOX

REMY IS UNFLINCHING. "Silas sees the marriage between you and Perri as a done deal, Knox."

"Silas can fuck off." Silas Fitzpatrick is the biggest manwhore on the planet. "Silas doesn't control me or my future. So he can stay the fuck out of it."

"Okay, then," Echo says gently, "Let's go back to Tatum. Or Vivi. Maybe you'll prefer one of them. They're both gorgeous, Knox."

"So's Malachi," I say. "You could marry him."

Echo makes a face. Malachi is the second-oldest Fitzpatrick. He's a loose player who gets arrested on a weekly basis. He seems to think he's above every law. Because of his money, he basically is. "Sure, he's hot, but Harlow Ashe spent two nights with him after the Island Festival last month and said he's completely twisted."

"Twisted is underrated," Wolf says darkly, sharpening

his hunting knife with the sharpening stone he always carries. "How's your list going, Blaise?"

She sighs. "About as well as Knox's."

If I marry a Fitzpatrick it'll be up to Blaise to marry a King. The Kings are the most gangster of our three families. The men are brutally cut-throat when it comes to business and everything else.

It's hard to know which one of the three of them—Enzo, Stone or Jagger—would be the worst. Enzo's a darkhorse, sort of mysterious and aloof. He's shady as fuck. But he's also CEO of King Enterprises and an investment genius, which might have its perks. We all study the markets and work to grow our investments, but Enzo seems to have an almost eerie knack. Remy consults him all the time.

Jagger is the youngest son, the wildchild of the King family. He's always making headlines for his reckless behavior and for the cavalier way he treats women. Not ideal in a husband—something I'm sure has crossed Blaise's mind. And Stone is probably the one I'd hate to see my sister end up with most of all. I don't know him that well but there's a cold, malicious side to him I don't trust.

We all lost count of their father Jethro's wives and mistresses a long time ago. Most of his children have different mothers. Their personalities are all very different but one thing they all have in common is that they're completely unpredictable. You never know what you're going to get from them at any given moment.

I can tell Blaise is worried. In her heart she has someone else in mind. But a marriage to Tristan Dempsey, an artist originally from San Diego who owns a gallery on Oahu's North Shore and has no ties to any of our three families, of course, won't honor the alliance.

"This is bullshit." I'm about to say I'd rather play Russian roulette with avoiding the curse than marry any one of the women on my list but I bite my tongue. Remy's pain is so close to the surface it would feel cruel to mention how things can—and do—go wrong when we mess with it.

"I know what we could do." Blaise does her best to lighten the mood. "We'll have a party. We'll invite the Kings and the Fitzpatricks. All the eligible bachelors and bachelorettes. We'll make a weekend out of it. Maybe it'll happen naturally. Maybe there are sides to some of them that we don't know well enough to fully appreciate. Maybe a few people will click and we can figure out a way to do this without dooming two of us into forced marriages."

Remy considers this. "That's a good idea. It's worth a try."

Blaise is the perfect person to plan a three-day party. She has the organizational skills of an army general. "I'll email Silas and Enzo. We'll plan it for next month. Under a full moon," she says.

"A full moon?" grins Wolf. He's a loose cannon, but also the most loyal person I know. Maybe he'll save me after all. "Bring it on."

"I'm going to Vivi's birthday party on Friday night," Echo tells us. "I can talk to them about it then, depending on who's there."

"Good. Then we're done here." Remy heads for the door. "Until then, the arrangement stands, Knox, unless a better match is made."

Remington is the oldest and in the unwritten laws of our family heritage, it means he has the power to make these decisions. But there's no way I'm marrying Perri Fitzpatrick. I know it'll cost me before I even say it. I get the feeling we *are* going to have to fight it out at some point. Probably sooner rather than later. "Like hell."

9

Cassidy

Ohhhhh my Goddd. Hell yesssssss. Woooooowww.

There's no better feeling in the whole freaking world than riding a perfect wave before the sun is even up, when the tropical Hawaiian water is as shiny as liquid metal, tinted with splashes of gold from the first sliver of the rising sun, then getting carried all the way to the end of it like the sea has provided you with your killer rush and is now gently delivering you to calmer waters.

Or something like that.

I get poetic when I surf and it can't be helped.

Riding the wave as far as it will take me, I paddle to shore and carry my surfboard up the sand.

It's my favorite time of day, when the world is quiet and only the most soulful of the surfers are around.

But I don't want to be late. It's my first week at my new job and we've been told to get there early today for a glitzy event at some super-rich family's party.

I've spent the past two years cleaning hotel rooms and I can officially say it is the most unglamorous job in the world. The things some people get up to when they're on vacation in paradise are downright shocking—and I'm hardly naïve when it comes to the worst of human behavior.

A few weeks ago, one of the other cleaners, Maggie, who's become a friend, heard about a catering company that was hiring waitresses. We both applied and by some miracle we both got the job. We get paid twelve fifty an hour—the first time in my life I've ever gotten more than minimum wage—and the best part is, we get to go to luxury houses to see how the other half lives.

And, *wow*, do they live.

I walk up the dune and dig my backpack out of the sand, where I bury it in a plastic bag whenever I go out surfing. Everything I own fits into this backpack. I'd wear it on my back *while* I was surfing if I could. It's the only time I let it out of my sight.

But I need to surf. Surfing keeps me sane.

I take out my towel and dig around in my bag for my sleeveless yellow sundress. Drying myself off, I slip the dress over my bikini.

I stuff my hair under my sailor's cap, some left-behind souvenir from a hotel room that never got claimed.

Unzipping the small inside pocket of my bag, I find my gold pin, making sure it's still here. Running my fingers over the raised ridges, I turn it over in my hands, like I have so many times before.

My mother's pin. The one and only thing I have of her.

My mother left me in a laundry basket on the front steps of a social services office when I was—they had to guess—around four months old. With a note pinned to my blanket.

Her name is Cassidy.

I still have the note, laminated now so it doesn't fade.

The pin is shaped like a golden feather. The initials CMK are etched into the gold, along with a number. 544/65872094. I memorized it a long time ago but I have no idea what it means. It's not a phone number or a social security number. It's not an address or a bank account or a passport number. I've checked out all those possibilities but nothing fits.

Just another mystery in a sea of mysteries.

I don't have a birth certificate or a family or even an identity, aside from the one invented for me. My first name *is* Cassidy, that much seems to be true. Some case worker gave me a birthday, a middle name and a last name before handing me over to foster care. I was given the same initials as my runaway mother and my birthday was listed as July 4th.

Cassidy Meadow Kelley has a certain ring to it, I guess.

I check my phone for messages.

> Make sure you get here by 8 am sharp.
> The vans are leaving at 8:15

We're all doing double shifts today. It's been interesting so far to visit the multi-million dollar homes we've been working in.

According to Maggie, today's event is next level. Some birthday party of an heiress at her family's super-luxe Waikiki family compound.

I text my boss.

I'll be there by 7:45

I take out the small leather pouch that holds my knife and I strap it securely to my thigh, where it can't be seen under the skirt of my dress. It's a habit. An unfortunate side-effect of my upbringing or lack thereof: I don't take my own safety for granted. When you're completely alone in the world and you're young, female and broke, bad shit tends to happen from time to time. I make sure I'm prepared for it.

10

Cassidy

I WALK along the beach to where Crew is setting up his surfboards for the day's lessons. He teaches absolute beginner tourists who'll pay a hundred dollars an hour for the privilege of balancing on the sand for half a day before paddling out and falling off a couple of times. Then they can go back to Chicago or wherever and tell their friends they're surfers.

"Catch any good ones?" Crew has dirty-blond dread-locks and bright green eyes.

"They were all good ones." Every wave I've ever caught is a gift. It's the only place I feel free.

Crew lets me borrow his surfboards in exchange for the one day a week I do for him—Mondays, which I get off from my other job—waxing the boards and cleaning up the shed he rents where he stores them.

"You got any plans for tonight?" Crew is always asking me out.

I'm not interested in dating. Not him or anyone else.

I've occasionally wondered if there's something wrong with me. I've never had the slightest urge to get close to another human being. Maybe because I was abandoned so young and I've spent so long fending for myself. Maybe I've become closed off. I don't know.

The less philosophical reason is that there's just too much I need to do before I even think about getting attached to someone who might hold me back. I got dealt a hand in life that most people wouldn't choose. *I* wouldn't have chosen it, not in a million goddamn years. Of course I wouldn't have. But it's my life and there are good things about it too. Surfing. My new job. My few acquaintances that might even be called friends.

But most of all there's a big-ass, very-steep mountain that consists of all the things I need to change. Hard, monumental things like trying to scrape together enough money to eat. Finding a safer, better place to live. Getting out of the hole I've been in my whole life. Things that require grit, blood, sweat, tears and maybe even a small amount of luck. I'm pouring my heart and soul into the first four and praying like hell for the last one—which, for me, tends to be elusive.

I'd been through a dozen foster homes by the time I was ten. I ran away from the worst of them when I was sixteen and never looked back. I didn't want to be a burden or an afterthought or, far worse, some loser's prey. I decided I'd rather take my chances on my own.

I used the only money I had to buy a tent and a

sleeping bag. And I set up camp at the edge of the tent city tucked just behind the main tourist area of Honolulu. It moves and it changes but it's still there. You might see the edges of it on the way to your Waikiki resort when you get driven in from the airport.

My entire life has been spent within a fifteen mile radius of the place I was dropped off as a helpless baby by the person who was supposed to love me most but instead left me without so much as a last name or a clue about who I am or where I came from.

Actually, there are a few clues.

The three initials, embossed onto my gold pin.

The mysterious number. *544/65872094.*

And my tattoo.

It's a small, intricate, circular design inked between my shoulder blades. I've spent most of my life trying to keep it hidden. I know it's there. What I don't know is who put it there or what it means.

Who gives a four-month-old baby a tattoo?

And why?

I've never trusted anyone enough to ask about it. And I've never been able to find out what it symbolizes. A google search doesn't give that kind of information, at least not that I could find.

I've wondered if it's some kind of family crest or the mark of a secret society. Anything that might link me to ... *belonging* to someone or something.

No such luck. I'm as alone as I've ever been and, even though I'm resilient because I've had no other choice, it's a detail that claws at me. I've always had the feeling that the tattoo is trouble. Something dark. If I needed so desperately to be given away, the reasons behind my mother's choice to run must have been bad ones. In my mind, the two things have always been linked.

What does the symbol mean?

Why was this mysterious mark inked onto me?

Was it her that did it? Or someone else?

Why did she leave me and where did she go?

11

Cassidy

BEING ABANDONED AS a baby falls into the category of getting dealt a shitty hand.

Luckily for me, I'm a born optimist. In my bones I know my future has more in store for me than tent cities and low wage jobs. I have no intention of *keeping* my shitty hand. I decided a long time ago I'd play it all the way to a full house of aces and kings.

I finished high school, found a job, then another job, and moved into a tiny studio apartment that's awful but at least it has walls and roof. My next goal is to earn enough money so I can find something better.

The apartment I'm living in now is depressing as hell. I also have neighbor problem. Dash, who lives in the apartment next door, collects my rent in cash for the land-lord and he's not to be trusted. It makes me uneasy that he has his own set of keys. It's why I carry my belongings with me wherever I go.

I live in one of the most expensive neighborhoods in the United States, but there are still plenty of dives. I happen to live in one of the diviest dives in town. The only upsides are: it's not a tent and it's temporary.

Which is why I'm working seven days a week and have as long as I can remember. I'm determined to crawl my way up life's ladder, with bloody fingers if I have to.

Touching the lives of the rich and famous makes me feel like I'm getting closer to where I belong, even if I'm only serving their food and cleaning up after them. It feels like I'm at least heading in the right direction.

"I'm working tonight, Crew."

"You work too much."

I smile at him, because he says the same thing every day. Crew got dealt a shitty hand in life too. He once told me his parents died in a car crash when he was seventeen. He lived in his van for a few years and worked in a surf shop. One by one he bought all the old surfboards they were getting rid of and set up his own little business. I know it's not always easy for him to make ends meet. He seems mostly content with where he's at right now, which is another reason I don't want to date him. I could never be content with scraping by with just enough to survive. I'm doing exactly the same thing, of course, but the difference is, I'm not content with it. Not even close. "I'll see you tomorrow morning."

His first customers are starting to arrive so I walk up to the surf club. I pay two dollars for a shower, put on my uniform and pin my hair up.

Then I walk the six blocks to Perfection Catering.

They're already loading up the vans parked out in front. I show my ID to the driver and get into the van, where Maggie has saved a seat for me. She's as Irish-looking as a person can get, with bright red hair, mint-green eyes and a sprinkling of festive freckles across the bridge of her nose.

"I can't believe we're going to *Seven Mile Beach*," she gushes.

"What's Seven Mile Beach?"

"Are you kidding me? It's only the most expensive residence in the United States. We're working for the Fitz-patricks today. It's Vivi Fitzpatrick's twentieth birthday party."

12

Cassidy

"Vɪᴠɪ Fɪᴛᴢᴘᴀᴛʀɪᴄᴋ." Doesn't ring a bell. "Should I know who that is?"

Maggie rolls her eyes, like she can't believe anyone could be so obtuse. "What am I going to do with you? The Fitzpatricks are celebrities. They own the most exclusive high-end hotels in Waikiki. Their resorts are where the tourists with serious money stay. They're booked out months or sometimes even *years* in advance." Maggie keeps up with all the latest social media gossip.

I, it has to be said, don't. "Why are they celebrities? Just because they're rich?"

"Most of them are also movie stars. Tatum and Malachi are the most famous but all five of the Fitzpatrick siblings have been in at least one movie or made cameo appearances on TV. Here, I'll show you their photos." Maggie knows I don't really have the time or the data to scroll the internet non-stop. She fills me in on all the gaps in my celebrity education.

"This is Malachi." She zooms in. "Isn't he absolutely gorgeous?"

I guess he is, in an internet-worthy sort of a way. He has black hair and white teeth. He's surrounded by beautiful women in bikinis smiling vapidly for the camera. "Yeah," I say, mainly to agree for the sake of agreeing. But I don't think Malachi Fitzpatrick would be my type at all, if I was to aspire to something like that. Not that I *have* a type, but still. You can tell at a glance he'd be outgoing and popular. Confident beyond belief. The life of the party. My polar opposite, in other words. I tend to keep to the fringes.

"Perri, Tatum and Vivi Fitzpatrick's follower numbers on Instagram are ranked one, two and three in the world." Maggie scrolls further. "Here's a photo of the three of them."

I point to the sister in the middle as she zooms in. "Is that Tatum?" I recognize her face.

"Yes. And this one's Perri. And that's Vivi on the right."

Vivi isn't smiling. Perri is wearing a lot of make-up. She's overly-styled and has a weird sheen to her, like she could be made of plastic.

I don't get a chance to ask Maggie more questions because we're driving up to a massive gate. We come to a stop and several security guards climb aboard. The van is searched and we all have to be checked with metal detectors to make sure we're not armed. Which seems a little over the top but I guess these celebrities can't be too careful.

13

Cassidy

WE FINALLY PASS the inspection and our fleet of vans gets waved through. A palm-tree lined entrance winds along a grassy slope overlooking a golden sand beach and the turquoise water. There are more vans and catering trucks already parked along the wide driveway, which circles a marble fountain.

Maggie and I are both wide-eyed as we drive into the compound. The house looks like a five-star plantation-style hotel with modern additions. There's a gigantic lanai and a glittering infinite pool surrounded by palm trees, modern furniture and neutral-toned loungers. The entire place gleams with money.

We're led inside, where the kitchens are bigger than the entire first story of my apartment building.

We're put to work alongside the army of staff that are already setting up the outdoor area with the tables, decorations, an outdoor up-market tiki bar and a giant buffet.

The day goes quickly. I follow along with all the orders we're given, preparing the food and putting together the platters. Once everything is ready, we're given a quick break to put on our serving uniforms.

The limousines start pulling up just after six o'clock. Maggie and I are given trays with flutes of champagne and told to stand near the entrance so we can serve the new arrivals. From here, Maggie fills me in on who's who.

"I love this job," Maggie gushes. Then her eyes go wide. "Holy shit, that's Jagger King!" A guy is stepping out of a white stretch limousine. He has straw-colored blond hair that catches the early evening sun. The rolled-up sleeves of his shirt show off his gold chains, his suntan and his tattoos. "God, he's so beautiful."

He really is. "Is he a movie star too? He looks like one."

"No, he works for his family," Maggie explains. "All the Kings do. They own banks, skyscrapers and basically half the real estate and businesses in Honolulu. If the Fitzpatricks are the Hollywood of Hawaii, the Kings could be described as the Wall Street."

"He doesn't look like a banker."

"That's because he has so much money, he can look however he wants." Two other people get out of the limo. "There's Stone," Maggie whispers excitedly.

Stone is tall and lankier than his brother. His sable-brown hair is artfully mussed-up. He's wearing sunglasses and black clothes. While Jagger comes across as cool and relaxed, Stone's expression is more serious. There's a reckless, almost-sinister edge to his vibe.

"And there's Aurora." Maggie is totally starstruck.

Aurora has dark red hair and a sexy, femme fatale look. She's wearing a red dress, if it could even be called a dress. It's more like a shred of ripped fabric that's covering only the most necessary areas.

"None of them look anything alike," I whisper.

"Their father Jethro has had a bunch of wives and mistresses, so most of them have different mothers."

"Wow."

"Raven and Stone are the only ones that have the same mother. All the others are half-siblings. Stone is only, like, a month or two older than Jagger because their father's wife and mistress were pregnant at the same time. Can you imagine?"

Not really, no. "How do you know so much about them?"

"Because I follow all of them online, of course. And so much gets written about them." She gives me a patient, that's-so-obvious smile as she continues. "I read somewhere that Raven and Stone's mother, who was Jethro's second wife, tried to *kill* the mistress, who's Jagger's mother. Even though he had all these women, apparently Jagger's mother was the one true love of Jethro's life. But both the wife *and* the mistress ended up dying in mysterious circumstances. No one's ever been able to figure out exactly what happened. Isn't that wild?"

"That can't be true."

"It is! I read about it online."

"Did she? Did she kill her?"

"No one knows for sure."

Yikes.

The Kings are coming up the steps. Maggie and I watch them as they help themselves to champagne. Up close, they're even more striking. Their clothes and their obvious, glittering wealth give them a power that's hard to describe. Jagger is the most physically stunning, but all three of them have a magnetic, sparked presence, like if you touched them they might give you an electric shock.

As Jagger takes a champagne flute from my tray, his gaze lands briefly on my face. His gold hair catches the light almost theatrically but his irises are a very dark brown. As our eyes meet, something about him seems almost weirdly ... *familiar.*

But why would it?

I most definitely have never met Jagger King. Maybe I've seen a photo of him somewhere before. He winks at me before sauntering off into the growing crowd.

14

Cassidy

Maggie exhales a shaky breath. "Did you *see* that? He looked right at you!"

There's some commotion as more people make their entrance behind us, from the interior of the house.

"It's Perri and Vivi!" Maggie exclaims with hushed awe. "Vivi is the one in purple."

Both women are dark-haired and exotic-looking. They're wearing the most to-die-for outfits I've ever seen. Vivi's is a purple sequined short-sleeved crop top and matching tight-fitting, barely-flared pants—which I might possibly have sold my soul to own. Vivi has unusual amber-colored eyes, noticeable even from a distance. Perri is a few inches shorter than her sister. Her hair is pulled up into an elaborate braided crown with jewel-like beads weaved into it and she's wearing a fitted bright orange dress with feather detailing.

"Their *clothes*," I gasp.

"I know, right? All the designers are always lining up to dress them," Maggie whispers. "Oh, look, here comes Echo Ramsey."

A valet opens the door of the next car and a young woman steps out. "Who's Echo Ramsey?" I whisper back.

Maggie gives me a look. "You seriously must be living under a rock, Cassidy. You've never heard of Echo Ramsey?"

"Uh ... no."

"You've heard of *the* Ramseys, though, right?"

I could explain to her that I've been too busy laying low, working seven days a week so I don't starve, trying like hell to pull myself up by my bootstraps so I don't have to go back to living in a tent, sharpening the kitchen knife that's strapped to my thigh at all times because I never know when some down-on-his-luck drunken desperado—or my meathead neighbor who happens to have a key to my apartment—might have less-than-honorable intentions, and since there's no one around to help me or protect me, I have to be on guard every hour of the day and night.

But I don't.

"The Ramseys live on Kauai," Maggie's patiently explaining. "All three families are interconnected. There are a lot of marriages between the families and they own businesses together. The Ramseys are more reclusive than the others."

"Why?"

"They just prefer to stay out of the limelight. Their house is like a castle. It's surrounded by acres of land and high, guarded walls. I've heard it's like an absolute fortress, but inside there's this beautiful haven, with all kinds of orchards and botanical gardens. The Ramseys live like they're still on the frontier. They ride horses. They hunt and fish. They grow crops and they live almost entirely off the land."

"Wow." I imagine what that must be like. To catch your own fish or pick fruit off your very own trees.

"My friend's cousin went to a party there once. She said they all look like supermodels."

"Echo Ramsey sure looks like one."

"Totally. I mean, *look* at her."

Echo is willowy thin with dark, glossy long hair that's beautifully cut. She's almost ethereal-looking, like she could be half fairy or a nymph who just wandered in from a magical woodland. There's a quiet gravity to her. It's the groundedness of someone who *belongs* and who walks around every day feeling the effortless security of that. You can tell she's loved. You can tell it holds her up and shapes the way she looks at the world. I have a radar for that kind of thing because it's so absent in my own life.

Damn it.

My eyes sting.

But I shake it off.

God, it's been a while since I got emotional about my lost family. Something about Echo Ramsey makes me feel things I usually keep locked away in my heart.

"Blaise Ramsey is stunning too," Maggie says. "They all are. I've seen the occasional photo of Remington, in the city. He's the oldest. He's on the board of some of the businesses the families co-own. He's huge and built like a fighter. So are Knox and Wolf. They train in MMA, I've heard. But they hate publicity. There are a lot of cousins and extended family too, like a clan, but it's the five siblings that get talked about most."

And now I'm curious. "What about the other two? Knox. And Wolf." They have unusual names.

"Apparently Wolf is crazy and, like, *armed*. He's some kind of weapons expert or something. I don't know much about Knox. My friend's cousin said he was the most gorgeous of all of them. He's seriously hot and he spends most of his time swimming and hunting. He's sort of wild and outdoorsy, like a tropical island version of a hot mountain man. He's hardly ever seen. I've never seen a picture of him. But according to my friend, all the Ramsey men are absolutely lethal—I mean, I don't know why you'd describe someone you just met as *lethal*, but that's what she said."

"Wow," I say again. It all sounds so wildly romantic, I think. Keeping to yourselves. Swearing loyalty to your clan.

Growing up like I have, I've always coveted the idea

of a *haven*. What would that be like, to belong to a place that's guarded and beautiful and filled with people who know you and who care about you enough to keep you safe?

I wish I could find out.

15

Cassidy

My own life is as devoid of wild glamour or fierce loyalty or botanical gardens as it's possible to be.

But there's no use crying about it. I tried that a long time ago and it never helped.

The place is filling up now and we spend the next few hours serving the guests. We're run off our feet. There are champagne fountains and a live band who are apparently number two in the charts right now. The guests and the hosts are making the most of it.

Maggie points out Malachi and Silas, the oldest Fitzpatrick siblings. They're both surrounded by harems of women. The one named Tatum couldn't be here tonight, according to the speeches. She's on location shooting a film.

I might envy them if their world wasn't a million miles from my own. There doesn't seem like much of a point to be jealous of people like this. These are the chosen ones who were born under the luckiest stars there are.

But I do feel my grit kicking in. I'll never have *this* life but I can have *a* life. One that's better and more beautiful than the one I'm living now. All I have to do is make it happen.

Later, when the night is lit with a full moon, glowing bulbs and scenic fire pits that reflect off the surfaces of the pools and the ocean, I'm clearing one of the tables. I hear a low conversation.

I know by now that the two women sitting at the next table are Echo Ramsey and Perri Fitzpatrick.

Perri is beautiful, but it's a much more manufactured beauty than Echo's. It's the type of beauty that washes off. Her makeup is smudged and she's crying. She's spent most of the evening talking to Echo. Vivi joined them for a while. She was here when they sang happy birthday but disappeared soon after the cake was served.

"He'll agree to it, though, right, Echo?" Perri is practically pleading. There's an edge to her desperation that gets my attention. It's forceful.

"He's still talking it over with Remy," Echo says gently. "But it's definitely a ... possibility."

"But who else would he choose?" Fresh tears wet Perri's flushed cheeks.

"Nothing's been decided yet, Perri. It'll be decided when you all come to Kauai next month."

"Why won't he reply to my messages or answer my calls? I just want to *talk* to him about it."

"He hardly ever answers his phone." Echo is trying to reassure her. "For any of us. Unless it's an emergency."

"This *is* an emergency," Perri sobs. "It's my *life* we're talking about and I want *him*."

A few of the other servers are bustling around me now and I follow them with my tray of glasses into the kitchen. I'm a little disappointed I'll never know what—or who—they were talking about.

By the time all the catering equipment has been cleaned and loaded up, it's almost midnight. We climb back into the vans. The Fitzpatricks tipped us so well, my boss, Eleanor, hands out fifty dollar bills to each one of us.

Wow. I'm grateful. This will get me that much closer to finding a better place to live.

"Anyone up for a poker game tonight?" asks one of the other servers, on the ride back. His name is Ben. He once mentioned that he's taking a few classes in marine biology at the university, part-time. He's grinning at me and waving his fifty dollar bill. He's been friendly to me since I started this job. "We play at a the Irish Rover every Friday night, Cassidy. Just down the street. You and Maggie should come along."

"Not me," Maggie yawns. "I have a date with my three-hundred thread count Egyptian cotton. I'm heading home." Maggie lives with her parents in a three-bedroom townhouse in Kalihi, she once told me. She has an older brother who works construction. She has a dog named Bear.

The thought of her, going home to her stable family

and her locked doors ... it feeds another wood chip onto the warm flame in my heart that's been gaining momentum lately. I'm not sure why.

The luxury of the people's houses is feeding it.

The white-gold glint of Jagger King's hair is feeding it, go figure.

Echo Ramsey's comfort in her own skin is feeding it.

Fifty dollars would double my savings and get me a week or two closer to a new apartment.

Or it will buy me a seat at the poker table with these college boys who play for fun.

For better or worse, I happen to be somewhat of a card shark. When you hang out with the homeless and displaced for years on end you tend to pick up a few tricks. I have a knack for it, I've been told.

And sometimes you have to take your chances.

Two hours later, I'm sitting at the poker table with four of my workmates. Three hundred and ninety-two dollars is sitting on the table, along with a Swiss watch, a half pint bottle of Jack Daniels, a gold ring and a plane ticket to Kauai that leaves in three days.

Imagine that.

After everything that's happened tonight and all the things Maggie and I talked about, it feels like a weird twist of fate.

It's a beautiful haven, with all kinds of orchards and botanical gardens.

I don't dare even hope for it.

It's Ben's deal. Five card draw with sevens wild.

I can tell by the unmistakeable glow of eagerness in his eyes that Ben's hand is a good one. "How many do you want, Cassidy?"

All I have is a pair of fours. And nothing to lose except my last fifteen dollars.

I place three cards face down on the table and slide my money into the middle. "I'll take three."

Ben deals me three cards. As he finishes dealing to the others, I pick up my new cards.

I stare at them for a few seconds, wondering if my eyes are deceiving me.

Holy shit.

This kind of thing doesn't happen to me. Ever.

It's two fours and a seven.

Five of a kind.

I don't look up. I keep my expression bored, aiming for an edge of disappointment. The exhaustion is easy enough to summon. "I'll see you."

Ben smiles. He puts his cards on the table. It's a full house, queens high. "Read 'em and weep."

One of the other guys groans. All of them fold, one by one.

Ben starts to reach for the pot but I place my cards on the table. *Read* these *and weep, sunshine.* "Five fours."

Ben glares at my cards. "You've got to be fucking kidding me." He throws his cards down, pissed off. It's his father's watch I just won.

For a second I wonder if I'm dreaming.

This is the luckiest score of my entire life.

I slide the watch over to Ben. "Keep it." I give back the ring. I would never want to keep someone's jewelry, knowing how important my pin is to me.

But I'll take the whiskey.

I'll definitely take the money.

And I'll take the plane ticket.

16

KNOX

"*Fuck*, Knox."

Wolf and I are in the ring. I'm covered in sweat and so is he. He's slippery as a greased pig but I manage to get him to ground and hold him, landing a decent uppercut.

I can admit I'm taking my pent-up rage out on him. I figure he deserves some of it. It takes all my strength but I get him into an anaconda vice grip and slowly tighten my hold.

"Not so tough now, without your Widowmaker or your Glock," I taunt him.

"I can't bail you out if you kill me," he gasps.

"You weren't planning to anyway." I squeeze harder.

Wolf groans. "If I'm dead you'll never know."

"All right, Knox," my cousin Leo says from the corner. Leo spent two years in Las Vegas competing in the UFC. He met and married a doctor named Hana. Last year they decided to come back to Kauai and settle here.

Hana now runs her own practice here in town and Leo coaches us. "You're fired up today. And you're on a winning streak."

"Depends on how you look at it," I grunt.

"Let him go," Leo says. "Maybe you should think about going professional, Knox."

I can't think of anything worse than performing for rabid crowds like some kind of goddamn show pony. After a few more seconds of satisfyingly kicking my brother's ass, I release him.

I climb to my feet and Wolf lays there catching his breath. Reminding myself again that my doom isn't *his* fault and in fact he's one of two people on the entire planet who can potentially save me, I offer him my hand.

Wolf takes it and groans as I pull him up. "You're either a world-class talent or the life sentence hanging over your head is as good as a goddamn steroid infusion."

"I'd go with option two." I almost feel bad about about his bloody lip and the bruise forming across his cheekbone. "You're going to have a decent shiner by morning."

"Not your fault, brother."

This almost makes me smile. "Isn't it?"

"No. It's great great great grandpa and his cronies' fault. Oh, and the hot golden angel who appeared to them in what I can only imagine was a drug-induced vision of biblical proportions."

"Yeah. If only *I* could have one of those visions."

Wolf laughs. "It's not over 'til it's over, man." As though he's reading my mind.

Which makes me wonder if maybe Wolf has an ace up his sleeve.

I can only hope.

"I'm going down to the beach," I tell them, heading for the door.

"Think about it, Knox," Leo calls after me. "I could call the guy who used to manage me. His name is Bulldog."

"Of course it is. And the answer is no."

I leave them to it, making my way outside. To the trail that leads around the lake, past the gardens. To the walled pineapple plantation. Along the ridge and down the slope. Through the lowlying rainforest and into the cove where my house sits on rock and stilts, perched over the water next to a stretch of sand.

Inside, I take my phone out of my pocket. The screen is full of messages.

Perri.

Perri.

Perri.

I have no idea how she got my number. I never gave it to her.

I open one of them.

> Silas said he talked to Remington. He
> said it's all arranged. I can't wait to see
> you again Knox. I can't wait for ... all of it.
> Call me. Please? Perri xxx

Fuck.

What if I can't do it?

What if I can't bring myself to say the vows that will bind me for a lifetime to someone I don't love and never could?

A divorce from vows forged by the Angel's Curse isn't allowed.

Am I dooming myself to a life of regret so I can keep my family safe from the tragedies that seem to hound us, and haunt us?

Unless fate has an ace up her sleeve—*please have an ace up your sleeve*—the answer to that question is yes.

17

KNOX

I DELETE the messages from Perri, then power my phone off and leave it on the table.

I grab my speargun and go out onto the deck.

The sun is setting.

I stare out at the vermillion sky and the blazing water, tinted red by the sun like the blood of my own bleeding heart.

I wonder what would it *feel* like to fall in love.

The bond of it.

The absolute certainty that transformed my staunch older brother into a mess of adoration.

I might never know.

Odds are I *will* never know.

But maybe this is for the best.

Look what happened to Remington in the end, after all. And our parents. Maybe *love* is the curse.

I'm realistic. I'm duty-bound. I'll do whatever I can to

protect myself from a loveless marriage. But I won't condemn my family.

I stare up at the first evening star. I always think of my parents when I look at the stars.

If this really is my destiny, so be it. If it isn't, show me. Put that destiny in my path. Help me recognize it. Give me a sign.

My mother used to keep a journal. Over the years, we've all read at least some of it. Blaise and Echo pour over it and quote from it from time to time. I haven't read a lot because it somehow feels invasive but one thing always stood out to me. She called my father her north star. She wrote that her world revolved around him and there wasn't a damn thing she could do about it.

She thought everyone has a soulmate.

I'm not so sure.

I kick off my boots and drop my weapons belt. I arm my gun and dive into the water.

I think about letting go.

Swimming out and never coming back.

Letting the sea take me.

But that would only pass the curse on to Wolf or Echo.

It's not something I would ever do.

Maybe I should go for Aurora King. The thought makes me feel slightly sick. I'd probably catch something on our wedding night. It's written in the alliance docu-ment that the marriage must be proven to be consum-mated. I have no idea how they even confirm something like that in this day and age. Either way, no one seems at all dedicated to the "purity" of the alliance marriages.

Living with the Kings sounds so fucking unbearable. They're the most unhinged of all of us and they live inside the thick haze of their own self-importance.

Tatum Fitzpatrick could be a better option. A marriage in name only. She'd spend her life on location, jet-setting around the world. We'd hardly see each other.

Or timid little Vivi. But then I'll have to live with not only a wife who's terrified of me but also her sister, who would probably murder me in my sleep if I choose Vivi or Tatum over her.

I swim alongside a school of to'au, spearing one.

Soulmate.

Is there really such a thing?

The lucky ones are the people who find theirs, like my parents did. Even though tragedy struck them—her, my father, Remy—at least they knew what it *felt* like to fall for that one person who you knew in your heart was the one, unconditionally.

The unlucky ones are the people who wander through their whole lives and never know. The ones whose paths never cross with the one they were meant for.

To me, that feels like the biggest curse of all.

18

Cassidy

BY THE TIME I leave the bar, it's just after 3 a.m. In the end, I won a grand total of four hundred and fifty-eight dollars.

I still can't believe it.

Things like this don't happen to me.

The cash is rolled into a wad and zipped into a pocket of my dress. Yay for dresses with pockets. I stashed the plane ticket in the hidden compartment of my bag, along with the two other most coveted things I own. My pin and the laminated note. *Her name is Cassidy.*

Sure it is, Mom. Now if you'd only given me a few more key pieces of info about who the hell I am, it really might have come in handy.

I spend around thirty seconds wondering if I'll even use the ticket. It's daunting as hell to think about flying to a completely different island, to start a completely different life.

It's a one-way ticket.

You can always come back, I tell myself.

But who am I kidding.

Of course I'm going to use the ticket.

And why would I *want* to come back? I live in a dump, I work fifteen hours a day and the only things in my life that give me tiniest bit of happiness are my forced positive outlook on life, a few borrowed surfboards and my stolen hour just before sunrise.

I have no idea where I'll end up or what I'll find on Kauai, but when something *this* random and out of the blue falls into your lap, I figure the universe is trying to tell you something. Luck isn't the kind of thing that shows up on my bingo card all that often, so this score feels important.

This is my chance to take a leap of faith.

Making my way back toward my apartment, I feel a sudden wave of relief, that I'll soon be free of this place. I freaking hate where I live. I'm scared whenever I'm there and I never sleep well because a part of my brain is always aware that I might be in danger. That someone might break in at any moment. Every bump in the night is jarring and I spend most of my days exhausted because of it. The threats always feel like they're close by.

I'm used to that feeling, but it's getting worse.

It's hot in the city and the moon is full tonight. Moody clouds shine with an actual silver lining. Maybe it's a sign —of what, I have no idea.

I feel spooked, like storms are brewing.

I turn the corner and see a small crowd of people out in front of my apartment building. The building where I live looks like one of those old motels you see in nineties movies where drug deals go wrong. Which basically sums the place up. I can hear voices and music.

Shit.

My douchebag neighbor is having a party.

Dash works as a bouncer in one of the downtown clubs, so he usually gets home around this time of night. I know this because he cranks up his music and the walls are paper thin. He parties all night and sleeps all day.

Dash prefers to hang out on the seedier side of life. Everything about him and his entourage is exactly what I'm trying like hell to distance myself from.

Living next to Dash is a constant reminder that I'm lost, that I have no family and no protection. That I'm vulnerable. He also reminds me that I have a long way to go in life. I live next door to a thug and a loser. I like to think I'm better than he is and that my future is a lot brighter. But sometimes, late at night when I'm exhausted and strung out, it's hard to do.

But now I have my ticket.

Dash is one of the reasons I've been desperate to move. He's also one of the reasons I always carry my knife.

I don't trust him.

I think about walking in the other direction. I could sleep on the beach for a few hours until it's time to get ready for work again.

But my clothes are dirty and my spare, clean uniform is hanging up in my tiny bathroom.

Maybe they won't notice me. I'll be quick. I'll pack up the last of my stuff and I won't come back here. I'll just disappear, never to be seen again.

Trying to be as quiet and inconspicuous as possible, I walk past the small crowd to my door. I see Dash, standing with a group of guys who all look like bikers or hitmen. Before I can sneak inside, Dash calls out to me. "Hey, Cassidy."

Damn it.

One of other men talking to Dash is watching me. He's tall and dark-haired. He's surrounded by people that almost look like bodyguards. He's wearing a black t-shirt and has a lot of tattoos, including a distinctly designed bow and arrow dripping with red ink-blood on his muscular upper arm. I notice it because Dash recently got the same one.

Fishing around in the front pocket of my bag for my key, I find it. But before I can unlock my door, Dash and the other guy come over to me. "I already unlocked it for you," Dash says, his words slightly slurred, like he's been drinking. He grins at me. Because he knows there's not a damn thing I can do to stop him.

Asshole. It's why I carry everything I care about with me at all times. I had a feeling he was going through my stuff when I wasn't around.

The other guy is broad-shouldered and dark-eyed. Not just dark in color but also in the expression behind them. He's got the look of someone who's capable of ... things I don't want to find out about. I can't help noticing that he's got a leather holster strapped across his chest, under his leather vest. I can see the glinting metal of his gun.

"Is this her?" he asks Dash.

Is this her? Dash has told this guy about me? Why? I don't like this at all.

"Yeah," Dash replies. "This is Cassidy Kelley. Cassidy, meet Axel Archer."

Axel Archer. The name is familiar, of course. And the tattoo makes sense now.

Arrow.

It's a group that gets talked about. They're some sort of crime ring. They're dangerous career criminals who commit the kind of felonies that get people locked up for life. Murders. Bank robberies. Kidnapping. Prostitution. Drugs. Weapons. You name it, and Arrow has their fingerprints on it.

They recruit people from the streets to join them. Axel Archer is the kingpin, but he seems to somehow escape the law. Because he gets his recruits to do his dirty work for him.

Dash's new tattoo must mean he's one of them now.

This is not good news.

I need to get away from here. Right fucking now.

19

—————

Cassidy

"CASSIDY KELLEY," Axel repeats. He leans a burly shoulder against the wall next to me, all cocky arrogance and barely-checked aggression. He's got the vibe of someone who's used to getting his way. And who won't take no for an answer.

Axel's eyes rove my face, and lower. I'm wearing my yellow sundress, which I changed back into after work. I'm glad to know my knife is strapped to my leg. At least I'm not completely defenseless.

I think about running but some sixth sense tells me they'd chase me.

Before I can stop him, Axel reaches to pull off my hat, like a bully in the playground.

"Hey—" *Shit.* My hair spills over my shoulders. My hair is long and so blond it's practically white. It always gets the kind of attention I never want. In another life,

75

the color of my hair might have been something I could have appreciated. In this one, it's a liability.

Axel stares at me wolfishly. "Damn," he drawls.

I guess that's his idea of a compliment, but I push past him, getting inside and slamming the door behind me. I lock it, knowing full well the flimsy locks—which they have the key for—won't keep them out for long.

In a rush, I start packing the things I might need.

A forceful pounding on the door makes me jump. "Axel wants to talk to you, Cassidy," Dash calls out. "He has an offer for you."

"Go away."

I force myself to ignore the stinging behind my eyes and the thudding pulse of my own fear.

As I pack as much as I can fit into my small bag, I hear the sound of a key unlocking my door. My heart practically leaps out of my chest.

Why didn't I trust my gut and stay away from here tonight?

Dash is a jerk and the kind of guy who was born to be someone else's dumb, eager pawn. Axel is clearly something else altogether. A predator. A deviant with an army at his beck and call.

The door opens. Axel's big frame fills the doorway and it terrifies me. This man is reckless. He has no fear and no limits, I can feel that.

I think about trying to rush past him but he closes the door and leans up against it. His voice is low when he says, "I want to talk to you about something, Cassidy. I'm about to make you an offer you can't refuse."

My terror is making me braver than I feel. "There's nothing you could offer me that I want."

Axel laughs darkly. "You haven't heard the offer yet."

I have a knife and I'll fight to the death, you asshole. I'll kill you if I have to.

I don't reach for my knife yet. I don't want him to know I have it.

Fury floods my veins along with adrenaline because I don't *want* to panic. This situation is the stuff of my worst nightmares. And I have a very bad feeling about what's about to happen next.

Axel takes a step deeper into the dim, dreary room and looks around. "I like what you've done with the place." Like this is all a big joke to him.

Holding my bag by the strap as casually as I can, I start to inch my way closer to the door. There's really no other escape route. The window in the bathroom is too small and too high. "I have to go."

Axel's mouth quirks. "So soon?" He's enjoying this game of cat and mouse. "Did you know I own this building?"

Will I survive this? Yes. I have to. I have a plane ticket. "No." I could tell him he's a shitty landlord but now's definitely not the time.

"Do you know who I am?" His voice is graveled and distinctive. He has a tattoo of another small arrow with a feather tail across his cheekbone. "Have you heard of me?"

I don't know if I should tell the truth or not. "Yes."

"I can offer you a way out of this shithole. We're looking for people like you. Dash said you live alone. He said you have a hard time keeping up with your rent. In fact, he told me this month's rent is late."

Damn you, Dash.

"It's not late. It's due today." I pull the wad of cash out of the zipped pocket of my dress and hold it out. "Here. This is more than I owe."

"I could give you so many better options than this place."

I force my voice to sound steady, like we're having a casual conversation and this aggressive, armed stranger hasn't just broken into my apartment and is now blocking my way out. "I really have to go now. I have a new job and I'm starting work early today. I don't want to be late."

There's a flatness behind Axel Archer's expression that terrifies me. A blankness that's entirely devoid of emotion. "Did you know our new recruits get paid in cash? I think we could come up with a number you'll be happy with. For someone like yourself there could be added benefits. A new apartment. An allowance. Your own surfboard."

They've been following me.

I reach for the doorknob but Axel's palm presses against the back of the door, holding it closed.

"Please," I hear myself say.

Please don't make me do what I can only hope and pray I'm brave enough to do.

20

Cassidy

AXEL ARCHER TOUCHES an end strand of my hair and I flinch. "Dash is one of my newer scouts," he tells me. "He told me about you. But he didn't mention how fucking gorgeous you are."

I shove the money at him. "Please. I need to go. Just take it and let me go."

There's a low chuckle that makes the tiny hairs on my arms lift. "I have another idea." Axel's fingers play with the zip at the back of my dress. I shrug him off as force-fully as I can but he pins me in place with the big bulk of his body, which is hard in ways I don't even want to think about. "I always get what I want, Cassidy. Remember that. Don't fight me."

"*Stop,*" I plead. "*Please. Let me go.*"

Axel pulls the zip of my dress lower.

"*STOP,*" I scream, fighting him with everything I have. "*Get off me!*"

He's so fucking *heavy*.

Axel's palm presses over my mouth to silence me. I abstractly comprehend that his hands are dirty. I try to claw at him but he's *unbelievably* strong. He manacles my wrists in one of his hands.

"I can make your life so much better than this," he growls in my ear. "All I'm asking for is a small ... down payment."

I can't move.

Help me. Someone. Please help me.

But no one will. No one ever does.

I'm so tightly pinned, I can't even reach for my knife.

God. I need to stop him. He's fumbling with his belt. He's pushing up the hem of my dress.

I hear a whimper and realize it's me. I hate the way it sounds.

I make the decision to never allow myself to be this vulnerable ever again.

I feel Axel's fingers unzip my dress halfway down my back. I try to punch him, but he's too strong. He's too close. *Holy hell, this is happening. There's nothing I can do to stop him.*

Axel suddenly goes eerily still.

There's a note of shock in his voice as his fingers touch the small circle that's inked between my shoulder blades. "What is this? You have a tattoo."

Axel's grip on me loosens as he studies the inked mark.

I take my opportunity. I reach for my knife.

I turn and, with all the strength I have, I plunge the blade into his stomach.

Axel is so shocked he takes a step back from me, holding his hands to his stomach, where the blood is already starting to pool.

"*Fuck.* You little—"

I bolt, grabbing my bag and opening the door enough to squeeze through.

I run like my life depends on it, because it does. I run to the corner and sprint through the back alley. My only advantage is that I know all the nooks and secret shortcuts in this neighborhood. It's where I've spent most of my life. And there are lots of them. Everyone wants an easy walk to the beach. There are pathways laced between every building.

My lungs are on fire.

I'm still holding my bloody knife in my hand. *I held onto it*, which seems sort of crazy but I'm wildly relieved to still have it.

I stick to the darkest route, weaving through secret pathways and dark doorways.

I can hear yelling from the next street over, but I find a hollow under the overhang of a parking garage and I squeeze through it, making my way to the next street.

And the next. Following the route like I already know where I'm going.

The last place they'll ever look for me.

The airport.

21

Cassidy

I walk for hours, staying off the main roads.

The dawn is beginning to paint Diamond Head with a lavender glow. It's about the time I'd usually be getting up to surf. Crew will wonder where I've taken off to.

I'm in Kalihi, I realize. I'm actually not that far from Maggie's house, not that I've ever been there.

I've never told Maggie where I live but people tend to pick up on it when you live rough, like I do. Some sixth sense warns the people you meet not to get too close. I'm an orphan. I'm profoundly alone. I was abandoned by my own family. That shit tends to dust itself onto your aura. It's detectable. Friends I've made along the way pick up on it. They're kind enough. They'll share a laugh with you and talk to you when you're at school or work because it's neutral territory. But they'll never invite you home or ask you to hang out with them and their close friends. That's just the way it is and I'm used to it.

My plan is falling into place, though, and I decide I'll let Maggie know she won't be seeing me again.

I see an ATM machine up ahead. I stop walking long enough to text Maggie.

> Something unexpected has come up and I'm leaving. Please tell Eleanor I won't be back at work. Please tell her I'm sorry I couldn't tell her in person. Take care, Maggie. I'll miss you xx

Then I text Crew.

> Hey Crew, I'm taking off for a while so I won't be able to help out on Mondays anymore, sorry about that. Thanks for hiring me. And thanks for letting me use your surfboards. I hope you catch all the best waves, my friend, and take care of yourself

I'll miss him and his hopeful green eyes. His friendship and his shed full of longboards kept me going through some difficult days.

Then I throw my phone down a small bank where it lands in a shallow creek.

Axel Archer has friends in low places. My phone cost me twenty-nine bucks and might not be traceable but I don't want to take the risk, just in case.

I check my pocket for my poker money but it's long gone. I dropped it in my rush to escape. And I won't get paid for my new job until next week. Even then, it won't be much. I've only worked there for four days.

I take out all the money in my bank account.

A whopping twenty-six dollars.

In the movies, the police or the techie criminals are always tracing people through their bank transactions. So I bend my ATM card in half and drop the pieces into the little slot by the cash machine that's supposed to be for receipts you don't want. In case Axel and Dash and their gang could somehow trace me.

Who knows if they're sophisticated enough to find me, or if they'll even want to. But, since I've stabbed their crime lord, I have a hunch I've now got a big-ass target on my back. Best to become as invisible as possible for a while.

I don't think it was a lethal wound. Axel Archer will recover. With a white-hot vendetta against me and a legion of thugs ready to do anything he asks.

Not a great situation.

I pull on my oversized gray sweatshirt. And I put on a beanie I bought at a thrift store for a dollar. It's one of those hats you can pull down into a face mask. A *balaclava*, the guy at the thrift store had called it, taking care to show me that detail. It could come in handy, he said. At the time I'd thought, *when the hell would something like this come in handy?* But maybe he was right. Maybe it will. For now I wear it as a hat, stuffing my hair underneath.

Pulling the hood of my sweatshirt up, shielding myself as much as possible, I keep walking.

Sticking to the meandering side roads and constantly

checking to make sure I'm not being followed, it takes me another hour to get the airport.

I've never been to the airport before but it's easy enough to find the terminal with the local departures. There's a flight that's leaving for Kauai in thirty-five minutes.

I walk up to the desk where a woman is typing into a computer. She glances up at me. The empathy in her eyes is the first thing I notice. I don't know if it will help me but I silently thank the universe for putting her in my path and I pray for one more lucky score. I *need* this woman's kindness like I need the air I'm breathing.

"Can I help you?" she asks.

I place Ben's ticket on the counter in front of her. "I have a ticket to Kauai that's scheduled for three days from now. But I was hoping there might be an earlier flight. It's an emergency."

She starts typing again. "Is it regarding a family member?"

"Um ... yes." I don't like lying, and I hardly ever do it, but I have a sudden flashback to the way Axel's shock stopped him for a few seconds, almost like he *knew* what the symbol meant. *What is this? You have a tattoo.* I think about what will happen to me next if Axel or Dash finds me. "My mother."

"I bet she can't wait to see you," the woman says.

I'm a little shocked when my eyes fill with tears. I haven't cried in a long time. But right now, I can't hold it in. Maybe it's because I haven't slept. Or because I can still taste the terror of what *almost* just happened to me. I brush the tears away. "Sorry."

She smiles and there's genuine emotion behind it. Maybe she has a daughter my age or a niece she's fond of. "I'll tell you what. Coach is full on this flight. I don't usually do this because we occasionally get last minute reservations, but we're going to start boarding soon and we still have four first class seats available. How do you feel about an upgrade?"

An upgrade? "That would be amazing."

"Do you have some ID?"

Shit. I don't have a driver's license. And I threw away my bank card. But then I remember my new ID for Perfection Catering. I pull it out. "Will this do?"

She looks at the ID. And the ticket. Then at me. My bloodshot eyes. The strung-out expression on my face. My second-hand, oversized clothes.

The clacking on the keyboard continues. "I'm going to pretend the name on this booking matches yours. If anyone asks, your name is Benjamin J. Reece. Because everyone needs a lucky break every once in a while, don't they, Cassidy? Some people don't get enough of them."

"I ... I couldn't agree more."

"Any bags?"

"Just this one." I turn slightly to show her my backpack.

"Only a carry-on, then." She prints out a card and hands it to me. "Here's your boarding pass. We'll start boarding in around five minutes. First class passengers board first so you can make your way over to Gate 3 right over there."

I've never had the stars align for me the way they are for this out-of-the-blue trip to Kauai. But I'll take it. "Thank you," I say, resisting the urge to give the lady a heartfelt, you-just-saved-my-life hug.

"You're welcome, honey. Have a nice trip home."

22

———

Cassidy

I BOARD the plane and a flight attendant shows me to my seat by the window.

I can't believe I'm on an actual airplane.

As I sit, the strap of my knife's holster rubs against my thigh. They didn't pat me down like they do in the movies, or make me go through a metal detector. Maybe because the inter-island commuter flights are more relaxed when it comes to security. Either way, I'm relieved. Because I've made it this far. And because I still have my knife. In case I need it. *Again.*

Another flight attendant offers me a glass of champagne, a single flute sitting on its own tray.

It's the first time I've ever been ... well, *served*. It's always *me* who's doing the serving.

It's a strange feeling but I take the offer, even though it's barely eight o'clock in the morning, hoping the champagne might calm my frayed nerves. It's insane when you

88

think about it, that this metal tube I'm sitting in is soon going to be flying over the *ocean*. The thought makes my stomach do a nervous little flip.

I take a sip of the bubbly liquid as more people file into the first class cabin.

I'm surprised when I recognize one of the other passengers.

It's Echo Ramsey.

She's wearing a white cotton sundress and a cute pair of wedge sandals. Her long dark hair is cut in a fashionable style. She really is stunning. You can tell her clothes are new and expensive but she wears them with an offhand, casual flair. She's waifishly slender but not frail-looking. The opposite, in fact. There's a willful confidence to the way she carries herself, like she could slay dragons if she had to.

Weirdly, this quality in her reminds me of ... myself. Except that I slay dragons because I have to while she slays them because she wants to.

I find myself wishing I could know her.

She slides her sunglasses up and takes the seat in front of me. She declines the flight attendant's offer of champagne and asks for tea.

Through the gap in the seats I can see that she's taking her phone out of her bag. She opens an app and touches a name on a list. *Blaise.*

A young woman's face shows on the screen and it's obvious the two are sisters. Blaise Ramsey is just as beautiful as Echo. She's sitting at a desk and there's a huge stone hearth behind her next to a wall of windows with a view outside of blue sky and rows of trees. I can even see the dots of golden fruit. They look like peaches. "Hey, honey. How was the party?"

I don't want to eavesdrop but I'm already riveted. Blaise's voice is comforting and kind, but also has that dragon-slaying strength behind it. She's not making small talk, she genuinely wants to know.

"It was okay." Echo is served her tea and she takes a sip. "Perri wouldn't leave me alone, Vivi disappeared for most of the night and Malachi was his usual lecherous self, but other than that it was fine."

"Are you on a commercial flight?" Blaise seems concerned about this.

"The private jet was having some maintenance done. I didn't want to wait. There's nothing to worry about. Security dropped me off and security will be there to pick me up. Remy arranged it."

"All right. But be careful."

It makes me wonder why they need so much security. Because they're celebrities, I guess.

I've imagined what it would be like to have a sister, of course I have. It's hard to imagine when you've never experienced it. The connection between these two women is fascinating me. They *care* so deeply for each other. The familiarity between them practically glows. I can only watch them with awe.

I don't usually dwell on the things that are missing from my life—and there are a lot of them—but something about these sisters makes me crave what they share, all the way down to my bones. *What would it feel like to have someone who knows you so well and cares about you so much?* The screen blurs and I realize my tears are welling up again.

Damn it. I really don't know what's gotten into me lately.

Maybe getting assaulted by a mob boss, stabbing him because you had no other choice, then barely escaping with what's left of your innocence could have something to do with it. Maybe fleeing to a place you've never been with nowhere to go and twenty-six dollars to your name could be a small part of it too.

I take another sip of champagne.

"What did Perri want to talk to you about?" Blaise asks Echo.

"She's obsessing about Knox. She wouldn't shut up about how she feels like they're made for each other and how he's perfect for her. But he won't answer any of her calls. She's freaking out about it."

So that's what she and Perri were talking about at the party. The brother named Knox.

"Maybe he'll come around by the time they visit next month."

"Yeah. Unlikely, but maybe. How's it going for you, Blaise? Have you come any closer to a decision?"

"Besides hiding out in the hilltop caves for the next ten years, no."

Echo smiles gently. "Those caves are actually really cool. Knox and I hiked up there to explore a few weeks ago. The caves are like a connected series of rooms. And there are these twin pools on the terrace just outside them. One has a little shelf you can sit on, like a seat. And a freshwater spring waterfall that feeds into it. There was even a small orchard up there with some papaya trees that were just starting to fruit. Some seeds from our trees must have been carried up there by the wind. I wouldn't have thought they'd take hold up there but they have. And the views out over the hills and the ocean are amazing."

"That sounds nice," Blaise says. *It really does.* "You didn't tell me you went up there."

"It was a random spur of the moment thing. Knox said it was beyond his scope and he wanted to go check it out so I hiked up there with him."

"Did you find anything?"

"No." Echo takes another sip of her tea. "It didn't look like anyone had been up there in a long time. But it was so beautiful. The place is like an idyllic hilltop wonderland."

"Well, if I disappear you'll know where to find me," Blaise says.

An announcement interrupts their conversation. *Please take your seats, ladies and gentlemen.*

"I better go," Echo says. "They're shutting the doors. I'll see you soon."

"Okay, honey. Love you, E."

"Love you too." Echo ends the call and the flight attendant talks us through a security briefing. Within minutes, the plane is lifting off.

There are several things that are basically transforming my life in this moment.

One, *we're flying.* We're ascending at a dizzying speed and I can see out my window that the ground is far below us now.

Two, something about the conversation I just overheard is hitting me right where I live. The sisterly love. The bond that just so happens to be one of the most beautiful things I've ever witnessed.

Three, the descriptions of a place that sounds closer to heaven on earth than anything I've seen or imagined.

I can see Oahu below us, the winding lines of the roads and highways, the golden stripe of sandy beach and the expanse of blue water, dotted with tiny white-capped waves.

Once we've leveled off, the flight attendants walk around with wheeled carts like it's no big deal that we're thousands of feet up the air. One of them notices me white-knuckling my arm rests and she smiles and offers to top up my champagne. I end up drinking it thirstily as I gaze down at the endless ocean and I'm glad to have it. It takes the edge off.

I'm *free*, I'm realizing.

Free from Dash and Axel Archer.

Free from the trench I've been trying to dig my way out of my whole life.

True, I have no idea what I'm going to do with twenty-six dollars, no job, no place to live and no plan.

It didn't look like anyone had been up there in a long time.

The place is like an idyllic hilltop wonderland.

No.

I seriously can't be considering trying to find some hilltop caves that I have no business being curious about.

There was even a small orchard up there with some papaya trees that were just starting to fruit. The views out over the hills and the ocean are amazing.

I've never had a view.

And I must be going crazy. I wouldn't even know how to get to such a place.

It's not a long flight. By the time I finish my second glass of champagne, I can see the green coastline of Kauai.

It's *so* beautiful.

The landing is terrifying but smooth and soon we're pulling up to the small Kauai airport.

I made it.

Now all I need to do is to figure out how to survive.

23

Cassidy

Echo is one of the first to disembark. A woman across the aisle gets off and I follow.

As soon as we're inside the airport, Echo is greeted by three very large security-guard type men. She doesn't seem to take much notice of them, scrolling on her phone as they retrieve her two bags from the baggage claim. Then she's ushered through glass sliding doors into a car that's waiting just outside. Once she's safely inside, the car pulls away.

There's no one waiting for me. Obviously. Which I'm mostly relieved about. At least no one is on my trail. Not yet anyway.

I look around, trying to figure out what to do next.

There's a magazine store with shelves of snack foods so I go in and use my twenty-six dollars to buy a bottle of water and all the food I can afford. Nuts, chocolate, dried fruit and energy bars. Twenty-six dollars doesn't go very far but the food should at least last me a few days. It gives me a buffer. Some time to at least figure out what to do and where to go.

Outside the magazine store, I notice there's a seating area with some iPads and seats.

Free Wifi! a small sign reads.

So I sit down in front of one of the iPads. The first thing I google is, **Axel Archer stabbed**. *Is he dead? Would he go to a hospital like a regular person or would he have some kind of underground doctor that could help him?*

There's a discussion on X about it. Turns out some of his recruits are online. Maybe Arrow wants to be accessible in case people want to join up with them. I scroll through the mentions of Axel and I'm able to learn that his wound wasn't fatal. He's going to live. He's healing as we speak and no doubt searching for the runaway who almost killed him.

I need to stay hidden.

Next I find myself googling, **Where does the Ramsey family live on Kauai?**

It's surprisingly specific, with a line drawn on the map outlining the huge Ramsey family ranch. On the satellite image, I can see a cluster of buildings. There's a road leading from the small main Ramsey settlement to an entrance gate that opens onto one of the main roads that circles most of the perimeter of the island. The ranch is outlined by what looks like a high stone wall. On the Ramsey's land, there's a long stretch of beachfront, with arcs of golden sand and also a series of sheltered, rocky coves.

I zoom in on the main cluster of buildings. Dotted trees form neatly lined rows and there are structures that look like greenhouses. These must be the orchards and the gardens. To the southwest of them, the terrain rises steeply.

I zoom in further. Would they be visible on Google Earth?

They hiked there so the caves can't be too far from their houses.

What are you even doing right now, Cassidy? What are you searching for?

And why?

Because I'm lost and I need a place to hide out for a while.

You can't live in a cave, *for god's sake. What's wrong with you?*

Everything about the caves and the way Echo Ramsey described them is digging into me in a way I can't explain. It's like the place is ... *calling to me*—which is ridiculous but that's how it feels. I have a wild curiosity to *see* them.

Maybe I'm losing my marbles. It's a ridiculous plan, to search for some hidden paradise tied to random people I don't even know. But I do. I want to touch the edges of what they have.

And the truth is, I have nowhere else to go.

24

Cassidy

I SCAN the landscape on the map. Past the line of the stone wall. To the steeper hills and the craggy cliffs.

I zoom in but the resolution isn't as clear.

But then ... *there.* High in the hills, maybe a quarter mile above the wall, there are two round natural pools. And what looks like the mouth of a small cave.

This is it.

I study the map and get a good feel for the lay of the land.

There's a town only fifteen miles or so from the Ramsey's gate. Princeville.

My decision clicks into place and it's surprisingly resolute.

That's where I'm going.

I'll hitchhike my way to the area. I'll hike my way up alongside the stone wall and I'll search for these caves. If I can even find them—*which I will, come hell or high water*—I'll look out at the amazing view. I'll sit in the pools. I'll eat a piece of fruit that I picked with my own hands. I'll stay there for a night or two until my food supply runs out. Then I'll make my way to Princeville and begin my job search.

I close out the map.

You're insane.

Maybe. But it's a mission that feels like it's been implanted onto my heart with a red-hot branding iron.

I exit the airport terminal.

The air is hot and the sun is bright. I start to take off my sweatshirt but notice that my dress is stained with blood. *Axel's blood.* So I keep my sweatshirt on and take off my hat, stuffing it into my bag. No one here knows me, I remind myself. I don't need a disguise. So I leave my hair long and loose. I try to smooth it, hoping I don't look too disheveled. Kauai will just have to take me as I am.

I follow the entrance road of the airport out to where it converges with the main road.

Sticking my thumb out, I start walking.

The very first car that passes me slows. The driver is an older man, maybe in his sixties, driving an ancient blue pick-up truck. He pulls up alongside me and his eyes are wide with a strange kind of shock as he stares at me.

Do I know him?

No.

Why is he staring at me like he's just seen a ghost?

"Can I offer you a ride, miss?"

"Where are you headed?"

"Wherever you need to go," he says.

Wow. People in Kauai are nice. "Do you know where the Ramseys live?"

"The Ramseys? Of course."

"If you could just take me as far as you can in that direction, I'd be grateful."

"I can take you all the way to the gate. It's no trouble."

I'm a little surprised by this stranger's generosity. "Are you sure? I wouldn't want you to go out of your way."

"For you, nothing's out of the way."

He's not saying this in a creepy way, more like he's mistaken me for someone important. "Well, that's very nice of you. If you're sure it's no trouble."

"No trouble at all."

"I'll, uh ... I'll climb onto the back if you don't mind." He seems kind but after the twenty-four hours I've had, I'd rather not take any chances.

"Of course you can. I've heard that's what you prefer. Here, let me help——"

"No. I'm fine." I make my way to the back of the truck, climbing aboard. Once I'm seated I give him a thumbs up through the back window of the cab and he pulls out onto the road.

That was easier than I thought it was going to be. And what did he mean by *I've heard that's what you prefer*? Maybe he's losing a few of his own marbles.

The guy drives straight through and even though it's breezy, the air is warm.

I'm not sure how long the drive takes. I don't have a watch or a phone. So I just enjoy the ride and the scenery. We drive through Princeville and my logical mind is saying, *just get off here. Ask the guy to stop. Start looking for a hotel or a youth hostel or a place that might potentially be hiring cleaning staff, and figure out where your next meal is coming from.*

But I don't.

We continue for a while until the truck starts to slow.

The driver pulls over onto the side of the road. Next to a high, smooth stone wall.

This is it.

The Ramseys' ranch.

25

Cassidy

I CLIMB OFF THE BACK, waving to the guy as I start walking away. From here, I can see the tall iron gate.

The guy calls after me. "You sure you don't need anything else?"

"I'm sure," I call back. "Thank you."

The driver toots his horn at me and turns his truck around, heading back in the direction we came from.

So here I am, standing in front of the gigantic gate of a family of complete strangers who don't know I exist. How on earth did I end up here, of all places?

My whole outlook feels strange and it takes me a few seconds to figure out why. I'm *happy*. I *want* to be here. Weirdly, I feel like my whole life has led me to this moment.

The gate is impenetrable-looking. Impressive but not ostentatious. There's no giant R or any way of telling who lives here if you didn't already know.

One thing that is obvious: no one's getting through that gate that the Ramseys don't *want* getting through that gate. It's around twenty feet tall and made of steel with sharp points at the top. The wall is high and thick with a subtle row of barbed wire running along the top of it.

They must really want to keep people out.

But where I'm going isn't trespassing. It's state land.

So I continue walking along the grassy strip between the road and the wall. It takes me a while to reach the corner. This place is freaking *big*.

From the corner, the wall winds away from the road, up the sloping hill, until it disappears over the rise of another, steeper hill.

What are you doing, you lunatic? Have you lost your mind? Why use up all your energy and the last of your food to hike up a giant mountain? What if you fall off a cliff or something? What if you die up there?

No one would even miss me.

It's that last detail that hits the hardest. I think about Echo and Blaise and how much they care about each other.

Is *that* what I'm looking for? Do I think I might somehow be able to know them or touch a piece of their lives by getting closer?

So you're a stalker now, just because two sisters were having a casual conversation you happened to overhear?

I don't know.

No.

I just want to see the place that someone as lucky as

Echo Ramsey would describe as an *idyllic hilltop wonderland.* She's *used* to wonderlands. Her whole *life* is a wonderland.

My quest to get to these caves has lodged itself into me and won't let go.

Fuck it. I'm doing it.

So I start walking up the hill, sticking close to the wall.

It's a grueling, steep hike through patches of thick rainforest and expanses of rocky slopes. I stop every now and then to have a drink and eat a handful of dried fruit and a few energy bars. No matter how much I eat I still feel hungry.

I'm tired because I haven't slept enough.

I'm pissed off because this is a crazy, possibly very stupid thing to be doing.

I'm emotional because I'm bushwacking up a steep hill on a strange island. By myself. If I fall or hurt myself I'll die out here and no one will ever know until all they find of me is a pile of bleached bones.

Okay, now you're getting melodramatic.

And it won't be long until it gets dark.

At this point I'm very glad that I've stuffed my whole damn life into the bag I'm carrying. What I realize is that a part of me has been preparing for this all along.

I have a flashlight, the sweatshirt I'm wearing, a beach towel, several changes of clothes, a toothbrush, a tube of toothpaste, three pairs of underwear, one spare pair of socks, a bar of soap, a brush, a raincoat, matches, some rope, a sewing kit, a light wool blanket and my knife.

I have my pin and my note.

I have whiskey and maybe two days' worth of food, if I can make it last.

So I keep going.

Reaching the summit of yet another steep hill, it gives me a view of some steeper rocks and cliffs further up. The sun is hanging low in the sky, tinting the whole world gold.

And there, high up, I finally see it: a cluster of caves.

Holy shit.

I found it!

I make my way over rocks, through shrubs and trees, along a trickling stream. I climb higher.

Until I arrive at the terrace where the two pools sit side by side.

Wow.

Echo Ramsey was right.

The view isn't just amazing, it's the most magical thing I have ever, ever seen. The green mountains and the rippled sea in the distance are painted all the colors of the rainbow by the melting glow of the setting sun.

One of the pools is being fed by a waterfall coming straight out of solid rock. The water is clear and clean-looking. Which is a good thing because my water bottle is empty. I hold it under the waterfall and refill it directly from the cool stream.

I drink the whole thing, insanely thirsty. If it kills me at least I'll die free.

I sit at the edge of the pool just to take it all in.

The relief is overwhelming. It's powerful and unexpected. It leeches into every corner of my soul, like a soothing tonic.

I wish I'd done this a long time ago.

It feels so good to be completely removed from my past life. The dinginess. The hopelessness. The grime. My apartment and my awful neighbor ... and his new boss. *The man who came very, very close to—*

But didn't.

I put it out of my mind.

I'm here now.

I watch the sun's edge dip below the horizon line and I make my way up to the caves. I'm covered in scratches and my clothes are dirty and torn. The sky is dusky now but there's still enough light to inspect my new digs. The first cave is like a small, cozy room. Along the closest smooth wall, there's a level, natural rock shelf.

Sitting just inside the doorway, I unpack a few things from my bag, placing my flashlight on the dirt floor next to me.

I take off my sweatshirt.

My ruined yellow sundress is stained and torn.

I peel it off and toss it a few feet away. In the morning I can take a bath in the pool and wash my clothes. I wrap my blanket around me, suddenly bone tired.

I reach into my bag, taking out my mother's pin, running my fingers over the little grooves of the golden feather.

What happened to you? Where are you? Why did you leave me?

The same old questions I'll never get the answers to.

The night sky turns purple, dotted with a million twinkling stars that feel like they're encouraging me, as though they're happy little friends who are glad I've made it this far.

Okay, I really am losing it.

I make myself a buffet of dried fruit, nuts and my last energy bar, washing it down with the cool, fresh water.

And as I stare out at the casting silver glow of the rising moon out over the waves, all the way to the horizon line, something else catches my eye. In the distance, down below me, I can see the flickering of lights, through the treetops.

The Ramseys' houses, maybe.

I could explore, just a little closer. Not too close, of course.

My eyelids feel so heavy.

I brush my teeth. Then I use my sweatshirt as a pillow and curl up inside my blanket.

Despite the hard ground, with my few supplies around me and my mother's pin on the little stone shelf within reach, this hard bed feels far more comfortable than any musty mattress ever has.

I realize now that freedom has power.

It gives strength.

I make up my mind to never allow myself to be as beaten down as I've been.

I'm as alone as it's possible to be.

But for the first time in my life, I don't feel lonely.

Cassidy

A BIRD CHIRPS, waking me. I open my eyes.

I gaze up at a rock ceiling and, outside, a bright blue sky.

Where the—?

Holy hell.

I flew to Kauai.

I got assaulted by my criminal landlord, who almost—

I stabbed him.

I'm in a cave on top of a mountain.

I'm safe.

I'm okay.

The sun is already high in the sky. I slept a long time.

I crawl out from under my blanket and realize all I'm wearing is a pair of panties.

It doesn't matter. There's no one else here.

I'm *excited*, I realize. To look around my new—temporary—home.

To start my new life. As a free person.

As a free, very hungry, very broke, very alone person whose survival skills in the wild are basic at best.

I ignore the little voice in my head that's pointing out the reality of my situation. I don't want to think too much about how dire it actually is. It's a stunning morning. I plan on making the most of it.

The light of late morning hangs romantically around the green, undulating peaks. I take a long drink from my water bottle. My stomach is growling insistently. I'm *starving*. I devour my last two chocolate bars.

Then I unpack my soap, my towel, my brush. I grab my toothbrush and my pile of dirty clothes. And I make my way down to the twin pools.

Each of them is around the size of a large jacuzzi. The water is clean and crystal clear.

So I strip down and lower myself into the one with the waterfall, sitting on the natural stone seat, letting the water cascade over me.

I scrub myself and wash my hair. The water's so refreshing, I feel like I'm in the process of being reborn. Into someone strong and capable, fully able to deal with the situation at hand.

Of course I can handle this.

I've handled worse.

I have to handle it.

Then I do my best to scrub my dirty clothes and I lay them out on a flat stone to dry.

As I let myself dry off in the sun, I brush the tangles

out my hair until it's silky and smooth. I need a haircut. It's been a long time since I cut my hair and it hangs almost to my waist. But that will have to wait.

I put on my bikini and pull on a pair of jean shorts and a white tank top. I clean the dried blood from my knife—*I can't believe I freaking stabbed someone with it*—and slide it into its leather holster, which I strap around my waist and tuck under the waistband of my shorts.

By the time I'm dressed I'm hungry again.

At this rate my food supply isn't going to last long at all.

I'm going to need more food.

A lot more food.

But I'm not ready to leave my cave yet.

It's then that I notice the fruit trees. There's a small cluster of them, just as Echo Ramsey described. They're scrubby and windblown in their sheltered cove. They're survivors who shouldn't be up this high but got blown here by a random breeze. Like me.

It's a stretch to call it an orchard, but Echo wasn't wrong. There are a few ripening fruits growing in clusters on several of the small trees.

I walk down to them and pick one. I take a bite and the juice drips down my chin. It's still warm from the sun and is without a doubt the most delicious thing I've ever eaten in my whole damn life. I eat three of them. There are ten left.

Around fifty feet away, there's a picturesque clearing

that's large and flat. I abstractly think about how it would make a nice site to build a house or pitch a tent.

Heading back up to the cave, I unpack the rest of my backpack, neatly placing all my few possessions on the rock shelf. I slide my full water bottle into the side pocket, and pack what's left of my food. And the rope. And an oversized long-sleeve shirt. And my beanie.

Remembering the distant lights I saw through the trees last night, I decide to see if I can find out where they were coming from.

I won't go too close. I'll keep a safe distance.

Making my way along the trail, I carve a groove in a tree. Every ten paces, I carve another one. So I can find my way back.

Good thinking, Cassidy. You're a regular frontierswoman.

Ha.

It's later in the day than I thought it was. Maybe mid to late afternoon.

Climbing up a steep bank, I reach another peak.

Holy shit.

Below me is an even better view.

Not just a view, but a discovery.

The mountain smoothes down to a huge, verdant expanse of rolling hills, sloping all the way down to a distant series of bays, each with its own golden beach. Buildings are dotted along the beaches and among the coves, and the whole area is surrounded by the high stone wall.

This is it.

The Ramsey estate.

27

Cassidy

I FEEL a little guilty for searching out the Ramsey haven like this.

Like I'm a thief or a spy.

But I'm not trespassing. I'm just enjoying the view.

Houses are clustered around the main street of the town.

The largest, highest-placed building is basically a castle, like Maggie's friend described. It's huge with modern touches, built of stone, wood and glass in a variety of architectural styles.

There are pools and a small lake on the western side of the castle, surrounded by palm trees and acres and acres of lush gardens and rambling orchards. Horses, cows and sheep graze in distant fenced pastures. I can see a coffee plantation, rows of pineapple plants, vast areas of organized vegetable gardens, avocado trees, a mango orchard, papayas, apples, fig trees. There's a row of banana trees and a grove of coconut palms, giving the gardens even more of a tropical paradise vibe.

My stomach growls at the sight of so much food.

Whoever described it as a haven wasn't kidding.

It's the Ramseys' own private world of idyllic perfection.

My brain is already formulating a plan.

Don't even think about it.

This section of the wall is around twelve feet high, give or take. What I'm wondering is if it's rigged with an alarm.

I want to find out.

No effing way.

If I trip the alarm, I can run back to the caves. I'll hide or I'll leave. I'll give up on this wild goose chase and I'll head back to civilization, where I belong. Done and dusted.

I could make a ladder.

You don't know how to make a ladder. You're not a freaking carpenter.

I have rope. I could build one. I could disguise myself.

This is a very bad idea.

If the wall isn't wired, I could climb over it. I'll make the ladder light enough to pull over the top so I can climb back out. I'll fill my bag with food in the dead of night. I'll be gone before they even know I've been there. They have tons of food. They'd never even notice it's gone.

You'll get caught.

I'm good at being quiet.

I'm fast.

I'm small. I'm as unthreatening-looking as a person can be.

And I have no other choice.

Of course you have choices. You can go find a job like a normal person would.

What if they're looking for me?

I stabbed *Axel Archer*, the notorious king of Honolulu's underbelly, who most likely has a network across more than just Oahu and who will no doubt be hell-bent on getting his revenge. The kind of revenge I don't even want to think about.

What if they retrace my steps? What if they talk to people and find out where I was working? What if they ask around and find out that I won Ben's ticket? Is that possible?

I don't know.

I think it *is* possible. Dash followed me before. He knew I went surfing every morning. It's not that big of a stretch to imagine he'd dig deeper to try to find out where I've disappeared to. He'll do anything Axel tells him to do. And it's more than likely Axel is on an absolute warpath.

I really, really don't want to be found.

I can either scale this wall and steal myself some food or I'll have to trek back down to the town before I starve. And risk being found once I get there.

Option one sounds a lot more appealing that option two.

If I'm going to be hunted or caught or even killed, I'd rather die right here in these beautiful mountains. At least my bleached bones will have a glorious view.

You're crazy.

Yes. I start looking around for some long, straight, sturdy pieces of wood.

By some miracle, I find some. Two long ones and four shorter pieces. I cut and wind the pieces of rope securely around each piece, tying tight knots until the rungs are in place.

There. I *can* make a ladder.

Testing it for weight-bearing strength, I tie more rope to the weaker areas to make sure it will hold. It's light enough to carry but strong and tall enough to get me over the wall.

Ridiculously pleased with myself, I look around, finding my path. Carrying the ladder, I start making my way down to the wall.

When I reach it, I cautiously prop my ladder against it, waiting for an alarm to go off. Ready to run.

Nothing happens.

So I carefully climb up. My ladder holds.

Even more carefully, I slide my hand over the top of the wall, feeling around to see if I trigger the sensors or radars or whatever.

Nothing happens.

Crazily happy about this, I climb back down, leaving the ladder in place.

My own unlikely portal into the Ramseys' paradise.

Then I make my way back up to the rocks where I can watch the scene until it's time for my raid.

I wait.

I eat some almonds.

I eat *all* the almonds. And the fruit.

I've eaten all my food. And I'm still hungry.

But by morning, if I'm lucky, I'll have as much food as I can carry.

Or you'll be dead.

I remember Maggie's descriptions of the Ramsey brothers.

Remington is huge and built like a fighter.

Wolf is some kind of weapons expert.

Knox is wild and outdoorsy, like a tropical island version of a hot mountain man.

All the Ramsey men are absolutely lethal.

Lethal, if I'm caught.

It's true, I don't love what I've become. Stabbing a man (even though I'm glad I did) and now stealing. But desperate times call for desperate measures. If Blaise or Echo Ramsey were in my shoes, I bet they'd do the exact same thing. Slaying dragons and all that.

It's still better than getting caught by Axel. If I'm still alive, at least I could potentially try to appeal to Blaise or Echo. I know they're caring.

For each other. Not for strangers who steal from them.

I wait, psyching myself up for what I'm about to do.

It's getting dark now and I can hear the faint beat of music playing. A group of people are gathering near the pools. Torches are lit, framing the pool area decoratively as night settles in. More people join the party and I can hear laughter and the clink of glasses.

I watch the moon rise. The stars begin to light up the sky.

In the city, you can't see the stars. Not like this.

Here, the whole sky is lit with them, like pinpricks into a layer beyond the sky that's as bright as the sun. It reminds me of a children's book I read once about how the stars are the memories of all the people who have lived and died. I loved that idea. I remember thinking at the time that some of them must be related to me, even if I never knew them. My biological grandparents might be up there—and my parents, who knows. Aunts and uncles and cousins. Tonight, it makes me feel less alone, like they're cheering me on, guiding me and lighting my way.

The party gets rowdier. People are swimming in the pool.

But after a while, the crowd slowly thins out.

I wait until it's quiet and dark and the only lights are the ones from inside windows.

It's time.

Pulling my oversized black shirt over my tank top, I wind my hair into a loose braid and tuck it under my hat. Checking that my knife is still tucked into its holster under the waistband of my jean shorts, I sling on my backpack.

My guess is that it's around 3 a.m.

I walk down the hill until I reach my ladder. Pulling the balaclava over my face, I adjust it so I can see. Then I climb up, easing myself onto the wall so I'm straddling it. It has a flat ridge along the top. I pull my ladder up. It takes some effort but I'm finally able to prop it against the inside of the wall, making sure it's steady and secure.

And I climb down into the Ramsey estate.

28

KNOX

"Ah, it's so good to be home," Echo sighs, sinking into one of the cushioned loungers by the pool, taking a sip of her glass of wine.

"You were only gone for one night." Wolf climbs out of the pool and shakes his hair over her, sending a spray of water all over her and our cousin Willow, who's sitting next to her.

"Wolf!" Echo squeals. "Can you please not be so juvenile all the time? What the hell?"

Wolf's laugh is infectious and it takes the edge off Echo's annoyance. I can tell she really *is* happy to be home after her night in Waikiki. She's in a good mood. It reminds me that I'll be leaving soon. Possibly to go and live out the rest of my life in the very place she couldn't wait to get away from.

"Nice shiner by the way, Wolf. Knox, can you please do something to tame him? You're the only one who can kick his ass."

"Remy can too." Wolf wraps a towel around his waist. "And occasionally Leo. Knox thinks he's tough but his win today was pure luck."

I give him a shove and he falls back into the pool. The girls scream with laughter. Wolf climbs out of the pool and throws his wet towel at me, spraying water everywhere, which causes more squealing and arguing.

Blaise shows up, along with Leo and Hana. My cousins Hunter and Zane and Zane's wife, Indie, are also there. Until the whole outdoor area is full of people.

There's music playing, alcohol flowing and everyone's having a good time.

I watch them, feeling slightly removed from it all. I'm used to the dread that hangs over my head like a black cloud these days.

Damn this hellish alliance.

If only we weren't shackled by such an outdated, crazy rule. Who would force their own family members into loveless marriages just for the sake of a pact that doesn't do us any good anyway?

Except that it does.

It keeps the wolves at bay. None of us can deny that.

Even me.

I stay for a while and have a few drinks with my family but I feel so fucking restless. My instincts are on overdrive. My fists ache and my senses feel like they've been plugged in to some cosmic current.

It's a strange feeling.

Like something's about to happen. Something that will change my life.

Either that or the ticking time bomb of my countdown is messing with my head.

The night is bright with fire and stars.

I decide I'll stay in my cabin in the orchards tonight. In case my hunch is right. Maybe something more sinister is out there. Maybe a threat is closing in. There's been no sign of anyone breaching our security but some sixth sense makes me want to stay close.

The party winds down and I make my way out to my cabin, which is small and basic and sits at the far corner of the mango orchard. I built it here because this was my favorite spot on the entire ranch when I was a little kid. My earliest memory was right here. Of my mother picking fruit from the trees.

Or maybe I imagined it.

Either way, there's something about the place that feels sort of sacred to me.

The cabin has a skylight that opens so I can lie in bed in the small loft and look up at the stars.

I climb up and lay there for a while, leaving my boots on and the belt I'm wearing with my hunting knife strapped to me. I don't know why.

But I can't sleep.

I can't shake the feeling that there's something or someone ... getting closer.

I manage to drift off for a while.

I'm in Honolulu. I'm at Seven Mile Beach. It looks different than it used to, though. It's smoking. The earth is hot. The pools are steaming. There's a river of lava flowing right past the pool. Perri Fitzpatrick is here. She's crying. She's pleading. But she's not the only one here. A girl, with long white hair, dressed in white, walks through the fire. She becomes one with it but it doesn't burn her. Do you know who I am, she says. Yes, I tell her. I know who she is. She's the Goddess of Fire and she's fucking gorgeous. She's the angel. It's her and I understand now why they would obey her. I'll do anything she asks. She's so beautiful, I'm on fire with it too. It burns me with a white-hot lust I can't control. I need her. I'll die if I can't touch her. Her dress is almost entirely sheer. She smiles at me. She crooks a finger at me. Come here, she says.

I wake with a jolt.

Fuck.

It's still dark. It's a hot night.

I'm covered in sweat. My heart's pounding in my chest.

My cock is rock hard and thickly, painfully hot. I free my cock and grip my full length but it's agonizing. It takes me literally three strokes and I'm coming hard. Hot ropes of cum spurt all over my chest and my stomach. I'm practically panting, catching my breath, waiting to come down from it as the last surges pulse hotly out of me.

Fucking hell.

That was intense.

The hot angel strikes again.

Now if only she was real.

It takes me a few minutes to get a grip.

There's no way I'll be able to get back to sleep, so I

get up and wander down to the lake. Dawn is starting to barely lighten the sky along the eastern ridge. No one else is awake and the trees shield me so strip down and wade into the water. It's the same temperature as the air. I dive under.

It feels good.

It cools me by a few degrees and I wash off the sweat and the cum.

And I feel better. The doom that's been hanging over me feels less oppressive all of a sudden.

I decide to make the most of the day. I've got my investments to check over and a cost benefit analysis case study to finish—one of the last few papers I need to complete for my MBA, which I've been doing online. Enzo King is actually teaching one of the classes after he got roped into a random teaching gig by his overbearing father. Some favor that needed cashing in. Then I'll give Wolf his rematch and maybe we'll go for a hunt.

I'm not dead or married yet. Might as well seize the day.

My dream was a fucking good one.

It's not the first time I've dreamed of her.

I'm walking back up the lake's sandy beach when something catches my eye.

Movement.

Someone's here. A small figure dressed in a long black shirt that's too big. Wearing a mask. Carrying a backpack.

A young teenage boy, maybe. I don't recognize him.

Beyond the kid, a homemade ladder has been propped up against the wall.

And it dawns on me. *He's an intruder.*

After a few seconds of frozen shock at the sight of me, the kid takes off, climbing up the ladder and pulling it up after him.

Yanking on my shorts and my boots, I grab my hunting knife.

And I go after him.

29

Cassidy

Two hours earlier ...

MY FOOT MAKES contact with the ground and I wait there for a few seconds, listening for signs of alarm. Guards or patrols.

What am I even doing right now?

This is crazy. I'm risking my life.

Still, this somehow feels like my safest option.

So I keep going.

I can't see anyone. A few lights are visible in windows of the castle in the distance and in buildings dotted around the landscape, but the night is quiet.

Looking around, I start to get my bearings. I'm on the far side of the lake, near a row of banana trees. I don't waste time. Pulling off a small bunch of almost-ripe bananas, I unpeel one of them, lifting my mask to take a bite. The sweetness of it is indescribable. I devour it and eat several more. I pick four more bunches, putting them into my bag.

Wandering further, I discover a cluster of apple trees. Carefully picking a dozen, I continue filling my bag, eating as I go. I'm so *hungry*. The fruit of these gardens is by far the sweetest I've ever tasted.

There's a vegetable garden next to the apple orchard, full of green beans. I pick handfuls, stuffing them into my bag. Further along, there's a row of avocado trees, laden with ripe fruit.

My bag is getting heavy now.

I'm deep inside the fortress, at the fence line of the mango orchard. I pick one of the fruits, allowing myself a minute to savor the ripe juiciness. I lift my balaclava further up so I can feast on it as I stuff several more of the mangos into my bag, which is now almost full.

Deciding not to push my luck, I begin retracing my steps toward the ladder. I'm surprised to notice the first light of dawn to the east.

I misread the time.

I've taken too long.

Walking more quickly now, I pull my face covering back into place as I hurry along the edge of the lake. My ladder is still propped where I left it.

But a sound makes me turn.

A splash.

I'm shocked to my bones to see someone walking out of the lake only a short distance away from me.

Oh my God.

He's big. Tall. And muscular.

Very muscular.

Like, absolutely cut.

He's not wearing a stitch of clothing.

Holy freakinggggh—

And he's looking right at me.

We both stand there in mute shock for a few seconds. But then he tenses, jolting me into action. I turn and run to my ladder, clambering up as fast as I can go, pulling the ladder roughly up behind me and jumping heavily to the ground on the far side, my bag of food still strapped to my back.

The landing knocks the wind out of me and I gasp for breath.

I leave the ladder where it lays and, even though I'm winded, for the second time this week, I run for my goddamn life.

I know he's coming.

I could see in his eyes that there was no way he wasn't going to chase me.

My legs threaten to buckle as I sprint up the steep slope. My back has gone numb from the weight of my load and my lungs are on fire as I struggle to get further up the hill.

He's following me. I can hear him thrashing through the brush.

He's gaining on me.

I'm getting close to the caves now.

So what? They're no safer than the place you just ran from.

Shit shit shit!

"Hey!" he yells, his voice reaching into my body and grabbing my heart. It's not just the rage in him that terrifies me but also the closeness. He's not far behind me.

I'm near my cave now. I'm almost at the pools.

Reaching the first pool, I stop. Because there's nowhere else to go. I drop my bag behind me and I turn to face him. I'm breathing hard.

He's maybe ten or twelve feet from where I'm standing, shirtless, dressed only in a pair of faded short black shorts that basically leave nothing to the imagination, and untied boots. His thighs are insanely muscular and he has a lot of tattoos on his legs, arms and chest. I can see a dragon, tribal patterns, inked words. In his hand he's holding a very large, very razor-sharp hunting knife that glints in the early morning sun.

He clearly outweighs me by around three to one and he's muscular as all freaking hell.

Help me.

For more than one reason.

He's ridiculously buff, in a way that's not only impressive but also ... I mean, holy hell ... it's downright beautiful. He could be a masterpiece sculpture carved by a genius's knife come to life. Which is a strange thing to be thinking about right now, considering he might be about to kill me.

Adrenaline is coursing through my veins but it's not the only thing coursing through me. I don't even know how to describe it. Fascination. Appreciation. What I'm witnessing here is an absolute specimen of male beauty in the prime of its life.

This isn't the build of Dash or his gym rat friends. This is a man who's ideally made and also toned to perfection by real, outdoorsy exercise. No doubt he's grown up swimming through the glittering ocean waves and hiking in tropical rainforests. Which he has, of course. There's something outrageously *natural* about him. He belongs to this place.

His hair is dark blond, the color of antique gold that catches the golden light of dawn, like the universe wants to show him off. It frames his stunning face in a wavy halo of wild disarray.

I'm not as scared of him as I should be. If anyone is going to do anything to me—even kill me—I want it to be him.

Even though he's a small distance away from me, I can see that his eyes are a vivid shade of blue. His expression is fierce—and fiercely … glorious. There's no other way to describe him. Everything about him is dazzling.

I have a feeling I know who this is.

He's the most gorgeous of all of them.

Knox Ramsey.

30

Cassidy

His masculinity is brutal and seasoned. I can practically feel the rolling waves of testosterone he's emitting as his chest rises and falls heavily from the chase.

I'm dizzy from my fear and from his blazing presence. He's outshining the rising sun.

"Who are you?" he demands. It's a command, that I give him this information.

I don't answer him. I'm still wearing my mask. I have no intention of giving up my identity. He might turn me in to the police. The last place I want to end up is in jail. It's a very easy place to be found.

"Where did you come from?" He takes a step forward. "Are you alone?" His voice is deep and mesmerizing, with a smoky edge. Even through my terror, I can't help thinking it: I like his voice. The husk of it is just as lethally alluring as the rest of him.

But I need to focus. My situation was dire before and

now it's much, much worse. I can't allow myself to be caught.

He takes another step forward.

I think about running but I know he'd catch me easily.

"Answer me," he booms. "Who are you?"

He's closing in on me. I panic, and pull my knife from its holster. If he knows I'm armed, will he let me keep the food instead of fighting me for it? *He* doesn't need it. He's got plenty.

But as soon as I do it, I instantly regret it, of course I do. It's easy enough to see he thinks my small kitchen knife is a joke. I can admit it looks sort of pathetic next to the huge, jagged hunting knife he's gripping in his strong hand. Plus he obviously knows how to use his far better than I do. This fact radiates off his big, sweat-glistening muscles. His stance is wide-legged and aggressive.

How on earth did I get myself into this mess? I'm on top of a mountain challenging a gigantic MMA-trained he-man to a knife fight. What the hell?

"You want to fight me, do you?" There's a note of jeering sarcasm in his question. Justified, possibly.

I don't want to die up here on this mountain, at the hands of this beautiful Ramsey heir. If I die now, I'll never be able to find out the truth about who I am. I'll never be able to build the kind of life I've always imagined I could.

"Show your face," he commands.

Can he be reasoned with? "Please." I try to make my

voice sound gruff, to disguise it. "I won't come back here. Let me go and I promise you'll never see me again."

A small crease quirks between his eyebrows, like he finds my request almost funny. "Take off your mask. You're not going anywhere until I know who I'm dealing with."

Neither of us moves.

"Who sent you?"

"No one sent me. I was hungry, that's all."

Clear confusion is written across his heartbreaking face. There are things about me he can't make sense of. His hair and his eyes are glowing with ferocity. *God, he's so beautiful.* "That's a fair reason, then. Show your face and you can keep the food. Take off your mask."

"I can't."

His mild amusement irks me. "Then I'll take it off for you."

I force myself to hold it together. I'm not prepared for the power of him. The sheer size of him and the violent allure. His chest is broad and muscular, his neck suntanned and corded, pulsing lightly with his heartbeat and a warmth I can practically feel. His tattoos are fascinating me. A dragon. Swirling spirals. The sun. Stars. The eight-pack of his abs are flat and defined. The unholy reveal of the V above his low-slung belt is blowing my mind. My gaze wanders back up to his face, which is sort of killing me. He's everything you wish you could have.

I can't possibly win against this god-like creature. You get the feeling fate wouldn't allow it.

"Here, take your food." I push at the heavy bag with my foot. As hungry as I am, I don't really want to die for ten mangoes and a few bunches of bananas. And I don't want to fight him. His weapon is obviously far more deadly than mine. Even if it wasn't, I wouldn't *want* to hurt him with my own small—but very sharp—knife. Damaging him would feel all wrong, like going against the grain of nature's order. "I won't climb the wall again. I promise. I'll disappear and you can forget you've ever seen me."

After a moment of intense scrutiny, like my disguise is no longer fooling him, he says, "Not a chance in hell. Show your face."

We stand there, knives raised, at an impasse of sorts.

Will he show me mercy? Will he have me arrested? Or will he kill me?

As if in answer, he takes a step closer.

And another.

I'd take a step back but there's nowhere to go. I'm trapped.

My heart is beating like a hummingbird wing.

He's almost close enough to touch me now. And his nearness delivers so much *feeling* I can barely breathe. I don't know how to react. His scent is intoxicating. Warm sun, worn leather, green grass and a woodsy smokiness.

He reaches with his hand, to pull my mask from my head.

I flinch.

What happens next is a blur. He misreads me, maybe, taking my recoil of self-preservation as an attack against him.

He strikes my knife with his knife, as though to knock it from my hand. But my recoil is lightning-fast and my movement repositions my weapon in a way he may not have been expecting. Instead of knocking my knife away, it strikes his, ricocheting at a forceful angle. His knife cuts through my shirt and slices into my upper arm. At the same time, my own knife sinks deep into his side, cutting a neat, long, horrible gash.

We're both surprised. I make a sound, a gasp of shock more than pain.

Correcting his mistake, Knox Ramsey strikes my knife with so much force it sends a jolt through me. My weapon goes flying and I can hear the clacking noise in the distance as it strikes rock near the mouth of the cave, far out of reach.

Stunned and grasping to hold onto consciousness, I fall to my knees as he stands over me. I can feel the warmth of my own blood wetting the sleeve of my shirt. His blood, too, is gushing from the deep slice on his stomach. *So much of it.*

"*Oh no,*" I manage to gasp.

What have I done?

I lay back as the sky spins.

Knox Ramsey kneels over me, peeling my mask up

and tugging off my hat. My hair loosens and spills across the ground.

His jaw drops. Whatever he was expecting, it wasn't this.

"Holy fuck." He stares at me for several long seconds. "You're a girl."

He fingers a lock of my hair, rubbing it between two fingers, as though fascinated by the feel of it, or the color. "Yes," I manage to confirm.

"My God," he gasps. "It's *true*."

I don't know what he means. I'm spinning.

"You can't be real." His expression is full of a strange sort of awe and that, combined with the outrageous magnificence of him, reaches into me, touching me in places I've never been touched before. It's *intense*, and I crave more of this connection with everything I have, despite what's just happened here, or maybe because of it.

"I'm sorry," I tell him.

He sits down next to me, heavily, setting down his knife. His stomach is now covered in blood and it's running freely from his wound. Much too much of it. I've really damaged him and I'm appalled that I could have done this.

"Angel. It's *you*."

What? Is he delirious? "No." *I'm the devil, for bloodying your perfection.*

"You should have *told* me." Like he's frustrated by my oversight. "Why didn't you show me who you were?"

"I ... I don't ..." I don't know what he's talking about. Maybe he's confusing me with someone else.

His hand grips my arm, where my sweatshirt is cut and soaked with blood. "Look what I've done to you. I've *hurt* you."

"I think I've hurt you more. I think you need a doctor." My voice sounds rasped and far away.

"Angel. I'm *sorry*. I'll fix it. I'll take care of you."

He definitely seems delirious.

I don't know if our injuries are life-threatening. Are there important arteries in people's arms? I have no idea. There are definitely important arteries and other necessary things in people's stomachs, though, and it's worrying me. I try to sit up but the world spins violently.

Knox Ramsey kneels next to me. The scent of him, of sun and salt and pure, uncut virility, now mixed with the iron tang of our mixed blood, makes me swoon for more than one reason.

He slides his hands under me and he lifts me. It's so easy for him, like I weigh no more than a child. "You shouldn't," I tell him, but it comes out as hardly more than a whisper. I'm desperately trying not to black out.

He carries me to the cave and lays me on my blanket.

Knox lays next to me. I can feel the heat of his big, buff body. He groans with pain as he reaches to take his phone out of his back pocket. It's one of those newest iPhones that costs the earth. Even his phone is covered in blood. *He's bleeding so much.* He checks the screen. "Fuck. We're out of range."

This is not good.

We lay here, dazed, sort of gazing into each other's eyes. The blue of his irises seems to pour into me, feeding me a comfort the likes of which I have never, ever known. Am I dying? If I am, I'm grateful that I can die in the presence of this beautiful stranger.

"I'm just going to lie here for a second," he says. "Then I'm going to take you home."

Home. I nod. In the swirl of my own dizziness, that sounds like such a good plan.

"I'm Knox." That rasp in his voice is more graveled now. "Knox Ramsey."

"I'm Cassidy." I don't bother with my last name. It's a placeholder. I don't know why but I don't feel like including it now. Not with him.

"The pleasure's all mine, Cassidy."

"I haven't given you pleasure, Knox Ramsey," I whisper back, regretting everything. "Only pain."

"If we live, that's something we'll have to fix."

"Yes," I hear myself say. "It is."

The darkness fringing at the edges of my awareness closes in.

31

Cassidy

My eyes open and it takes me a few seconds to figure out where I am. I'm trapped under a heavy weight, and my arm is throbbing.

I let my eyes adjust to the dimness.

The cave.

The chase.

The fight.

Knox Ramsey.

Oh my God. He's here. The heavy weight is … him. He's lying next to me, almost on top of me, with his big, muscular arm looped around me as though to keep me here.

Am I dreaming?

I watch him for a few seconds, completely mesmerized by how stunning he is. Everything about him is so unapologetically masculine. His square jaw, dusted with diamond-glinting stubble that matches the thick strands of his dark-gold hair. His lips are full and perfectly shaped. I can't help myself. Carefully, I reach out to touch the thick, silky strands of his hair, smoothing them back from his face.

I'm not dreaming.

He's real.

And he's heavy.

I try to move but I can't.

Outside, the sun hangs low in the sky. It's late afternoon, maybe four or five o'clock. We've slept for a long time.

There's a warm, slippery stickiness between us.

Blood.

Shit.

A lot of it.

I need to wake him. We need help.

It crosses my mind that if I go to a doctor or a hospital, I could be found by the people who are probably looking for me. But I can't worry about that right now. The more obvious concern is finding out how badly Knox Ramsey and I have injured each other.

"Knox," I say gently, trying to wake him.

He groans.

"Knox, can you hear me? Open your eyes."

His eyes blink open. His body tenses as he recognizes where we are. And who he's with. He stares at me intently. I'm kind of slayed by the way he looks at me. It's sort of ... adoring. Like he's happy to see me.

"Angel," he rasps in that way he has. Like he can't

believe I'm real. "You're so much more beautiful than I ever imagined."

He's very out of it. He's lost a lot more blood than I have. It's all over both of us. *God.* "You're going to be fine, Knox. Can you move?"

He stares at me dreamily. "Kiss me, angel. I want to feel you."

"I'm not an angel, Knox. You're alive. My name is Cassidy, remember? I'm going to take care of you. Everything's going to be okay."

"Cassidy," he murmurs. "I want to taste you. I've dreamed about you so many times. I just never imagined I'd actually *find* you."

I don't know if Knox will be able to make it down the hill in the state he's in. I don't know if I will either. But I need to try to get help for him. Once they find out what I've done, chances are his family will either lock me up or make me leave. We might only have this moment. And I have the urge to give Knox Ramsey whatever he wants.

I've never kissed anyone. Not even once. Not a single person.

I never had parents or loved ones. I've never bonded with anyone who cared for me enough to give them this part of myself. But now, with this dazzling stranger, I want to know what it feels like.

There are tears in my eyes as I do it. "I'm so sorry I hurt you. I should never have come here."

"Don't say that. I *need* you here. Don't you fucking leave me."

I'm a little surprised by his intensity. "I'm not going to leave you." I want to comfort him and heal him. Maybe I can, just a little, like this.

Very lightly, I touch my lips to his mouth. It's a soft, heartfelt kiss I can feel all the way to my soul. Which sounds strange but I absolutely can. I'm already connected to this stranger in ways that are more profound than I know what to do with. I want to touch him and know him. I want to give him everything he wants.

I mean the kiss to be brief and comforting, lightly curious. But the feel of his mouth against mine and the warmth of his breath on my face holds me there. I kiss him again, savoring the soft contact and the drugging taste of Knox Ramsey's perfect lips.

God, he's so beautiful.

He makes a sound that's half growl, half sigh. His strong hand slides to the nape of my neck to hold me in place. His grip reminds of how big and powerful he actually is. I feel the touch of his tongue. He licks into my mouth and it shocks me, this intimate fever, but the taste of him is already my new favorite flavor. I want more. He plays my tongue with his and I gently suck, drawing him deeper. He makes a low sound and moves as though to lift himself further over me. But then he groans with pain and lays back, his grip falling away. He goes still.

He's lost consciousness again. Tears sting my eyes because I need him to be okay.

I'm woozy as hell. But I'm able to lift myself enough, wincing at the searing pain in my arm. We're both covered in blood. It's hard to tell where his ends and mine begins.

I check Knox's wound, and—*holy hell*—it's bad. He's still bleeding.

Don't you dare die on me, Knox Ramsey.

32

Cassidy

I NEED to try to slow down the bleeding.

His wound runs in a diagonal line below his rib cage along his left side. It's deep but the edges are cleanly sliced.

I remember that I have a needle and thread in my sewing kit.

It's something I'm good at. Redesigning my second-hand clothes into things I actually don't mind wearing.

I need to do what I can to clean and protect his wound before I go for help.

Can I make it that far? Will they kill me when I get there?

I try not to think about that. First things first.

With effort, I peel off my shirt. The torn arm of it is completely saturated with my blood, and the front of it is wet with Knox's blood.

My cut runs the length of my upper arm. It's deep and jagged and painful. But it'll have to wait.

I manage to get to my feet but I'm unsteady. Once my dizziness passes enough for me to stand, I go outside and find my bag. My water bottle is strapped to the side of it. I pick up Knox's hunting knife. And I grab the clean, dry sweatshirt that's laid out on the rock where I left it after I washed it. Back in the cave, I get the sewing kit that's sitting on the rock shelf, along with the small bottle of whiskey.

Knox is still unconscious. Which is good because this will hurt. I cut my sweatshirt into long strips. Using the water from my bottle and the scraps of cloth, I clean the blood from his body.

His chest is powerfully built, the muscles sculpted and sun-bronzed. His stomach is flat and quilted with the defined ridges of his eight-pack and the ridged V that frames his lean hips. The saturated waistband of his shorts is slung low, revealing an arrow line of dark hair. He has a few scars. Small lines of paleness against the cinnamon of his suntanned skin.

I clean as much of the blood from him as I can.

Then, carefully, I sew his wound, pulling the edges neatly together. I pour small amounts of the whiskey along the length of the wound to do my best to disinfect it until he can be seen by a doctor.

The whole process is strangely exhausting.

I wish I could rewind time.

I wish I could heal him.

But I can't. I'm going to need to go to his family, no matter what it costs me.

After I've finished stitching him and doing my best to clean him, I lay a length of the cloth over his injury to protect it. I'd bandage him but he's too heavy to lift.

I've been so immersed in attending to Knox that I forgot about my own injury. But the pain flares now. My body feels unusually warm, almost tingly in places.

"I'm going to the pool," I tell him softly, even though he's still out. "I'll be back soon."

I go down to the water and strip down to my bikini. I lower myself in, quickly washing the dirt and the blood from my body. The water stings then cools the flaring pain in my arm.

I fill the water bottle with fresh water from the spring to take to Knox.

He's still asleep.

Then I stitch my own wound. It's so painful the tears blur my vision. I swipe them away to sew the final few stitches.

I'll carry his scar for the rest of my life. The mark of Knox Ramsey.

Like my other mark.

I concentrate on pouring a cap-full of whiskey and pouring it over my cut. The pain is so intense I almost faint again. But after a few minutes, the worst of the nausea and dizziness passes.

Checking Knox's wound again, I can see that the bleeding hasn't completely stopped but it has slowed.

I wrap the last remaining piece of my sweatshirt around my stitched arm, tucking it into place.

"Knox," I whisper close to his ear. "Wake up. Drink some water."

He groans and his eyes open.

"Here. Drink this. It's cold and fresh." I cradle his head in my lap and hold the water bottle to his dry lips.

He drinks some of it. I give him some whiskey too, hoping it might numb his pain. And a little more. I take a sip for myself. Then I set the bottle aside and I smooth a strand of his golden hair back from his face.

The expression in his eyes as he watches me is unfathomable. There's fierceness there, and something more. His fingers weave through the end locks of my hair. "Forgive me, angel. Please forgive me. I want to marry *you* instead."

He's very out of it.

I'm still cradling his head in my lap. The rough skin of his cheek barely touches the pillowy curve of my breast. I blush at the contact through the thin layer of my wet bikini, which is all I'm wearing. His breath becomes heavier and I can feel the hot strikes on my sensitive skin. Where his heat warms me, sensation gathers and pools, spreading and deepening in the low pit of my stomach.

Knox's rough fingers rove along my skin, pulling the fabric of my bikini top down, until my breasts are fully revealed to him.

I wasn't expecting it. It's so outrageously intimate. But I don't stop him. I don't want to. I *should* want to. We're strangers. But he doesn't feel like a stranger. He feels like … mine.

My breasts feel full and heavy. My nipples, so close to his mouth, bud into tight peaks.

The black pupils of his eyes have grown, almost swallowing the outer blue edge of his irises. This sudden darkening makes him appear all the more dangerous.

"You're so fucking *beautiful*," he says.

He weaves his fingers through my hair, holding me in place. His warm breath against the taut peaks of my nipples lights little fires along my bloodstream.

The sensation is insanely intoxicating. I'm dazed by everything that's happened, and that's happening now. Here I am, a runaway and a thief. In the past few days, I've stabbed two men, stolen as much food as I could carry and now find myself trapped with a very-muscular, possibly-dangerous Ramsey fighter who's just as likely to kill me as to save me. But the danger of him feels *good*. More than good. It feels like the most important thing that's ever happened to me.

"Feed me your beauty, angel." His voice is husky and deep.

Is it because our blood has mingled that I feel so connected to him already? I don't know. All I do know is that I don't want to refuse him anything. I can't. He feels too good. I lean closer, offering my nipple to his perfect mouth.

His mouth closes over the tight bud. I gasp as his tongue touches me. He pulls my nipple further into the hot velvet of his mouth, licking his tongue against the underside of the tip, biting gently with his teeth. The soft, scalding pressure funnels into my body, between my legs, where I get wet and swollen.

I moan as he moves to reach for my other breast. He holds the full weight with his large, rough hand, sending sparking pleasure through my body with the pinching, circling pressure of his fingers.

It stuns me, my reaction to him. I want him to do what he's doing. So much. He growls, gripping me, sucking my nipple deeper into his mouth. With no barriers between my skin and the slippery play of his tongue, the cravings of my body gain momentum. I've never felt so *alive* or so hungry to get closer. The pulsing ache in my breasts as he teases me with his teeth and his mouth swells and compounds to touch my heart, my soul and the soft, slippery place between my legs, over-whelming me.

As Knox's mouth feeds, a warm rush starts low in my belly, spreading in a hot wave of pleasure, which rises to an impossible peak, then shatters into an ecstatic over-load. My pussy clenches tightly, over and over, and I sob his name. All I can feel is the pull of his mouth and the soft, clenching core of my body.

How can he feel so good? Why is he the most beautiful thing that's ever happened to me by a magnitude of ten million?

I hold his head, stroking his hair, offering myself to him as he feasts on me, like I'm feeding him some kind of spiritual nourishment.

"You're a dream," he murmurs, "but I *feel* you. I've never felt so much. Do you feel me, angel?"

"I feel you, Knox. I feel all of you. Everywhere."

"Who knew death would be this beautiful?"

"You're not dying, Knox. You're alive. You're going to be fine." But the slur to his words worries me. His delirium is getting worse. His groans are double-edged. He needs to be careful not to rip his stitches, and the way his arm has looped itself around my waist is threatening to break their hold.

He's drifting again. His eyes close.

I put my hand to his forehead. He's hot. Maybe feverish. I know that the severity of his injury is the only reason I'm able to loosen his grip.

I'm struck again by the savage beauty of him. The sculpted brawn of his broad chest and the perfection of his big, muscular body.

Damaged now.

By me.

I know what I need to do.

I'm surprisingly unafraid. My new, wildly connective bond with Knox Ramsey has made me feel … not stronger, but strong in a different way. He's in me now. I can feel him. Like I've absorbed some of his life-force and it's coursing through my veins along with my own.

And I'm still rippling with the pleasure he gives.

I set some of the fruit, the water and the whiskey within his easy reach.

I lean close to his ear and whisper, "I'm going to go get help for you, Knox." I don't say *I'll do whatever I have to, to be with you again.* Or *I wish I could stay in this cave with you forever*. I guess it says a lot about my life when almost killing each other is the most beautiful thing that's ever happened to me. But it is.

Then I kiss his lips softly.

And I leave him.

Pulling my bikini top up, I find a the only clean piece of clothing I have left. A white cotton sundress I made myself out of a lace-trimmed tablecloth I paid three dollars for at a thrift store a few years ago. I liked the softness of the cotton. It's old and worn and a size too small for me now, but it's clean enough. It'll have to do. I try to smooth my hair with my fingers. I lace up my old black Converse high-tops. I grab a mango to eat on the way.

And I start making my way down to the walls of the Ramsey fortress.

33

Cassidy

My ladder is still there on the ground where I left it when I ran from him.

Propping it up, I climb to the top and pull it over, making my way down to the interior. I can see a small crowd of people in the distance, near the castle.

There are people getting into big, four-wheel-drive type vehicles, revving motorcycles and even a few people on horseback. A nearby helicopter's propellor is starting up. Like they're putting a search party together.

My heart is beating fast.

They'll listen to what I have to say, I know that much. They'll be searching for Knox. They'll be grateful for the information I'm about to give them.

But what happens then?

I don't know. If Knox dies or if I can't somehow stay with him, I don't know what I'll do. I don't want to analyze how tightly bound I already feel to Knox Ramsey.

Right now all I need to do is make sure he lives. I'll have to figure the rest out later.

When he's healed, will he be angry? Will he remember me?

I think about his kiss. His mouth on me. The fresh memory brings heat to my face. *The way he feasted on my breasts like I was feeding him. God. His mouth was so hungry. It was so unexpected. So mind-blowingly intimate. He felt so amazingly good.*

As I pass through the orchards, two young boys run over to me. They stare at me in a way I'm starting to get used to. With a shocked fascination. Like I'm a ghost or a vision.

"Are you the Goddess of Fire?" one of them asks me as they trot alongside me. The other one says, "She's the angel!"

First Knox and now these children? "I'm not an angel. *Or* the goddess of fire. My name is Cassidy."

"What are you doing here?"

But we're approaching the castle now and the group of people busy getting their rides ready all stop what they're doing to stare at me.

I'm a stranger. I'm trespassing. These details clearly register on their faces. They're confused about how I could possibly have gotten inside their walls. They're wary about possible danger. They're wildly curious. And they're wondering if I'm ... *the Goddess of Fire?* Whatever they've mistaken me for, I'm ruffling people. I fit a description that means something to them.

Two men walk over to me, with that same wary, spell-bound disbelief.

"Knox is injured," I tell them. "He needs help."

This gets their immediate attention. "Follow me," says the taller one. I wonder if he might be Knox's cousin. I can see the family resemblance. His hair is sandy blond, not as vibrantly gold as Knox's. His eyes aren't as blue.

Please be okay. I'm sorry.

I'm led along a wide path toward the castle. As we get closer, I'm in awe the grandness of the building.

What would it be like to live in a place like this? You must wake up every morning feeling like the luckiest person on earth.

One of the men, the darker-haired one, is talking on his phone as we walk.

"Remy, it's Nero. Yeah. We have a girl here who's breached the wall. She says she knows where Knox is. He's injured … I don't know. We're bringing her in. She's bleeding."

Am I?

I glance down at my arm. My makeshift bandage is soaked through with fresh blood.

The front doors are open by the time we reach them and I'm led into a huge entrance hall. Because the place looks like a castle from the outside, I might have expected dark, medieval-inspired interiors but, inside, it's surprisingly light and modern-looking. There are enormous paintings on the walls, palm trees in large pots, light-wood furniture and four massive leather couches circled around a glass coffee table. The stone floor is covered with giant Persian rugs. Through arched doorways, I can see tantalizing glimpses into other to-die-for rooms.

I've never seen such a beautifully designed, opulent space in my life. Still, it's the last place I want to be.

Has he woken up yet? Is he still bleeding?

I wish I was with him now.

But I'm the one who struck him down, of course. And when his family hears about that, there's no telling how they'll react.

There's a commotion as a group of people pours into the hall, led by a huge, striking man I can guess must be Knox's oldest brother, Remington Ramsey. His hair is darker than Knox's and his eyes are a distinct shade of lightning-bright gray.

At his side stands another brother. Wolf, I'm guessing. He's tall, slimmer than Remington but still outrageously muscular and athletic-looking. Wolf's hair has that same golden tint as Knox's but it's darker. His eyes are a bright, light blue, the color of glacial ice. My first impression of him is that he's aggressive and reckless. This effect is only magnified by the arsenal strapped to his body. Several belts are strung across his bare chest with knives hanging from them, along with pouches and pockets holding other sharp, lethal-looking objects.

Two young women rush through a nearby door.

It's Echo. And Blaise.

"*Oh,*" breathes Blaise.

All four of them are staring at me like ... well, like

everyone has since I arrived on Kauai. Since I stopped disguising myself and covering or tying up my hair.

I imagine how I must look to them. My hair is wild and windblown. My dress is worn and a size too small. My skin is covered in scratches. The bandage on my arm is soaked with fresh blood that's now dripping down my arm.

The Ramseys are all speechless for a few seconds. There's an intimidating hostility to both Remington and Wolf, but I get the feeling they don't want to offend me— or whoever they think I am.

"I'm Remington Ramsey. What's your name?"

"Cassidy Kelley."

They process this for a split second. "You know where Knox is."

"Yes. He's in the caves. The ones in the idyllic hilltop wonderland near the twin pools and the self-seeded orchard."

It sounds strange describing it like that now. Both Echo and Blaise stare at me with an edge of disbelief that borders on alarm. Because it's exactly how Echo described it.

Maybe it's the blood. The fear. The exhaustion. The lack of food. Everything feels dream-like and other-worldly, as though I'm watching the scene from some-where outside my own body. I've left a part of myself back in that cave and I'm unsteady on my feet. I force myself to stay strong. "He's wounded. He's unconscious and he needs a doctor."

Remington Ramsey reacts instantly, barking orders at some of the people gathered around us. "We'll take the helicopter," he says to them. "Get Hana. We'll have to find a place near the cave to land."

"There's a flat clearing that's probably big enough," I say. "Just below the orchard."

Remington stares down at me, his expression half enraged, half crazed with worry. Even so, he's got a steadying presence. You get the feeling that, as long as he's in charge, you'll get the best possible outcome.

Wolf, on the other hand, has a ferocity to him that makes me uneasy.

"You'll come with us," Remington tells me.

I nod, quietly elated that he'll allow this.

Thank you thank you thank you.

They're not going to cast me out.

I get to see him again.

My Knox. He's mine. I want to keep him.

34

____

Cassidy

I'm led outside and across the lawn to where a few other people are climbing into the helicopter.

I'm helped into it and strapped into one of the seats as the door is pulled closed and we take off.

Wow.

It's sort of terrifying but also amazing. We can see the entire estate from up here.

I feel a tug on my arm.

The woman sitting next to me is holding a large leather bag on her lap. She's unwinding my bandage. "I'm Hana. I'm a doctor." She's pretty, maybe in her late twenties or early thirties. "I can take a good look at this when we get back but for now I can at least put a clean bandage on it."

"Thank you. I'm Cassidy."

She sets the saturated bandage aside and starts wrapping my arm with a fresh one. "You stitched this?"

"Yes. It hurt."

She smiles. "I bet."

We're landing now in the clearing.

Remington and Wolf jump out as soon as we touch the ground. Hana and the others follow.

I'm struggling to keep up. These people are strong, well-rested and fit. They've obviously spent their lives being well fed copious amounts of nutritious food. I, on the other hand, haven't. I'm hungry, tired and weak. My arm is agonizing. And I'm still tangled up by having my world rocked by the most intense experience of my life.

Knox Ramsey.

I feel like an invisible rope is tied to him and looped around my heart. It's his pull that's guiding me along the trail more insistently than my own strength. *He's* the reason I keep walking. I want to get back to him in case he needs me.

He doesn't need you, I remind myself. I'm the intruder. The thief. The reason Knox is injured in the first place.

I trip, scraping my knee on a rock.

I hate that my eyes are leaking again. Everything hurts.

Climbing to my feet, I reach the entrance of the cave where Remington, Wolf, Hana and a few others are gathered around Knox. He's still either asleep or unconscious.

"Knox," says Remington, touching his hand to Knox's forehead. He glances at Hana. "He's burning."

Remington lifts the makeshift bandage I laid over Knox's wound. He and Wolf both exhale a low oath.

Hana kneels next to Knox. "Did you stitch this, Cassidy?"

"Yes. It was bleeding so much."

"Who fucking *stabbed* him?" Wolf asks, and I'm grateful Knox chooses that exact moment to show signs of life. He groans and stirs.

"Angel," Knox slurs, his eyes still closed. "Come back to me."

"Let's get him onto the stretcher," says Remington.

"*Angel,*" Knox groans again, louder this time. There's a frenzied edge to his husky voice. He thrashes and growls in pain as he does this. "I need you."

Remington's gaze slides to me. He nods his head toward Knox in a curt, commanding gesture. I'm being given permission—or ordered—to go to him. I crawl over to Knox. I touch my hand to his shoulder. His skin is on fire. "I'm here, Knox."

Knox's eyes open, and he blinks several times. He reaches for me, sliding his hand around the back of my neck. "Don't do that to me. Fuck. I thought I'd dreamed you. Kiss me again, angel."

"Your brothers are here," I tell him. "They're taking you home."

"Stay with me. Stay."

Will they allow it? Do I even want to go with them? Should I try to run?

I know I won't run.

They would easily catch me, if they wanted to.

And I'm not leaving Knox. He's doing that *thing* he

does, where he warms me with his magnetic energy, as though there's an invisible link between us that's alive and charged with something necessary. I'm so strongly drawn to this bloodied Ramsey brother, I can hardly breathe.

Remington is watching Knox. And me.

Knox's hand strokes my hair. "Beautiful, magical girl. Feed me again with your beauty."

"He's delirious as fuck," Wolf mutters.

"Don't you let her out of your sight, Remy," Knox yells feverishly. "She's *mine*."

Remy doesn't look at all pleased about any of this. "Let's go," he says.

35

Cassidy

I open my eyes.

Vague recollections come to me. Of doctors standing over me. Peeling off my bandage and sliding a needle into my arm, which hurt like hell. After that, I remember nothing.

I'm in a dark room.

Where is he?

Is he okay?

Will he remember me?

I'm in a huge bed. The most lavish, comfortable bed I've ever slept in, in fact. The sheets are white and soft and there's a pillowy comforter pulled up to my chin.

I sit up a little, letting my equilibrium settle more or less into place.

The curtains have been pulled closed and at their very edges, light seeps in.

I'm dressed in a short white babydoll-style nightgown with lacy trim, made of the softest cotton. And matching panties.

Wow.

On the bedside table there's a glass of water. I take a long sip and end up drinking the whole thing.

Checking my injury, I can see that it's been cleaned and bandaged. Properly, this time. Gingerly touching my fingers to my arm, it feels better. Not as sore and inflamed as it was on the trail.

I pull the comforter back and slide off the high bed. Opening the curtain a crack, I see it's daytime. I feel like I've been asleep for a long time. I'm several floors up. From the high-up vantage point and the pool area down below, I must be inside the castle.

The view is insane. The orchards and farmland slope down to the ocean. Dramatic clouds billow over the expanse of blue water in the distance. And the room, now that I can see it better, is beyond luxurious. The carpet is thick and soft, the furniture modern and expensive-looking. An open door leads into its own little bathroom. I walk into it, flicking on the light. The walls are marble tiles. There are shiny chrome fixtures and an enormous walk-in shower that looks like a car wash.

I stare at myself in the mirror for a few seconds. My hair is mussed from sleep, but someone must have washed it while I was sedated. I'm no longer covered in blood and dirt.

My blood. *His blood.* Its absence and *his* absence is making me feel panicky and strange.

Which is crazy. But at the same time the intensity of it is sort of killing me. I'm feeling it so hard.

We fought. We came very close to killing each other. Then we shared a moment, because we both thought we might die. Even though it was by far the most important moment of my life so far, it hardly means we're ... *together* in any way. We're strangers. Almost-strangers.

But that's not how it feels. Not at all. It feels like I've been marked by him and touched by him. Deeply and irrevocably. I'm his: this fact feels scarily real and there's not a damn thing I can do to talk myself out of that. I want him.

Will they let me see him again? Has he told them I'm the one who hurt him? What are they planning to do with me?

In the mirror, my eyes look spooked and wild. It's strange, but I haven't spent a lot of time in my life looking in the mirror. Mainly, I've tried to hide myself, and shield myself, because attention was always the very last thing I wanted. Living the way I have, it only brought me trouble.

But I study my reflection now. There's a row of bright, flattering lights above the mirror and I can see myself maybe more clearly than I ever have. My eyes are a very dark shade of brown. I have long, dark eyelashes and dark blond eyebrows. My skin is olive and tans easily. My hair is long and straight, naturally white-blond with honey-colored streaks. People have often commented about how the dark color of my eyes clashes with the light color of my hair. It's memorable, Crew once told me.

Most people can look in the mirror and see family resemblances to the people they love. Like Knox and Wolf and Remington can. Definitely like Blaise and Echo can.

It makes me wonder if I'll ever find out who *I* look like.

Most likely not.

And today's not the day to worry about it.

I need to find Knox.

I need to see him. They have to let me.

They don't have to do anything of the kind, actually.

More likely they're about to throw me in jail or kick me back out onto the road to thumb a ride to the next town.

There's a toothbrush still in its wrapper and a tube of toothpaste. I quickly brush my teeth. Then I splash my face with some cold water and smooth my hair as best I can.

Walking back into the bedroom, I notice my dirty, blood-stained white dress is draped over a chair.

I practically jump out of my skin when there's a sudden knock on the door. The door opens.

Echo Ramsey walks into the room. Behind her, I can see Remington and Wolf standing outside the door. From the look of them, it's clear the men are waiting for me but maybe have made a concession to not storm into my bedroom—at least for now.

I'm fascinated, like I was on the plane, by Echo's vibrant, willowy presence. She's absolutely gorgeous, in an off-hand, natural way. She's tomboyish and slim but easily one of the most beautiful people I've ever met.

"Sorry about the intrusion," she says to me. "It's been hell getting them to wait, but I told them you needed to sleep before they interrogated you. You must be Cassidy. I'm Echo, by the way."

"Is Knox okay? Please tell me he's okay."

"He's going to be fine. There was some pretty extensive internal bleeding but none of his vital organs were damaged, luckily. He's as strong as an ox and already giving them hell. The doctors said he needs bed rest—and good luck with that, I said—but he's going to make a full recovery."

The relief is indescribable. I have to stop myself from falling to my knees and sobbing with the overload.

"How are you feeling?" she asks. "You were so tired."

"Better now. Thank you."

"You've both been asleep for two days."

"Two *days*?"

She's carrying some clothes, which she lays onto the bed. "I brought you a few things to wear, since your dress is ... ruined." That's a nice way of putting it. *Old. Threadbare. Too small. Covered in blood.* "Are you willing to talk to my brothers? They're very ... insistent. Patience isn't something that comes naturally to them."

Am I willing? I didn't expect to have much of a choice, but I'll do whatever they ask. I just want to see Knox. "Of course."

"I'll give you a minute to change. Then we can meet out in the living room when you're ready."

"Okay. I won't be long. Thank you, Echo."

She leaves me to it and I pick up one of the dresses she's brought for me. It's a pink mini-length silk tunic that's beautifully cut. I slip off my nightgown. Echo overlooked a bra, so I pull the dress on without one. It hardly matters. The dress fits me, if just a little bit loosely. It's casual but, even so, it's the most beautiful piece of clothing I've ever worn.

It seems a shame to ruin the look with my old, worn-out dirty black high-tops, so I leave them off.

I open the door and walk into the expansive living area of the plush apartment. There's a wall of windows showcasing the over-the-top view. An open-plan, state-of-the-art kitchen looks like it's hardly ever been used. Several hallways lead out of the room and there are a few closed doors.

All four of them are here.

Remington is standing by the window. Wolf is leaning his shoulder against a wall. He's wearing his usual criss-crossing belts across his chest and, while he waits, he's sharpening a knife with a stone.

Both men are huge and they look out of place, too roughed-up and outdoorsy for this plush room.

Wolf glances up from his knife-sharpening as I walk

in. "She wakes," he comments, like my sleep has somehow been a luxury they've generously allowed me. His size and his fierceness are the first things I noticed about him, but there's a mischievousness to him that sits just under the surface. It's a playfulness with an edge, though, like a cat who teases its prey before killing it.

36

Cassidy

BLAISE IS SITTING on a bar stool at the huge central island between the kitchen and living area with a laptop. As I walk in, she closes it.

Remington makes the stilted introductions. "Cassidy, this is Blaise, you've met Wolf. And Echo."

Echo is sitting on the couch, scrolling on her phone.

"Is Knox here?" I can't help myself. I resist an urge to grab the front of Remington's shirt pleadingly.

Remington frowns at my question. "He's still sedated. He gets agitated whenever he comes to and they don't want him to rip his stitches or injure himself further."

Because he wants to see me.

I don't know how I know this but I do. From the expressions on their faces, they know it too.

"I have a lot of questions," Remington says. "But first, I want to thank you for coming to us. And for not leaving Knox to die."

"I would never have done that."

"Even so, we're grateful that you came to us when you did. But tell me this: what you were doing in the caves in the first place? Who are you, where are you from and why are you here?"

Where to start?

I decide to just be straight up with them. I get the feeling Remington Ramsey values honesty above almost anything else. And I need as much of his mercy as I can get. A lot of the decisions about my fate are in his hands. So I tell it like it is. "I'm from Honolulu. Near the canal. I've lived there my whole life. I won a plane ticket to Kauai in a poker game and I was on the run so I used it. I arrived here a few days ago. I had nowhere to go and no money so I climbed up to the caves. From there, I could see your orchards. I didn't have much food and I was, like ... starving. So I climbed the wall. I stole some fruit. I'm sorry about that. Knox saw me and he chased me back to the caves. That's when we fought."

"So it was you who stabbed him."

I take a deep breath. I don't want to make them mad, and this will. "I was wearing a mask over my head. He wanted me to take it off. I refused. He tried to remove it and I ... reacted."

"By nearly gutting him," Wolf comments, not without anger.

"We struck at the same time. I didn't mean to hurt him. I don't think either of us meant to do what we did."

Wolf's aggression has shifted gears. There's none of

that mischief in it now. "If Knox *meant* to seriously injure you, you wouldn't be standing here right now."

"I know," I say simply. That's kind of obvious.

Remy is pacing slowly in front of the wall of windows but it's Blaise who asks, "You say you were on the run. From who?"

"From ... my landlord."

"Why? Who's your landlord?"

"His name is Axel Archer."

At the name, all the Ramseys react. They clearly not only know who Axel Archer is, but they see him as a threat. Maybe *the* threat. They tense and I can see rage in Remington and Wolf's expressions. In Echo's, it's something closer to fear.

I guess it makes sense. Arrow is a crime ring. The whole reason to *be* a crime ring would be to try to steal, cheat or bribe your way into the kind of lifestyle and wealth the Ramseys have. Maybe they're one of Arrow's targets. The reactions in this room makes it clear that it's a real possibility.

Because, clearly, there are threats. The walls and the security and the weapons make that more than obvious.

"Are you an Arrow recruit?" Remy asks darkly. "Is that why you're here?"

Wolf's hand moves to the gun that's holstered to the belt around his waist. Where it rests.

"*No.* I'd never even met him before. I got back late, after the poker game. They were there. I was trying to get away from them. I was leaving. But Dash——my neighbor

—had a key. And I realized then that he's a recruit. I saw that he had the same tattoo, of a bloody arrow, that Axel has. He gave Axel the key to my apartment and that's when Axel ... he came in. Before I could get out. He wanted to make me an offer. He said he would pay me to join them but I told him no. He was trying to ..." It's hard to say the words. But they're all waiting for me to continue. "He tried to force me to accept his offer." I hear the catch in my throat at the memory and my eyes are tearing up—*damn it*—but I keep going. "So I stabbed him. In the stomach. Deep. He wasn't expecting it. That's how I got away from him." *If I hadn't had my knife ...*

But I don't bother spelling that detail out.

After several long seconds of intensity, Wolf laughs. "Shit. The angel has claws. Two in one week. Any others we need to know about?"

I brush my tears away impatiently. "Why does everyone keep calling me an angel?"

"We'll get to that later," Remy says gruffly. "Does Axel know where you are? Does he know where you've run to?"

"I don't think so. I threw my phone into a ditch and I destroyed my money card before I got to the airport so they couldn't trace them. The name on the plane ticket wasn't mine and the lady didn't record my real name." Or, as real as my name gets.

"Good girl," Wolf murmurs.

This detail is important to them. Blaise adds, "So

there's no way they could know that you're here in Paradise."

"I don't think so."

"How did you know about the caves?" Remington insists. "Did you come here with the intention to breach our walls? Were you seeking us out?"

"No. I ..." I hate myself now for doing it and I can only imagine how they see me. But, still, I can't quite bring myself to regret any of it. And I'm not going to lie to these people. I already have too much respect and awe for them. I wish I was one of them. I want them to be able to trust me. So I give them the truth. "I overheard Echo and Blaise describing the caves and the pools. And the orchard on the mountain. I was on the same flight."

Echo's watching me.

"I'm sorry," I tell her. "I overheard you talking to Blaise. And I had nowhere else to go. I wanted to see what an idyllic hilltop wonderland looks like because I've never seen one before. I was thinking I could hide out there for a few days before hitchhiking to Princeville and finding a job."

Wolf's hand is still resting on his gun, I can't help but notice. "I bet you wouldn't have any trouble getting a ride."

I'm not sure if that's a compliment or not.

"Go on," says Remy.

"But then, from up there, I could see your gardens. Everything was just so incredibly beautiful. There was so much food and I ... I thought I might be able to take some and you wouldn't even notice. Because there was so much."

"Where's your family?" asks Remy pointedly. "Do they know you're here?"

"I don't have one."

"What do you mean you don't have one?" Wolf drawls.

"I'm an orphan. I was abandoned by my mother when I was only a few months old. I don't even know my real last name."

"Really?" There's pity in Wolf's question, like he considers this a great loss.

I've told these Ramsey siblings more about myself and my life than I've ever told anyone. For a second, I have a weird urge to show them my tattoo. My darkest secret. I don't know why, but I get the feeling they would know what it means. They would have knowledge about the entrenched histories of these islands, the secret societies, the family crests and so on. They'd have reasons to learn about things like that.

But I can't bring myself to do it. What if the mark is the symbol of something bad, like I've so often feared? What if it means I *am* part of Arrow, somehow tied to it through my mysterious bloodline or my unknowable past? Or something worse?

A loud thumping noise interrupts us.

A bang from behind one of the closed doors.

A crash.

A groan.

Something smashes.

"*Angel.*"

Knox.

He's looking for me. He's calling to me.

"Shit, he's awake," Blaise says.

More banging noises and a growl of pain.

Louder this time: "*ANGEL!*"

The door swings open, slamming against the wall from the force of it.

Knox is standing there, like a big, muscular golden bear. His dark blond hair is a glorious mess.

I gasp lightly. Because I can't help it.

I'd almost forgotten how ridiculously beautiful and *built* he is. My reaction to him isn't something I can control. His pull is like that of a supercharged magnet.

I have this crazily strong craving to touch him. To lick his skin and taste his mouth. *To offer myself to him like I did in the cave.*

His blue eyes blaze as he sees me. I can tell by the starry look in them that he's still medicated. Like in a three-sheets-to-the-wind kind of way. All he's wearing is a pair of boxers. The bandage wrapped around his stomach is stained with a dark line of fresh blood. A tube is hanging out of his arm, which he notices and yanks out.

"*Knox,*" Echo scolds him. Because that would have hurt.

Before I can even react to him, he closes the distance between us and I'm surrounded by an all-encompassing clinch against his big, fiery body. He buries his face into my hair, weaving his fingers through it almost painfully, inhaling deeply, holding me close as though trying to pull me into himself. He's so much bigger than me it's like being wrapped in his hard warmth. "Thank *God*. You're here. Do you know how long I've been *searching* for you? I fucking *need* you, angel."

I don't know what's happening. Or why. Or how I could possibly find the words he just spoke—and everything that came before them—enough to fall sort of cataclysmically in love with Knox Ramsey.

I know he's delirious. I know once all the drugs wear off and he's back to full health he'll probably wonder who the hell I am.

Still.

No one's ever needed me before.

37

KNOX

I HALF-SIGH and half-growl into her hair, breathing lungfuls of her scent. Because she smells so fucking good. "My angel girl."

I gaze down at her and my brain sort of short circuits because she's here and she's *real*. Her hair is white-gold and her eyes are full of sparks—just like the legend says.

I can *feel* the burn of it. I'm on fire with it.

The pull of her is next-level. I've never felt anything like this before in my life.

I asked for a sign and they gave me one. Maybe this means ... I don't know what the fuck it means. The most beautiful girl I've ever seen isn't an apparition at all but a living, breathing, lethal little nymph who has literally walked straight out of my wildest fantasies.

The last few days are a blur. I'm not entirely sure which parts are real and which parts are a dream. I was so out of it in that cave. But one crystal clear memory slices through the haze—of her. Keeping me alive. A kiss. Feeding me her perfect breasts and those sweet, juicy nipples. Her soft moans as she came, just from the greedy hunger of my mouth.

I'm starstruck. I'm also—*hell*—getting hard just thinking about it. Which—considering the way I'm dressed and also the way my hyper-vigilant family is gathered around me like they're worried I'm about to fall over —isn't ideal.

"The fight was my fault." I misread her. I took her for a scared kid, not a fighter on the offensive. The way she sunk that knife makes me think she's used it before. Most likely defending herself.

Now she's got me.

"Knox, you're not thinking straight—" Remy starts.

Wolf interrupts him, half under his breath, "Rem. Let him have this. He's about to get fucking marrie—" I break my hold of the girl just enough to cover Wolf's mouth and give him a shove, keeping her tucked against me. Why the fuck would he say that?

But I'm distracted.

Cassidy.

Who is she?

Where did she come from?

I have a million questions.

But first, I need to get rid of my family. "As touching as all this is, I can survive the rest of the day without the four of you micro-managing every fucking thing. I appreciate the love, but you're all officially dismissed. Blaise, can you organize for some food to be sent up? We're starving. And get them to send up a couple of bottles of champagne too. We're celebrating. Because we're *alive*."

"Knox, you're not supposed to drink while you're on—"

"Out. All of you. *Now*."

They're all worried and I guess it's fair enough. The whole knife fight on top of a mountain followed by a dramatic rescue mission was a lot.

And now this.

This completely unexpected stranger with the platinum hair and the dark, soulful eyes that watch me like she's as fascinated by me as I am by her.

I know what Remy's thinking. I know what all of them are thinking. But I need some time to deal with this gargantuan curveball.

We still have time.

38

———

KNOX

"Knox, you're still bleeding," Blaise says.

I look down and she's right. It's soaking through the bandage wrapped around my stomach. "I've had worse in the sparring ring. Hana said it'll bleed for a while when I do anything strenuous."

Like I'm about to.

"We need some time," I say, and they finally take the hint.

"I'll have some food sent up," Blaise says as they all start making their way toward the door. "And I'm getting Hana to come take another look at you."

They finally leave and the two of us are alone together.

She's quiet. Taking everything in. Like she's just landed and needs some time to adjust.

I stare down at her for a long moment. I still have my

arm wrapped around her waist. I can feel the silk of her hair on my skin.

I really can't believe this.

I glide my thumb along her cheekbone. Her eyelashes are long and dark. Her lips are full but delicately shaped and rosy pink. The exact same color as her nipples—a color I'll never forget as long as I live.

Making an angel come while you're bleeding out in a cave has a way of imprinting itself onto your memories. "Are you all right?" I ask her.

"Yes," she says, glancing down at her bandage. Then at mine. "I'm sorry I stabbed you."

"I'm not sorry you stabbed me."

A hint of humor dances in her eyes. "You're not sorry I accidentally almost killed you?" Her voice has the slightest smoky edge to it. It's the sweetest, sexiest thing I've ever heard.

"No," I confirm. "Because if you hadn't, I wouldn't have been able to kiss you."

A warm blush touches her cheeks and what I'm realizing is that my girl is sweet but also feisty. Which I already know. There's a wild strength to her. She's as ravenous as I am. She's remembering how good it felt. "It was a good kiss."

"I can do even better when I'm conscious."

She smiles and I can't resist. I lean in and I softly brush my lips against hers.

She barely sighs and her lips part. I slide my tongue into the heaven of her mouth.

Holy fuck, she tastes good.

I deepen the kiss, needing more, already addicted.

We both jump at the loud knock on the door.

"That was quick. I hope you're hungry." I reluctantly let go of her and wrap a thick blanket that's hanging over the arm of a chair around my waist. My cock is thick and heavy between my legs and my boxers aren't quite up to the task of concealing all that.

"Hungry doesn't even begin to describe how I feel," she says.

I grin hotly at her. This girl might just be my soul-mate. There's an intriguing mixture of street-smarts and total innocence to her that fascinates me. There's so much I need to learn.

I open the door and a couple of our kitchen staff wheel in several trays piled with food. There are platters with sliced roast beef, bread, fruit, cheeses, dips, sliced vegetables and olives. Plates are loaded up with chicken wings, french fries and hamburgers. There's a pizza, two bottles of champagne on ice, an apple pie and a chocolate cake.

"Whoa," Cassidy gasps. Her eyes have lit up at the sight of so much food.

One of the cooks hands me a folded up piece of paper before they leave. "From Hana," he tells me, closing the door behind them. I unfold the note and read it out loud. "You're a terrible patient, Knox Ramsey. I told you to stay in bed. I have other patients to see before I can get to you but there are clean bandages on the dresser in your room. Wrap it tightly but not too tightly. I'll check on you later. GO BACK TO BED. ~Hana."

"I can help with your bandage," Cassidy says.

"Hana said you did a good job stitching me up."

"I know how to sew."

"Is that right." I don't really ask it. I'm ridiculously mesmerized by everything she tells me. It's amazing how the smallest details about a person can be so interesting.

"I make some of my own clothes. I like designing things."

"So does Echo. She designs a lot of her own clothes."

"Really?"

"You could take a look at her machines if you want. She loves talking about what she's working on."

"I would ... love that." There are unspoken words I know she's thinking. *Is she staying? What's going to happen next? How much time do we have?*

I know what Remy's answers would be.

My problem is, I don't know if I can live with Remy's answers. "First up, though: food. I hope they've brought enough."

Cassidy's laugh sort of slays me. "There's enough here to feed an army." She picks up a piece of the chocolate cake and stuffs half of it into her mouth.

"Really? You're starting with the cake?"

Her eyes close like she's having an orgasmic experience and I feel the sweet look on her face all the way down to my thickening cock. "*Ohmigodthisissooogood.*"

She's curvy but thin. Too thin. Which I plan on fixing.

She devours the rest of the cake as I pop the champagne and pour two glasses. We're already doped up to the eyeballs but who cares. I almost died two days ago. *And the angel is in my room,* gorgeous and real and stuffing her face in a way that's getting me hot as fuck.

I hand her a glass. She takes it and I clink mine against hers. "To angels."

"And devils," she grins, taking a bite of pizza.

I grab a slice. We haven't eaten since before our confrontation at the caves. Before we "met" at the lake. Who knows how long we've been out. Two days, at least. Maybe three. I remember dreaming of her. Calling out to her. Wanting to make sure she wouldn't leave me.

"So, where should we start?" I say.

"What do you mean?"

"I don't know a single thing about you. Except that your name is Cassidy. And that you made me a promise in that cave I'm going to have to hold you to."

"What promise?" But there's the light blush.

"First things first. Where did you come from? Why were you living in the caves? How did you get there? Where's your family?"

"That's a lot of questions."

"How about we start with this one: who are you?"

39

KNOX

"You know my name," she says. "Cassidy."

"I don't know your last name."

"I don't have one."

I take another bite of pizza, narrowing my eyes. "So we're playing games, are we?"

"The social worker named me Cassidy Meadow Kelley. I was abandoned by my mother when I was around four months old with a note that said, 'Her name is Cassidy,' pinned to my blanket with a gold pin." A flash of panic crosses her face. "*Oh no.*"

"What?"

"My pin. I left it in the cave."

I want to smooth the little furrow between her dark blond eyebrows away. "It'll still be there. No one goes to those caves."

"They're the only things I have of her. The note and the pin."

"What does it look like? I can have someone to go up there and get it for you."

"It's a golden feather with the initials CMK and a number etched onto it."

"What's the number?"

"I've never been able to figure out what it means."

"Can you remember it?"

She nods, taking a bite of a french fry.

"Tell it to me."

"544, dash, 65872094. I've checked everything I can think of but I've never been able to crack the code."

"Say it again."

"544/65872094."

"Sounds like a safety deposit box number. We have a few of them."

Her dark eyes are wide. "Really?"

"They usually start with three numbers, then a dash, then eight more."

She's quiet for a few seconds, processing this. "How would I find out?"

"I'm sure we can figure it out. Enzo would know."

"Enzo King? I've heard of him."

"He'd definitely be able to trace that number to whatever bank it's associated with."

There's an intensity to her that's deep, like I've just said something that has shaken her, or changed her life. "I can't believe it. I've been trying to figure out what that number meant my whole life."

"Maybe we can figure out what the M and K of CMK stand for too. I'll help you."

Tears fill her eyes. Which hits a dark place inside me. I can't handle her tears at all. I take her hand across the table and it's small and so delicate it makes me feel like a feral wild animal who's sharing a meal with a soft, perfect heavenly being.

I take her hand and pull gently. "Come here." My voice sounds graveled and deep. It's spellbinding to me, how her eyes are so dark and her hair is so light.

She comes to me and I carefully pull her down so she's sitting on my lap. She hardly weighs anything. It's got to be obvious to her that I've got a raging fucking hard-on but it can't be helped.

"Thank you so much, Knox. It's ... a lot. To think that I might finally be able to get some answers to questions I've had for a long time."

"It's all right, angel. I'll do anything you ask me to."

"Why does everyone keep calling me angel? What does that mean?"

"It's from the legend."

"What legend?"

"The Goddess of Fire. Your resemblance is sort of ... exact."

Her smile is sardonic. "The Goddess of Fire?"

"Yes."

"I've never heard of her."

"You must have."

"No. Never."

"The Goddess of Fire wanders across the islands of Hawaii. Some people call her the White Lady. Our family calls her the Angel."

"Why?"

"I thought everyone knew this legend. We all learned it as kids."

"I never really had ... people ... to tell me stories or read to me. I'm an orphan. I was raised in foster care and none of it was all that ... well, good. At all. I spent a lot of time running away."

I hold her face with my hands. She's not crying but she's feeling it. Her life has not been easy, I can read that in the sadness. And I'm going to fix her.

Fuck the curse.

"I'll tell you the story." They wouldn't have put *the literal angel* in my path if they didn't want me to have her, and protect her. And to keep her. "And you do have people now. You have me. Because once you stab me, heal me then kiss me, you own me. I'm afraid there's no getting rid of me now that we're bonded in blood."

She bites her lip at the memory. But there's a hint of a smile there too and I think I'm in real trouble here. I don't want to curse us, or anyone else, by loving something I can't have. But my mind is working on several levels.

There has to be a way.

Even if it means defying my fate, I have to find a way.

40

KNOX

"WHAT HAPPENS IN THE LEGEND?" Cassidy asks.

"The angel has white or white-blond hair. She's as gorgeous as you'd expect an angel to be. She travels around, sometimes hitchhiking."

"Hitchhiking?"

"Yes."

"I hitchhiked from the airport."

"Yeah?"

"The man looked very spooked. He took me exactly where I asked him to."

"Of course he did. If you don't give the Goddess of Fire whatever she wants, she causes heartbreak. Or catastrophe. She can light fires with her fingertips. But if you please her, she'll leave a trail of magic that will enchant your life."

"Wow."

"Where did you fly in from?"

"Honolulu. A few days ago—or however long it's been. A week? Anyway, Echo was on my plane and I heard her talking to Blaise about some caves that were an idyllic hilltop wonderland because Blaise wanted to hide from something and Echo said she'd hiked up there with you. She said there were pools. And a view. And I had nowhere to go. So I went there."

"You went to the caves because you had nowhere else to go." Goddamn it.

"I found them after the man dropped me off and I hiked up to them. I explored a little. And that's when I saw the orchards inside your walls. There was so much food and I was so hungry. So I climbed over."

"How did you know which part of the wall wasn't rigged?"

"I didn't."

"We're going to have to beef up our security." But I'm glad now, that we left that section unwired, because it was too far off the beaten path to worry about. "Why did you come to Kauai?"

"I won a plane ticket in a poker game."

Of course she did. Luck brought her to me. Because I *asked* for her to be brought to me. You don't grow up hearing about five generations of curse-obsessed ancestors without believing in the power of it. "So you're a card shark?"

"I got lucky."

"How'd you get so good with that knife?"

She closes off a little. I've touched a nerve. "I told all this to your brothers and sisters already."

"Told them what?"

"I was ... on the run."

"On the run? From who?"

"From my landlord."

"Why? Who's your landlord?"

She pauses, like she knows she's about to get a reaction. "His name is Axel Archer."

And it does get a reaction. "*Axel Archer* is your fucking *landlord?*" I tense up at this information. "Are you an Arrow recruit? Is *that* why you came here?"

"*No*, Knox. I'd never met him before the night I ran from him."

I stare into her eyes for a long moment. I'm already connected to this girl in ways I'm not sure what to do with. Except by making her mine in every possible way. I'll kill that fucker if he's touched one hair on her head. "It wouldn't matter if you were, angel. I'll fight for you no matter what you are."

A tiny furrow appears between her eyebrows, like she can't believe I've just said that. "I'm not a recruit, Knox. He made me an offer but I refused."

Axel Archer is a lowlife piece of shit drug lord criminal with a huge grudge. And I don't know if I want to hear the next part of this story. Because *she's mine*. She's meant for me. I brace myself. "What offer?"

"A new apartment. A so-called better life. I told him no. I tried to leave. He ..."

I need to know. "He what?"

"He broke into my apartment. He had a key."

I can't breathe. "Please tell me that's when you used your knife."

"It is. I stabbed him." *Thank fuck.* Because I'd end up dead or in jail getting revenge. "In the stomach. Deeper than ... well, deeper than I stabbed you. I don't know if I was trying to kill him. Mostly I just wanted to get away from him."

"And did you?"

"Yes."

"Good girl. That's good."

"He was so shocked."

Despite everything, and mad with relief, I almost laugh. "I bet."

"I ran. I went straight to the airport. And that's how I ended up here."

I hold her face and I softly kiss her lips. She tastes like sugar and starlight. She tastes like my wildest dreams. "You're safe now. I'll make sure of it."

Cassidy's eyes are deep pools of emotion. She kisses me again. For a few seconds I just let her do this. Without devouring her. I'll get to that soon enough. My cock is a throbbing beast of agony but I'm falling in love as much as I'm on fire with lust.

"Do you want to know something crazy?" she asks softly.

Do I? "Okay."

"The kiss."

"What about it?"

"It was my first kiss."

She's ... *untouched?* "Yeah?"

"Yeah."

"Ever?" There's a surge of wild relief, of course there is. But then again, she's my dream come true. It almost seems like I should have known. *She's for me and only me.*

"Ever. I just turned twenty-one—well, according to the birth certificate they made for me. Sort of late for a first kiss."

"We can make up for lost time. You and me."

"Knox?"

"Yeah?"

There's gravity to whatever she's about to ask me. "Who are you marrying?"

Goddamn it, Wolf.

You, I want to say. *I'm marrying you.*

"Our family has ties to two other families. Remy is discussing it with the others. But nothing's been decided yet." Or, almost nothing.

It's a few seconds before she speaks. "I had a job before I left Honolulu, working for a catering company."

I watch her eyes and I wait to hear where she's going with this. She touches a strand of my hair, playing it with her fingers.

"I'd only worked there for a few days. There was this party at the Fitzpatricks. It was Vivi Fitzpatrick's birthday."

"Echo went to that. You were there?"

"I was one of the servers."

I can only imagine what she might have overheard. "How was it?"

"It was good." She doesn't elaborate, and I fall a little harder for her for that reason alone. There's a perceptive intelligence to her that somehow matches my own. We're on the same wavelength, already, in so many ways. And she's telling me that she knows at least a small part of the story. I'm almost glad.

I pick her up and there's a spear of pain from my injury but not much. There's hardly anything to her, like she *is* half ghost or apparition. I'm going to change that. Her life has been hard but that part of it is over. I'm here now. She's going to get everything she needs and even more of what she wants. "I think we should start making up for some of that lost time. Right now. I don't want to waste time. Not with you."

Her fingers are still weaved through my hair and she kisses me as I carry her into the bedroom. The blanket I wrapped around my waist falls to the floor.

I hardly ever sleep here. I prefer the beach house or my cabin in the orchards. But it's a nice apartment with a king-sized bed and all the mod cons.

I place her gently on the bed. After our time in the cave, it feels so natural for us to be together. There's no hesitation or doubt. We can feel our bond and we both just want to get closer. There was never any ice to break for Cassidy and me. We jumped straight into the fire.

"Sit down and I'll unwrap your bandage," she says.

So I sit on the bed and pull her between my spread knees so she's standing between them. She's so small compared to me. So petite. But at the same time she holds a power over me that feels almost shockingly absolute.

I don't know if it's the whole angel thing, but I would literally do anything for her. It doesn't feel like we just met. It feels like I've known her my entire life, in my dreams. Now that she's *here* all I want to do is touch her and taste her.

"I'm going to take off your dress. I want to see you while you heal me, like you did before."

Her cheeks get that warm pink flare as her eyes meet mine. There's so much fiery depth to them. Her hair catches the low, golden light of the lamp. I swear this girl has an aura. A halo. I guess it's not surprising.

"I'll heal you, Knox. I'll give you everything."

Fuck yeah. "My angel is pleased with me. She's enchanting my life."

I place my palms on her thighs, slipping them under the hem of her short dress, lifting it higher. I'm careful because her arm is sore but she barely winces as she raises her arms and I pull the dress off over her head.

All she's wearing is a pair of white panties. Her skin isn't pale. It's golden, a shade darker than her hair.

I slide my palms along the skin of her hips, then her stomach, feeling her smooth warmth. Her breasts are full and fucking perfect, bouncy and plush with those pink nipples beading into taut buds, begging to be sucked.

She's so damn gorgeous it's killing me.

My cock is fully, insanely hard, thick and rigid and halfway up my stomach, only partly concealed by my boxers. I can feel the wetness of pre-cum coating the head.

I take her breasts in my hands, gently squeezing them together so her nipples are close to my mouth. I lick one, swirling my tongue around it slowly as it tightens. I feel feral, almost dizzy with need. She tastes like nothing I've ever experienced.

There's an edge of insanity to this desire. I would kill or die to have her.

She touches her fingers tenderly to my face as she offers her nipple to my mouth, watching my eyes as she does this. There's a newness to this for her, I can see that, but not a shyness. Whatever she's thinking, it's cut with soft, hundred-proof lust. Her panties are wet, clinging lightly to the puffy pink outline of her pussy and the tiny nub of her clit.

Holy fuck.

But then she gently pulls her nipple from my mouth. She begins to unwrap the blood-soaked cloth from around my stomach. "See, you are healing." Her hands are soft, careful miracles. She winds the fresh one around my body, fastening the end so it's secure.

"Because of you."

She laughs. "It's because of me it happened in the first place."

"No, that was because of me. I didn't gauge my opponent correctly. I underestimated you. But I won't make that mistake again."

Her smile lingers, and I watch her, mesmerized by everything about her. The pale goldenness of her hair. The mind-numbing fullness of her breasts as she moves. The flare of her hips and the plush curves of her body. The faint grooves between her ribs are the only imperfection. They show me what she's been lacking. Her journey to find me hasn't been an easy one.

"Your family is kind," she says.

"Sometimes. I think they're half terrified of you. In case you light fires with your fingertips."

"I promise I won't."

"You already have." And I can't take this anymore. I pick her up and carefully lay her down on the bed. I straddle her, crouching over her, holding my weight. I don't care about the pain of my injury. I'm more concerned about the pain of my fucking cock. I'm so damn hard all she'd have to do is touch me with her cool fingers and I'd come all over her.

Her lips are already parted. I slide my tongue inside, kissing her ravenously.

I kiss my way down her neck, biting and sucking my claims like a fucking vampire. Marking her. Devouring her.

"*Knox*," she gasps and squirms with need. "You feel so good."

"Because we're made for each other."

I take her nipple between my teeth, then lick with my

tongue until her taut bud is all wet with it. I swirl the liquid with my fingers as I take her other nipple in my mouth, sucking deeply.

She moans my name, grabbing fistfuls of my hair almost painfully. I like it.

My girl is feisty.

But I'm feistier.

I move lower, licking a trail down the concave plane of her stomach and along the angular jut of her hipbones. I'm going to feed her. Until she's round with health and the baby I'm going to put inside her.

You're marrying someone else.

I shove the thought from my mind.

No.

I'll never be able to do it.

Not now.

I slide my fingers over the saturated cotton of her panties and she gasps.

"Look at you. You're so wet for me, baby. I'm going to take these off now. I need to taste your juicy pussy. Let me kiss you."

"*Knox,*" she gasps, pushing at my head. "What ... ?" Like she's never heard of such a thing.

"That's right, baby girl. I'm going to kiss you and eat you and make you come. Let me taste you." I pull her panties off with my teeth as I kick off my boxers. Then I push her thighs wider, pinning them.

"Knox, you can't—"

I lick her, delving my tongue into nirvana. She's slick with cream and I feast on her in greedy mouthfuls, never leaving her. Getting her ready for me.

I'm more than addicted, I'm *home*. This is where I want to live my life and plant my seed. Right here.

Her soft moans almost undo me. I'm almost coming.

I fuck her with my tongue, stroking and exploring with my fingers to give her every possible pleasure. I lick her open, like a flower, feeding on the nectar that's all for me. Circling her clit with my tongue, I play her nub with light, teasing flicks. Then I suck it gently into my mouth, increasing the suction as I slide two fingers into the insanely tight constriction of her body, curling them to find the most sensitive places, working the slippery friction.

Her thighs quiver. I keep my rhythm, forcing her pleasure higher until she's crying out, gripping me and writhing against me as her pussy starts to spasm. I use my thumb to tease her orgasm higher as I thrust my tongue deep inside her.

I can taste her pleasure.

And I am so fucked.

The flavor of her bliss does something to me. It changes me.

I hardly know her and yet I've known her my whole life.

I've just met her and yet she owns me, body and soul.

If we're cursed then so be it.

If it takes her first then I'll follow her.

Because what I'm realizing is that heaven on earth is worth any price.

41

Cassidy

I'M FLYING. I'm floating. I'm *coming* so hard I honestly don't know if I'll survive it. The pleasure is extreme, cascading through my body in tidal waves that start where his hungry mouth and his magical fingers play me, and burn through me in hot bursts, over and over. I'm moaning his name.

"That's my girl," he murmurs against my blissed-out pussy. *"You taste so fucking good. I'll break every rule for you. I'll die for you."*

He makes me come again.

And again.

Until I'm boneless and spent. But also energized with a full-body glow.

I'll never be the same.

Knox Ramsey is mine.

Even if I get cast out and wander the earth for the

rest of time, he'll still be mine. I'm so in love with him that my heart and my body ache with it.

There's a part of me that wonders if he's obsessed with his vision of me. His dream or his legend. I decide not to care if it's a fantasy he's in love with, or what he knows about who I am that he's so far discovered. Which isn't much. We've known each other only days. But there are times in life—and I've never experienced one until now—when something feels so good and so right that it overrides every doubt and all hesitation. We both want this in a way that feels extreme and extraordinary. We know our time together might not last.

And I've already decided. My physical being won't *let* me refuse him, I need him too much. I want to feast on him and take him inside me with a hunger that's new to me. I'm losing my mind.

As he lays next to me I push him onto his back and climb onto him, being careful not to hurt him as I softly, at first, kiss his mouth. His face is wet with my own plea-sure and it's insanely, wildly intimate.

I lick his plump bottom lip, tasting our mixed flavor, dipping my tongue into his mouth which he takes and slides against his own. He tastes like lust. He tastes like dreams coming true.

I kiss my way down his big, buff body. Biting softly and licking his skin. I'm fascinated by his hard, sculpted muscles and the broadness of his shoulders. The dark bronzed color of his skin. He's such a masculine creature.

No one ever tells you that lust is as spiritual as it is

voracious. I'm on fire for him. I want to give him every-thing I have. I want to eat him and drink him and give him the kind of pleasure that will change his life.

So I kiss my way down his chest, swirling my tongue around his nipple, which makes him groan. I lick him and kiss him with teasing, biting nips, down his stomach to that tantalizing V and the line of dark hair.

My pussy is wet and still rippling. My breasts feel full and my nipples are sore and sensitive from his greedy mouth. I rub them tenderly against him as I feast on him.

"*Cassidy. Oh, fuck.*" He seems almost overcome. "*You feel too good.*"

He's breathing heavily, watching me. His ocean-blue eyes are feral and lust-drugged. His fists are clenching into the covers of the bed like he's laid up on a torture rack.

Moving lower, I stop when I reach his gigantic cock. For someone so worldly in so many ways, I've never been … up close and personal with anyone. Not at all. You don't grow up like I have without understanding a few things. But I've spent my whole life running.

Until now.

I take his thick shaft in my hands and he's heavy. So incredibly big and hard. It's surprisingly silky. There's creamy wetness coming out of him and I glide my tongue across the fat head of his cock, tasting him. It's salty and addictive. I want more.

I lick him tenderly, trying to get more of the liquid to come out of him. Then I take him deeper, easing his cock into my mouth. There's so *much* of him, I can only take less than half of him. I grip him as I lick my tongue along the ridged veins on the underside of his cock. I suck on him as deeply as I can.

My fingers rove and explore.

He's mine. All of him. There's nothing I won't do.

I keep working my rhythm, milking him as I grip and stroke and suck hard.

His cock starts to jerk in my mouth and I'm suddenly flooded with thick throbs of hot, jetting cum. *His seed. It's mine. I love it.*

I drink him thirstily, taking him in lusty mouthfuls as it spills down my chin.

I love him.

He keeps coming and I swallow more, until the pulses calm. Then I lick him clean, kissing his barely-softened cock.

"Angel." His voice is rasped and raw. "Come here."

I climb up next to him and he wraps his arms and legs around me, staring deeply into my eyes.

"You're mine," he whispers.

"And you're mine," I whisper back.

It feels devastatingly true.

Please, please, let it be true.

42

Cassidy

I wake to the sound of voices.

I'm in Knox's bed, tucked in and crazily comfortable, wrapped up in soft cotton sheets and a plush comforter. He's gone.

The bedroom door is closed and I can barely make out the conversation happening on the other side of it. But as I listen more closely, I can hear what they're saying.

I hear Knox's voice. Already, his voice is deeply familiar to me.

Wolf's has a distinctive huskiness to it. And a more joking tone. "I've never seen you so content to stay bedridden before, brother."

"That's because my bed has never been so comfortable before," Knox drawls.

Remy's voice is low and gruff, as though the topic annoys him, "Either way, the sooner you're on your feet, the better." Then, after a lengthy pause, "You can't keep her, you know that, Knox. She'll have to return to Honolulu and you can see her there, if you choose to, after the wed—"

"Nothing's been decided yet." I'm learning this reply is Knox's go-to, whenever the topic is brought up.

"Knox, you'll honor your duty as a Ramsey by securing the alliance and keeping the best interests of your family—and yourself, as well as Cassidy—by marrying Perri Fitzpatrick. It *has* been decided."

There's a tense silence.

Remy's voice is quieter when he continues but I can still hear the low tones of his command. "Unless you prefer to marry Tatum, Vivi, Raven or Aurora, your wedding to Perri is going ahead. You can decide the date. You can decide which one of them it's going to be. But it *is* happening. We can't risk anything less."

"Risk has taken on a whole new meaning." There's a defiance in Knox's voice that I can feel. In my heart. And in the warm, soft core of my body, where I can still feel his lingering effect. We slept wrapped around each other. He woke me in the night to feed on my pleasure again. *His greedy mouth, so beautiful. So dirty.* I get wet again just thinking about him.

I thought he might ... take it further.

I would have let him.

I *wanted* him to slide that huge, thick cock inside me. I know he wanted it too—he whispered the words—but he held himself back. He made me come again with his mouth, then he rubbed his big cock against my still-rippling pussy, spilling his cum all over my stomach and my breasts, rubbing it onto my skin as though to mark me. I'm still covered in a sticky film of it.

God. He may as well have branded my heart with a red-hot branding iron.

I can feel his blood in my veins. And I can feel his seed nourishing me like a superpower. He's in me. I crave more of him like a drug.

"The Fitzpatricks and the Kings will arrive here a week from Friday and the plans will be finalized," Remy continues. "Until then ..." His voice lowers further. "... take what you want of her. But it can't last, Knox, not as anything more than a fling or a mistress. You know that. Don't fight it."

"I agreed to try," Knox tells him. "I agreed to consider my choices, out of respect for you. And for all of you. But I never actually agreed to marry any one of them." His tone sounds almost dreamily resolute when he says, "Remy, she's *the angel*. It's a *sign*. Come on, you must see that. I feel like ... Cupid's arrow has pierced my heart."

I can hear Wolf's low laughter. "That was Cupid's *knife* that pierced you. And you can be glad she missed your heart."

"Knox, be reasonable." Remy is pissed off now. "She's not the angel. She's a lost waif who happens to vaguely fit the description."

Knox doesn't seem to have heard him. "Maybe

having her turn up like this, just out of the blue, maybe *she's broken* the curse. Did you ever think of that?"

"You're still out of it from the blood loss and the drugs," Remy insists, and I can hear movement. "We'll talk more about this once you've regained your sanity."

I hear the door slam and it's quiet. His two brothers have left.

The bedroom door opens and Knox comes back in.

The outline of his huge shoulders and his wild golden hair makes my heart skip a beat. *He's so freaking beautiful.*

"Hey, angel."

"Hey, devil."

He pulls back the covers, staring down at me. I'm glad to see there's a hint of lightness in him, maybe at my endearment, despite the talk he just had with his brothers.

Slowly, he glides his warm hand across the coated skin of my stomach, cupping my breast. "I've made a mess of you." He takes my nipple between two fingers and squeezes, rolling it with his fingers.

I'm wet and I want him. "Make more of a mess of me."

"My angel's a dirty girl."

"I'm keeping my promise to you, Knox Ramsey. Promises inked in blood are real. I'll give you as much pleasure as you want." Then I whisper a challenge to him, because it's the only thing I can feel. *"Do it."*

His expression turns dark, sort of ragingly but quietly furious. I know why. He wants me as much as I want him. But if he takes me, it won't be something he can do only once, or when he's allowed to now and then because of the constraints imposed by whatever rule or alliance he's bound to.

He scoops me into his arms. "We're taking a shower. Then I'm taking you down to my beach house."

"I can walk, Knox. You'll tear your stitches again."

"Fuck the stitches." He carries me into his bathroom and turns on the shower, setting me carefully onto my feet on a fluffy bathmat. As he waits for the water to heat, Knox kisses me. He's angry and twisted up about the conversation he just had, I can feel that. There's a looming deadline and a fate he doesn't want, hanging over his head. I'm not sure if I can change that but I figure it's worth a shot. More than worth a shot. Knox Ramsey has become everything I want. Our bond was forged in blood and sealed with fire. And my grit feels close to the surface. I want all of him. I don't care what it costs me.

I let him kiss me, giving as much as taking, until the bathroom is full of steam and he pulls me under the jets of the shower. They're coming from the ceiling and the walls and they feel sensuous on my heated skin.

His low growl is full of agony. "Do you know how fucking beautiful you are?"

I understand agony. I also, because of him and for the first time in my life, understand ecstasy. I take the soap and I glide it across his eight-pack, under the stripe of his now-wet bandage, easing his huge, engorged cock away from his stomach to do it. Then I soap up his chest, loving the feel of his hard pecs and his strong, inked shoulders.

Inked.

But my hair is down.

Will I show him?

He's already told me he doesn't care what I am. But what if it's something unforgivable? His family is obsessed with curses and rules. To them, I'm already something to be used and then cast aside.

Knox and I might only have a few days together before they convince him I'm a temporary distraction from his duty.

So I keep it hidden.

They can try to convince him that I'm not his destiny.

But *I* can try to convince him that I am.

I take his hard shaft in my careful, soapy fists, sliding them along the thick, slippery length of him. Letting my fingertips tease as my nipples glide against the hair-roughened surface of his chest. I gasp because he feels so good.

I know he's conflicted by things I don't fully understand.

But *I'm* not conflicted.

I want to offer myself to him. And make it clear to him that I'll give him anything and everything he wants.

I turn, still holding his hard cock in my fist. From behind, I guide him so the broad head of his cock slides against the lips of my pussy, just holding it there. It presses thickly but he doesn't enter me. Not yet. Then I arch my back so his crown slides to the cove of my ass. It prods me there and he goes still. He's so hard I know he's close. I move, arching back and forth, so his big cock slides silkily between the cheeks of my ass.

"Fuck, you're so damn *hot*, baby girl. *Mine*."

"I'm yours, Knox." *I love you.* I almost say it.

But of course it's too soon. The bigger part of me doesn't care. Not at all. I've never in my life experienced the kind of joy, luck, beauty, desire and everything else that goes along with being in the presence of Knox Ramsey.

I *do* love him.

I love that he's shown me how good life can actually *feel*.

I turn again, soaping up his length even more. I grip him harder and slide my hands along him faster, cupping him then gripping his cock in slippery, squeezing tugs. More pre-ejaculate spills out of him. He's close. I'm almost shocked by how easy it is to get him off. I know how. I can give him the most intense pleasure he's ever felt because I *want* to. So much.

It's my new purpose in life. And I don't care how that sounds when I say it in my own head.

He's worth it.

He's the brightest star.

And he has the biggest, most beautiful cock. I mean, come on.

I love it when he comes.

His hand presses against the sandstone wall of the shower. He stares down at me in that way he has, like he's still not sure if I'm real. He wants to kiss me as he comes so I give him my mouth and I suck on his tongue as I take him over the edge.

Knox comes *hard.*

His cock bucks in my hand and his cum shoots in thick ropes all over my breasts and my stomach.

I can sense as I squeeze him that it's so intense for him once he's coming, it's almost too much to bear. So I lighten my grip as I keep tenderly working him. A fresh throbbing rush pulses out of him and I can't resist. I bend down to him and I let it jet into my mouth, sucking lightly on the fat head of his cock as the last few bursts coat my tongue.

It takes him a minute to recover but once he does he removes one of the shower heads, which is attached to a European-style hose and he sits on the stone bench of his shower, pulling me onto his lap. He positions my legs so I'm sitting with my back against his chest, my legs spread over his knees.

"My Cassidy girl. You're the hottest little angel in the whole damn world. I'll never get enough of you."

I almost say, *take more of me. Take all of me.*

He holds the shower jet between my legs so the warm current pulses over my clit as his rough, thick fingers slide inside me. He's more forceful this time. More insistent. And the sensation takes me to the height of pleasure so quickly I can barely handle it. I cry out as his fingers thrust into me and the warm water massages my clit until my whole body is shaking. The pleasure is too much, cascading through me in a Niagara Falls of clenching, spasming beauty.

It lasts a long time.

Like all the climaxes do, it changes me.

The bond feels stronger. And deeper.

I'm limp in his arms. My pussy's still rippling its bliss in soft clenches, from my inner muscles all the way to my fingers and toes.

Knox drops the shower head and just holds me for a while.

"I'll figure out a way," he murmurs. The air is thick with pleasure and emotion. "You're gorgeous, angel girl. You're so much better than the dreams. This can't possibly be a curse, it's too beautiful. I'm keeping you, angel. I love you. I've always loved you."

43

Cassidy

KNOX IS LEADING me by the hand through a rainforest, which opens out to a sandy trail along a cliff. "Where are you taking me?"

"You'll see." He grins down at me, then continues to lead me along the narrow trail. He's happy. As soon as we started this walk and the further we go along the trail, he's losing that edge of dread that's so much a part of him when he's in the castle.

He feels free here, it's easy to see.

The Three Little Words thing keeps warming me with its memory. I don't know how to feel about falling in love so fast. And I still wonder, even though our drugs have mostly worn off by now, if he's seeing me as a fantasy instead of a real person. It's something to think about, sure. But at the same time, we can both see our bloodbath meet-cute for what it was: a love at first sight baptism by fire.

Either way, we're healing now, and against the backdrop of his tropical rainforest natural habitat, he's a gorgeous sun god.

He's wearing a pair of swim shorts that show off his strong thighs and his tattoos, his thick leather weapons belt and his work boots. A clean bandage is wrapped around his torso, but it's stopped bleeding. His brawny muscles are tanned and strong and I can only stare at him in awe as we make our way down the path toward a small sandy bay. I have never met a more physically beautiful human being in my life. He still has the power to stun me with it.

His dark-gold hair is wavy and windblown.

Knox is carrying a large backpack full of food that he had someone pack for us.

All I'm wearing is the short tunic dress Echo lent me and my old sneakers. My bikini is long gone and my old clothes disappeared, maybe to be cleaned or repaired. Or thrown away. Everything else I own is still up in the cave.

Including my pin.

I should remind Knox that we need to hike up there to get it. But something about doing that brings up questions I'm not quite ready to face. *How long am I staying? What happens when our time runs out?*

And the day is too beautiful to worry about anything but the clear blue water and the arc of golden sand below us. And—*wow*—the house I can see around the bend.

"Knox," I gasp as it comes in to full view. "This is your *house*?"

"This is my favorite place on earth. Right here."

The house is two stories. The rear half sits on smooth rock and the front half on high stilts. A huge deck extends out over the water. It's surrounded by its own little grove of palm trees. Next to the house is a sandy beach that extends along the length of the small bay. "It's so perfect."

"It's paradise," he says simply. We get to the house and Knox opens the door and leads me inside.

I'm officially in love with it.

Inside, the house is cool and rustic. It's open plan with a kitchen along the back wall and a wooden island between the kitchen area and the huge lounge. Chunky leather and wood furniture fills the space. There are ceiling fans shaped like thick wooden palm fronds. The entire front wall is made of wood-framed glass folding doors. Knox pulls them all the way open.

The deck is the same size as the entire interior of the house. There's a table and chairs, a row of unlit torches, a fire pit, stands for fishing rods, an outdoor kitchen and a lounger that's almost the size of a bed. Under the eaves, there are some shelves with stacks of towels, fishing equipment and wood for the fire.

There's a wide staircase next to the kitchen and on the opposite side of it, an open door leading into a modern bathroom.

"Can we stay here for the rest of time, just you and me?" I don't believe it could happen that way, but I've never felt so damn *happy*. Just to be in this dreamy place. With him.

He sets the backpack on the island. "Yes. Do you want to see the upstairs?"

I smile at him and he laughs. "Yes."

The stairs lead up to a huge bedroom that's the same footprint as the lower story. The only furniture is a king-sized bed, two side tables and a huge couch that faces the ocean with a long, low coffee table in front of it. There's a high-tech telescope by the window and a door leading into a huge master bathroom. The bedroom has the same folding doors as the downstairs, and Knox slides them open.

Up here, there's a smaller balcony that runs the length of the room with a round table and a single chair. I go out onto it and stare down at the glimmering turquoise water.

Knox comes to me, picking me up and kissing my lips.

"I love your house," I tell him.

"I love that you're here with me. Who knew my very first visitor would be the angel herself."

I bite gently on his bottom lip and he bares his teeth at me. I can't stop another laugh from bubbling out of me. *I'm so in love with him.*

I didn't even know I was capable of love. Or to fall so *deeply* into it, so mind-bendingly quickly.

Of course I'm aware of the reality: he's supposed to marry someone else. He's duty-bound by some entrenched family alliance that can't be broken.

But she's not here now.

I am.

And I'm going to do everything I can to keep him. Which means the next few days, or however long we can stay in this perfect place, are all about loving him with everything I have. Because I don't know if I'll ever get another chance.

He sets me down. "How about a swim? I'll take my speargun. We'll catch lunch."

We go downstairs and as he unlocks and arms his speargun, I unpack the bag and put the food into the stainless steel fridge. "I don't know if I could ever get used to this."

"Get used to what?"

"So much *food*. There's at least a week's worth in here for a family of four." After so many years of going without, it feels crazily luxurious.

"You'll get used to it. Come on, angel." Knox goes out onto the deck. He kicks off his boots and lays his holster belt on the outdoor table.

I follow him, slipping off my sneakers. "I don't have a bathing suit."

So he comes over to me, takes my mouth in a scorching kiss, and slowly peels my dress up over my head, tossing it onto a chair. "Then I guess you'll have to swim like this." He grins and dives into the water.

I dive in after him.

I feel like a mermaid.

We swim through schools of fish and past colorful coral reefs. I see a sea turtle in the distance.

I think about what Remy said to him. *It can't last, Knox, not as anything more than a fling or a mistress. You know that. Don't fight it.*

Would I be willing to become his freaking *mistress*? Could I share him with his *wife*? Would that be better than having nothing of him at all?

No. Not in million years.

I could never share him. I don't want to be his bit on the side. I want to be his whole world.

I've only known Knox Ramsey for a week or something close to it. The first few days are still a blur. Watching him now as he swims and spears a fish, though, I know that if I can keep him, he'll be the love of my life. If I can't, he'll be the one that got away and that no one else will ever compare to.

And if I *can't* keep him, then the next few days with him will be the best of my life, I know that. I can feel it. Which is intensely sad.

I don't know if I believe in soulmates or love at first sight. Except that I do. Because everything about him is better than what I might have imagined, if I'd ever dared to dream so big.

Either way, I'm going to make the most of it.

He spears two more fish and we swim back to the house. I climb up the ladder at the side of the deck and Knox climbs up after me, looping an arm around my waist as he presses his face into me from behind, licking my clit then delving his tongue inside me. *"Mine.* I want you to go and make yourself comfortable on that lounger. Don't bother getting a towel. I need my fix."

I'll give him his fix. And I'll get my fix.

But what I want next is something he hasn't given me yet.

I want him to make love to me. I want him to take my virginity.

Will he? Or is he holding out on me because he's about to get married to someone else?

We spent two nights in his bed and I lost count of all the orgasms he gave me with his mouth.

He's a big, lusty animal but he's made no move to seal our bond in the most profound way of all.

I lay back on the lounger, relaxed in a way you can only be after a good swim and the warmth of the sun on your skin. "Knox?"

"Yeah?"

"Am I really your first visitor?"

"Aside from my family, yes."

I want to bait him. "So you don't bring your girl-friends here?"

He gives me a look, which turns hot and dark as I bend one knee just slightly. "Not a single one."

"Do you ... have a lot of girlfriends?"

His smirk is self-satisfied. "Are you jealous?" This pleases him.

"Does that mean yes?"

"No. It doesn't mean yes. I don't have girlfriends because I live here and most of the people that live in

Paradise are related to me." Dropping the fish into the sink of the outdoor kitchen, he scoops ice from an ice-maker that happens to be located under the sink and pours it over them. He dries his hands with a towel and walks over to me.

He gazes down at my naked body.

I'm still wet from the water but also wet because I can still feel the effects of his tongue prodding into me from behind.

"But you've ...?" It's a hard question to ask.

"But I've ...?"

"You've been with lots of women."

Knox smiles lazily, kneeling in front of me. "What are we talking about here, honey?"

"How many?"

"How many what?"

"How many women have you been with?"

His tongue laves slowly over my pussy. "I've been with ... a few. But rarely for more than one night and never without a condom. Any other questions?"

"Did you love them?"

The hot strikes of his breath stoke my lust even more. "No. I didn't love them."

"But you *made* love to them."

Knox Ramsey's blue eyes are sparkling. "You're jealousy is getting me hot, angel."

"You're not going to tell me how many?"

"I didn't keep track."

He's evading my questions, but of course I don't

really want to know how many other women he's slept with. The fact is: he slept with them. And he won't sleep with me.

I'm surly. And so turned on I feel restless. And reckless. I *want* to rile him and provoke him. My pussy feels like a warm, wet, ripe fruit, sweet and hot with need. "You liked them better than you like me."

His head tilts as he gazes up at me, and his blue eyes flash. "No, Cassidy. I didn't like any of them enough to spend a second night with them. You, on the other hand, are breaking my heart."

My eyes sting. I don't want to cry but it hurts, all this love I have for him. Why does this have to be so complicated when, to me, it doesn't feel complicated at all?

I want him, that's all there is to it. I want him to be my first and my last. I want him to be my only, for the rest of time.

But he won't give it to me. I can feel him holding back.

He frowns and lays his big body next to mine. He touches his finger to my tear, licking it. "Angel tears are something I simply can't tolerate. Tell me what's wrong."

"You don't want me like you wanted them."

The look on his face is one of slow understanding. "You're crying because you think I don't want you?" His sudden, low laugh turns me on even more.

He kisses my eyelid, then the other, so my tears wet his lips.

My tears seem to have struck something in Knox,

some animal desire or protective flare. There's a new ferocity in his kiss that makes my heart beat faster. Something in him has turned, almost like he's beginning to allow himself to act on his own desperation.

Knox lifts me and carries me inside the house and up the staircase to the bedroom. He lays me down on the bed.

His rough hands cup my breasts. He swirls my nipples between his fingers and thumbs, gently tugging and squeezing. It's almost painful, scalding me with prickling, deepening heat. His blue eyes are darker than I've ever seen them.

"My Goddess of Fire gets whatever she wants. But be warned, baby girl." He sucks my nipples carelessly, almost manic in his lightness. "Once we do this, there's no turning back. We'll be bound forever. You'll be mine and I'll be yours. It's the only way this can happen. Our fates will be sealed no matter what the consequences. Are you ready for me, angel girl?"

44

Cassidy

"I WANT YOU," I whisper. They're the truest words I've ever spoken.

Knox kisses my lips and I can taste the salt of my own tears. He frees his gigantic erection—*oh, God*—and kicks off his swim shorts. "It would be so easy for me to prove to you that I want you more than I've ever wanted anything in my life, Cassidy girl. And I don't know if I can take this anymore."

I gasp as he pushes my legs wide, licking lustily into my softness, wetting me with the messy strokes of his tongue. "If you insist on breaking down every defense I have with your tears and your plush, wet, ripe beauty, then you give me no choice. Is *that* what you want? Proof?"

I can only sigh my response.

"Are you ready for me to prove how much I want you, angel?" As though to emphasize his question, he sucks hard on my clit until I cry his name in a whispered moan.

He climbs up my body, supporting his weight above me, positioning himself.

"You want me to take you like this?" I can feel the broad end of his immense cock pushing between the slippery lips of my pussy, barely entering me. His size and his strength give him total control. Where his cock is just beginning to force its way inside me, there's a stretching, life-changing burn. *He's so freaking big.*

He roughly spreads my legs wider.

"You want to know why I've waited? Why I didn't take you as soon as I saw you? Do you have any idea?"

"No," I whisper.

"No? I'll tell you why. You need to understand that once I'm inside *you*, angel, I'll have no choice but to fuck you so deep and so good that I'll fill you up with my hot, gushing cum. We'll be forever joined. I don't want barriers, not with you. I don't want to hold back or wait or do anything but fuck you senseless and give you everything I have. Because you're the one. I knew it the second I saw you. Because I've been looking for you my whole life. It's the only way I can do this, so you need to be absolutely sure."

I tilt my hips up to him, because I *am* sure and because my body does it for me, until he's pressed even more strongly against me. *Inside me.*

Knox grips his thick length. My inner muscles clench on the emptiness. I think I might die from raw need.

"I've never had sex without a condom." His voice is low, almost crooning, as he rubs my clit with the fat, silky head of his cock. "I didn't want to be bound to them in that way and beyond that moment."

The caresses become more slippery. I can feel the first quivers of my looming orgasm.

"With you, angel, I won't want to separate myself from you. I'll want to possess you completely. I'll want you to take all of me. My big, bursting cock, my cum, the baby I'll put inside you, all of it. Because you're the one I want."

I run my fingers over the coiled muscles of his back, clinging to him, digging my fingernails into his skin to pull him closer.

"So you better be damn sure before you invite me in like this. Things will get complicated. It could kill us both. But I'll fight for you, I promise you that, angel. If you're sure you want all of me, then I'm all in. But you better be very sure you want me to take you nice and hard and deep and to make you come like *this*, Cassidy girl. Because it'll be game on."

His cock slides a fraction deeper. Even though I'm wet beyond belief and almost about to come, the burning, stretching sensation is dizzying.

"You're sacred to me," he continues, and his voice is husky with emotion. "You're the one. My sunlit angel. My Cassidy. Mine."

He pushes deeper, working his lazy rhythm. Out, then

in, just a little deeper. And a little more. *Oh God, he's so thick.*

"Is this what my angel wants from me?" He bites the soft flesh of my earlobe between his teeth. "Say it to me."

"*Yes, Knox,*" I gasp.

"You want me, and *all* of me? Once I start, see, there's no going back. And it'll hurt you, angel. There's nothing I can do to stop from hurting you, at first. But then everything I do will give you pleasure. As much pleasure as you can handle. Is *this* what you want me to do?"

I sob from the strung-out need of my body. "*Please, Knox.*"

He drives deeper inside me, and there's a sharp pain as he breaks through the fragile barrier of my virginity with one deep thrust. I cry out and he catches my moan with his kiss. He holds himself still, kissing me tenderly, until I begin to relax.

"That's the only pain." He smoothes my hair back from my face. "Are you ready for as much pleasure as you can handle?"

"*Yes,*" I gasp as he pushes deeper into me. I feel my body resisting him. He's too much.

"Relax for me, baby girl. Let me in." Kissing my mouth, murmuring sweet words as he fucks me more aggressively, until I can feel my inner muscles taking more, spanning his heavy invasion bit by bit.

He pushes my legs even wider, settling deeper with a forceful thrust that makes my vision blur. His soft-edged groan hums with finality and I know that he's fully inside me now.

It's uncomfortable, this extreme fullness of him deep inside my body. I wriggle, trying to find the pleasure. I tilt forward and back, just barely, feeling our wetness begin to soften the tightness.

Knox pushes his face into my neck. He makes a sound of quiet agony, like a muffled growl.

"Knox?"

He doesn't answer immediately. "You feel too good, angel. You're so fucking tight. So beautiful. I can barely hold onto this."

What we're about to do—in fact, what we're *doing*—is obviously a big deal. There could be consequences. Very big ones. I don't mention it to Knox now but I know it's unlikely I'll get pregnant. I don't get my periods regularly because I've spent a lot of my life hungry and underweight.

Even if I did get pregnant with Knox Ramsey's baby, I wouldn't mind. I *should* mind. Of course I should. Our future is very uncertain.

I'm not actively thinking that I want to be bound to him in this way.

Or maybe I am.

Maybe we both are. He's as much a part of this as I am.

Would they let me keep him if I was carrying his child?

I know he'll fight for me. I know he'd fight for us.

And it's enough.

He lifts his head and looks into my eyes. His slow smile is heart-breaking. "I'm inside my angel."

"My Knox," I gasp. "*Knox Ramsey* is inside me."

He kisses me and his mouth is hungry and possessive, his tongue licking into my mouth as he thrusts his big cock in a conjoined rhythm.

"I want to feel you come around me," he growls. "I want your pleasure to release me."

"We'll burn together."

"We'll die together," he says.

It's then that the discomfort begins to turn. The rubbing, burning friction of his extreme fullness inside me seems to sprout little wings that soften the pain into something else altogether. All sense and all feeling concentrates where my body is so tightly gripping his deeply nudging strokes. It hurts but at the same time nothing has ever felt this good.

Knox hears the tone of my soft exhale, reading the response I'm beginning to feel as he thrusts faster, deeper, finding the perfect balance of flesh and feeling. He keeps his pace steady, rooting out the ecstasy.

My legs are fully bent and wrapped around him. I'm pinned under him, held down by him, impaled by him. His mouth takes mine. I can only submit to him. He's all I can feel.

As soon as I embrace this total submission, a warm current begins to fill my body and my mind. It begins in my soul, it seems, coiling both into and out of the center of me. Knox's deep strokes entice it and force it higher and higher, melting me until there's nothing left of me except this overwhelming, devastating pleasure. The rising tide consumes me in a white-lit explosion of bliss, which holds and glides in an expanding swell.

As though to capture Knox Ramsey inside me, my body clenches tightly around him in welcoming bursts, pulling at the length of him in rhythmic squeezes, over and over.

Knox groans a mindless, low growl. I've never felt so much beauty and happiness as his big cock bucks deeply inside me, rubbing me with his throbbing length and setting me off again. My pussy clenches tightly in sync with the jerks of his cock as his cum pools hotly into me, flooding me and killing me with vibrant sensation. Long, lush, brimming shudders consume us both as we fuck and writhe and groan with the overload.

It's a long time before either of us can move or speak. We stare into each other's eyes, dazed and entwined. So completely connected in every way it's possible to be.

45

Cassidy

"I ONCE READ in this book that you can only truly know yourself if you ask yourself three questions."

Knox is laying on his stomach on the lounger and I'm straddling his back, rubbing suntan lotion onto his brawny shoulders. His eyes are closed and he's sleepy and relaxed. I lean closer to kiss his shoulder blade. It's late afternoon and the sun's glimmering reflection off the water paints our skin with languid flickers of blue. "What are the questions?"

"What do you believe in?"

He's quiet for a few seconds. "Family. Home. Having hot sex with the most beautiful girl in the world all day and all night."

I smile as my fingers glide smoothly over his back. I knead my thumbs into his muscles, massaging him with careful strokes. "I don't know about the first two but you're very good at the third."

"I'm good at all of them. You'll see."

We talk like this. Like we're together. More than that: like we're *staying* together and there's nothing that can change that. We've spent a whole week here, making love almost constantly, swimming, fishing, cooking, making love again, looking up at the stars, and talking about anything and everything.

Our skin is sandy and tanned. Our hair is bleached from the sun and the saltwater.

I never knew it was possible to feel so good or so content.

And I was right. It has been without a doubt the very best time of my life. By a country mile. I'm deeply, irrevocably in love with Knox Ramsey. To the point where I don't know if I can live without him.

I've made a point of not thinking about what happens when we leave the beach house, when he gets called back to the castle to talk to his family about what comes next. For now, we're pretending—or *I'm* pretending—that there's not an ominous deadline waiting for us at the end of the trail back up the hill.

"What's the next question?" he drawls.

"What do you hope for?"

Another long pause. "To spend the rest of our days doing exactly what we're doing right now. To marry you. To raise our little beach babies right here in this house. If I asked you to marry me, angel, would you?"

"Hmm," I say, caressing his lower back and gently squeezing his perfect ass. "Maybe."

He smiles but his eyes are still closed. We both know it's too soon to be talking about things like that. We also both know I'd marry him in a heartbeat. "You might have to," he says lazily.

I whisper it. "We're playing with fire." No doubt about it.

"I would expect nothing less from the Goddess herself."

This is what we do. The playful banter and the carefree love, like there's not a thing in the world to worry about.

Am I crazy to trust him and to want him this much? Have I lost my sanity, craving his sweat and his cum like they're my own lifeblood?

"Guess what I'm writing." My heart is stricken with love and my body is fiery with lust. My pussy warms and moistens. I draw the lines of a K across his back.

"Knox." His laughter is low and rumbling. "That's too easy."

I draw a C.

"Cassidy Meadow Kelley."

"I wonder what my real name is."

He barely turns to me, opening one blue eye. "I'm going to help you find out. We're going to trace that number and we'll figure it out."

Everything he says is exactly what I want to hear. Sometimes I wonder if any of it will come true. "Try to guess this one." I write an I. Then an L.

He flips over, adjusting me so I'm straddling his waist.

His bandage is gone now. Both our wounds are healed over. His is still red around the edges but it's less and less painful for him. "I love you," he grins up at me, holding my hips with his strong hands.

"I was writing, I *like* you," I laugh.

Knox laughs too and I tickle him. He squirms and grabs my wrists in an unbreakable hold. "No you weren't. You were writing, I love Knox Ramsey more than anything else in the whole fucking world."

"You're so full of yourself," I tell him, wriggling my hands free, gliding my fingers over the seeping head of his cock, which lays thickly against his stomach. He's rock hard, as usual. It's been an hour or so since we last came. My pussy wetly cradles the base of him.

We've spent most of our time naked or occasionally wrapped in a towel or the tie-dyed sarong I found in one of his closets. We make love many, many times a day. "I'd rather if *you* were full of me." His rumbling low laughter at his own joke rubs against me, easing my pleasure closer.

God, I love him so much.

"I'm surprised you have any luck at all with lines like that," I tease him, swaying against him, rubbing my pussy against his hard, silky length, moistening him with my own constant need for him.

"You'd be surprised. My girl loves my bad jokes and my big cock."

"Does she?"

"Fuck yeah. She can't get enough."

"Maybe because it's so perfect." I swirl the slick wetness on the engorged head with my fingers. "What else does she like?"

"She loves sliding her sweet, wet, pink pussy down onto my fat cock and riding me hard. She's a very dirty girl."

"Is that right?" I press the head of his cock against my pussy, letting him slip thickly inside me. I lower myself down onto him.

Knox grips my hips and thrusts deep, letting out a deep groan.

I grind onto him, squeezing him with my body as I bounce up and down. I work him, riding his cock lustily. "What else does she like?"

He sits up a little and grabs a handful of my hair. "She *loves* getting fucked deep and hard until I'm pumping her full of my hot cum. She *craves* it because she's a hot, greedy little minx." Looping his arm around my waist, he bucks his big cock deeper. "And she *feels* like nothing else on this earth."

I roll my hips, sliding up and then all the way down the full length of his thick, slick shaft. Each time I'm fully seated, I grip my inner muscles around him. The gliding friction as he fucks me and caresses every sweet spot I own with his big, driving body tips me over an impossible edge.

I see stars. I *feel* stars as my inner muscles clench tightly around him, over and over, pulling voluptuously at the huge length of him.

Knox erupts inside me, and the force of his jetting release sends me spiraling into another, even more intense orgasm. The pleasure courses through my body, as though I'm riding his energy. It spools into me, filling me with warmth and love and life.

We're still coming, staring deep into each other's eyes. I can see his own desperation there, equal to my own, like we might die if we can't stay like this, feeding off each other's pleasure.

"What's the third question?" he murmurs, kissing my lips, swirling his tongue over mine.

"What do you love?"

"That's easy. My angel girl. She owns my heart."

"And you own mine, Knox Ramsey."

But will it be enough?

Cassidy

ON THE SEVENTH DAY, Knox's phone rings. We've just come in from an early morning swim and I'm slicing some pineapple for our breakfast when *Remy* flashes up on the screen of his phone, which is sitting on the counter.

Knox walks over and picks it up. "Hey, Rem."

It's not on speaker phone but I can hear Remy's deep voice. "You okay down there? Haven't heard much from you."

"We're good. What's up?"

"I've got some news I think you and Cassidy are going to want to hear."

"What news?"

"We need to talk, Knox. Why don't you come up." It's not a question, but a gentle, firm command.

"Sure. We'll be up in an hour."

"Good. Okay. See you soon."

Knox ends the call.

"Everything okay?" I ask him.

"He wants to talk to us."

I guess I should be encouraged by the "us." At least Remy's not ordering Knox to send me back to Honolulu. Or maybe he is.

Would I go?

No.

Could I live in the caves?

Or here at the beach?

If they force him to make me leave, I don't know what I'll do. I don't have a Plan B.

You're a fool.

Maybe. I'm a fool who's so freaking in love all I can do is hope. And if I crash and burn, then at least I know what if feels like to fully live.

I like to think Knox wouldn't allow them to cast me out. Especially considering what we've been doing for the past week. Specifically, having sex—very unprotected sex —basically around the clock. We spend most of our time connected.

Something you should have thought of earlier, of course.

I don't think it's likely I could get pregnant, since I haven't had my period in three or four months, and even before that, they weren't regular. I looked it up online once and it said that, if your body doesn't "trust" that you have enough nourishment to grow a baby, it'll shut that option down until you do.

But I'm eating so well now. I can feel that I'm already starting to fill out.

So why am I playing with fire with a man I've known for less than three weeks?

Because I love him. *Because I want Knox Ramsey's baby. Because it would link us irrevocably. Because it would be a piece of him that would always be mine. And it would mean I was no longer alone.*

None of these are good reasons, obviously. I'm a lost soul with no guarantees. I'm being more than careless. I'm hoping for far too much.

Just like your mother did. And look how that turned out.

"Hey." He tips my chin up with his finger so I'm looking into his azure eyes. He lifts me easily and sets me on the island. He stands between my spread knees. A towel is loosely wrapped around his waist and his big, heavy cock is jutting through a gap in the towel. Knox pushes the short skirt I'm wearing up to my hips. I'm not wearing anything underneath. "Angels should never frown. What's going on inside that pretty little head of yours?"

"Nothing." But he's too perceptive.

He holds my face. The rough surface of his thumb, like a cat's tongue, gently skims my cheekbone. "Cassidy?"

"Yeah?" But I'm still frowning.

"I'm not going to let anything happen to us, okay? I mean it. I haven't told you everything about the alliance. I haven't told you about the superstitions that surround it and the reasons why the arranged marriages are some-thing my family takes seriously. Because I didn't want to spoil our time together. And it would have. But you need to know this: I'm willing to take any risk for you. We're meant to be together, we both know that. I'm working on it. Don't doubt me."

"I'm not doubting you, Knox."

"Good." His kiss is erotic in its lightness as he guides his cock to my pussy. He pulls me forward as he feeds his thickness into me. I'm not even fully wet but he feels *so insanely good*. He pushes the elastic neckline of my dress down to my waist. "Put your arms around my neck."

I do and he slides himself in, then almost all the way out, then in, even deeper. He does it again, gripping my ass as he fucks me slowly, gazing into my eyes. The climax rises and crashes quickly, milking him lovingly. Knox comes hard, deep inside me. Until the only movement is the secret ripples of our overflowing connection. My thighs are slick with it.

"*My angel*," he growls. "*Mine*."

In some ways I wish it wasn't as true as it is.

He lifts me down and sets me on my feet. Trickles of his cum drip down my legs. He pulls my dress back up over my shoulders, smoothing it. "You're beautiful, sweet-heart. I like the dress."

I found a needle and thread in a drawer in his master bathroom and made a cute sundress out of the tie-dyed sarong I found.

"Now go get any stuff you want to bring," he says. "We're leaving."

"Okay, boss."

He grins, but there's gravity to it. The outside world is breaking its way into our bubble.

His phone pings again.

They want him back.

We pack up and make ourselves presentable. Since I don't have any other possessions, after Knox pulls on some clothes, we make our way up the trail with nothing except the bag we brought with us, empty now since we've eaten most of the food.

Which makes me think about my pin again. And my note. I need to go get them. Or ask Knox to have someone get them for me. I know they're most likely safe where they are, since no one ever goes to the caves, but still. I've been so distracted I've hardly thought much about the two things that were always the two most important things in my life. But now isn't the time to bring it up. Right now I have bigger problems, namely whether or not I'm going to be forced out of Knox Ramsey's life.

I'm emotional about leaving.

Will I ever come back here?

Will it happen like he says it will?

I take a last look down at the golden bay and the turquoise of the ocean water before we take the turn that leads us back through the rainforest and up the steep incline toward the castle.

There are thunderclouds gathering to the east. Storms are brewing.

They're all there. Remy, Blaise, Wolf and Echo are all

in the big, open room with the fireplace and the view of the peach orchard, which they use as an office.

All four of them watch us as we walk in. The beachy look of us. The way Knox's hand grips mine. The easy intimacy of our closeness. I can feel that our body language communicates the intensity of the bond we feel.

"What's so urgent?" Knox asks them.

Blaise is half-sitting against a giant desk. She turns a laptop to face us. "This interview aired on the inter-island news last night." Knox and I walk closer. I can see a man on the screen of the laptop. The video has been paused.

Oh no. My stomach does an awful little flip. "That's the man who picked me up when I was hitchhiking. He's the one who gave me a ride."

On the screen, the man is standing next to his old blue pick-up truck. The caption says, *Jack Lum, Farmer.* A news reporter is holding a microphone up for him to speak into.

Blaise touches the play button.

"Oh, I saw her all right," says the man. He's animated. He's excited to tell his story. "I'd just dropped my son off at the airport for the seven a.m. flight to Hilo. A flight from Honolulu had just arrived and there was some traffic so I waited until most of it cleared out. I was heading home, driving along, minding my own business. And *there she was.* Her hair was blowing in the breeze and I couldn't believe my eyes. The *White Lady,* standing there on the side of the road with her thumb out, just as clear as day. She was looking for a ride, just like you hear about. She had long, very-blond hair. It was almost white. She looked like she might be in her late teens or maybe twenty. She was wearing a gray hooded sweatshirt over a yellow dress. And a backpack. And black sneakers. She looked like she'd been traveling for a while. Because that's what she does, isn't it? Her clothes were worn and dirty. There might have even been blood on her dress. I'm telling you, *it was her*. It could only have been her. I told her I'd take her anywhere she wanted to go. Of course I did."

The woman who's interviewing the man asks him, "Where did she want to go?"

"She asked me if I knew where the Ramseys lived. I told her I did. So I took her all the way to their gate and as soon as we got to it, she hopped off the back and disappeared. Because that's another thing she does, isn't it? She was the prettiest thing I'd ever seen. Absolutely beautiful, in a way that could make you believe that heavenly beings really *do* exist. Polite, too. But she had that fire in her eyes. Determination, that's what it was. The *Goddess of Fire* herself, I'm telling you it was her. I never in a million years expected to see her with my own eyes. But it could only have been her."

Blaise pauses the video. "Cassidy, do you think Axel Archer would recognize that description of you?"

I can see by the look on Blaise's face, and even more on Echo's, that they're worried.

"Yes," I tell them. "If he sees that, or if Dash—my neighbor who's one of his recruits—sees it, I think they would know it was me. It was the same outfit I was wearing when I ... when I ran from them."

Remy and Wolf look pissed off.

And Knox—Knox looks furious. His grip on my hand tightens almost painfully.

What have I done?

47

Cassidy

I've brought my own danger to the Ramseys.

I'd tried to cover my tracks but I never knew about ... the legend. The very last thing I expected was to be mistaken for some legendary, magical *goddess*.

But if this was on the news, I have no doubt that Arrow will know by now that I'm here inside the Ramsey compound, or close by. They'll be looking for clues and this huge target will have landed right in the middle of Paradise. Axel will come looking for me, I know he will. I could hear it in his voice. *What is this? You have a tattoo.* My hunch is that he knows what my ink means and—whatever it *does* mean—it's something he wants.

I could show it to them now. I've artfully kept it hidden from Knox this whole time. Carefully keeping it covered. Because—in the same way he doesn't want to talk about his family alliances or the arranged marriages

—I didn't want it to spoil our time together. I didn't want it to be a reason he might distance himself from me in any way whatsoever, when so many other things threaten to do that for us. And now hardly seems the time, since my choice is clear.

I've created the ultimate conquest for Axel Archer—inside the walls of Paradise.

I've brought the threat to them, the very last people I would ever want to hurt. This place has been nothing but a magical sanctuary for me. I can't bear the thought that this peaceful, beautiful place might be targeted by blood-thirsty criminals—because they want to get to me.

What if they're able to breach the walls, like I did? What if Axel comes after Blaise or Echo, and threatens them like he did to me? What if he uses his gun on one of the people in this room? *What if it's Knox?*

I couldn't bear it.

"I'm sorry," I tell them. "I should go. I don't want them to come looking for me here. I had no right to put you in danger like this."

I swear I can feel my heart literally breaking as I slide my hand from Knox's grip. It *hurts* but at the same time I feel surprisingly numb.

What if he gets killed because of you?

Knox grabs my arm. "What the hell are you talking about, Cassidy?"

"I mean I need to leave! I need to get far away from here, in case they're searching for me. I should never have come here. Let me go."

Knox's grip on my arm doesn't release. Instead, he grips me even more tightly, with both hands. It's painful, because of the injury he gave me only weeks ago.

"*Please.*" I'm staring into his crazy-blue eyes. I feel frantic. And devastated. "I'm not going to put you at risk. I can't. Not when it's my fault."

"What are you even saying right now, Cassidy? It's not *your* fault they tried to get to you. It's theirs. It's fucking *his* fault."

"If I go now, I can hitchhike away from here. There'll be another news story of me heading in the opposite direction. So they won't come looking for me here."

"*No.*" Knox is enraged. "That's not going to happen. Don't even think about doing that, do you hear me? If they come here looking for you, then we'll fight them. We're ready. That's what our walls and weapons are designed for. It's why we train. It's what we prepare for. Paradise is well protected. And so are you."

"I don't want you to fight for me!" It's bad enough I've scarred him with my own knife, damaging him and almost killing him. I can't let anything else happen to him. Not when there's something I can do about it. "I have to go."

I hate that there are tears in my eyes. Of frustration. And regret. That I've brought this to them.

It's Echo who surprises me first. "You can't *leave*, Cassidy. Absolutely not. You'd be caught. If you stabbed Axel Archer, he's going to want some serious revenge."

And Wolf. "As much as I think you'd give Axel a good

run for his money, you're better off right here." He flicks a thumb toward Knox. "If you can bring *this* boy to his knees, you're clearly a force to be reckoned with. And so are we."

I'm amazed that they would offer this. "I couldn't handle it if anything happened to any one of you because of me."

Even Remy chimes in. "And *I* couldn't handle it if Arrow could better any one of us. They're a bunch of vagrant kids from the streets led by a thug who thinks only of his own best interests."

"Besides," Knox says, "if you ran, I'd follow you. And my family would follow me. So you'd be putting all of us in a lot more danger by running. I don't want to hear any more talk about running. Are we clear?"

"We can all see it, Cassidy," says Blaise. "The connection you and Knox clearly have. Don't make him chase you, okay? It's too risky. At least here we're prepared for them."

What *I'm* not prepared for is ... the care. Their protective instincts. The way they've made me feel almost like I'm one of them. After a lifetime of feeling so desperately alone, it's overwhelmingly ... *beautiful*. I'm not just in love with Knox Ramsey, I'm in love with his whole family and his entire world. "But ... are you sure?"

Knox's palm slides around the nape of my neck. He leans in and touches his forehead to mine. "Of course we're sure. Don't you dare leave me. I'd follow wherever you go."

"I don't want to leave you, Knox."

"Then don't. Promise me."

"Okay."

"Okay?" It's a growl and a command. And a plea.

"Yes, Knox."

"We're going to go and tell some of the others to start getting some things ready. You stay here with Blaise and Echo. I'll be back. Promise me you'll be right here."

"All right, Knox."

"Good girl."

With that, Remy, Knox and Wolf leave.

"Wow. He's *so* in to you," Echo grins at me, despite the drama. "That's a cute dress, by the way. Where'd you get it?"

I'm still reeling. "I ... I made it."

"Really? Did Knox tell you I also sew and design—"

"Listen, you two," interrupts Blaise. "You can talk fashion later. Cassidy, would you be willing to show me exactly where you breached the security? There's a gap and we're having it wired, but I'm not actually sure where the unsecured part ends."

"Of course I can. Do you think—?" I hesitate.

"Do I think Knox will mind if you leave this room for a few minutes to show me? No. Because it'll help make the perimeter that much more secure." Knox mentioned to me once that Blaise is the smartest person he knows and I can see that about her. She's clearly some kind of tactical expert. "I've also been scanning the internet for signs that there's anyone talking online about you and where you are. I haven't seen anything. They'll probably find out, but I can't see any sign that they've found out yet."

I take a deep breath with relief. "I'll show you where I climbed over."

Blaise stands. She's slim and has an athletic build. "You coming, E?"

"Sure."

The three of us walk out the side door of the office, into the orchards. Through the avocado grove to the mango trees. The sky is overcast now. The air feels heavy and electric, like it's about to rain.

"There." I point to it. The ladder is still propped up against the wall where I left it. All those day ago when I came to tell the Ramseys where Knox was. That feels like a long time ago. So much has happened to me since then.

But as we're nearing the ladder, I can see pale, thin vertical lines on the wall. It takes me a few seconds to realize that the lines are ropes that have been thrown over.

Nearby, there's movement.

I see a shadow.

A shadowy figure.

It's someone dressed in black.

Two people.

Six people.

Six *big* people.

All three of us sense the danger at the same time.

They're surrounding us.

We've made a critical mistake.

Because the people closing in on us aren't Ramseys.

48

Cassidy

MY MIND BLURS WITH PANIC.

I recognize one of the men. "Dash?"

"Cassidy. You didn't really think you could escape us, did you?"

I turn but Dash and one of the other men grab me forcefully.

"Get the other two," he orders the others.

Echo screams but the sound is cut short by one of the men who grabs her and covers her mouth with his gloved hand. She squirms and hits him hard enough that he grunts in surprise and releases her.

Blaise does some sort of karate move on one of the men and he falls into a groaning heap. She pulls a knife, holding it close to another man's face.

These Ramsey women are bad-asses, is what it boils down to.

And so am I.

But the man Blaise is threatening holds up a gun. He clicks off the safety catch and aims it directly at her. "Don't make me use this, sweetheart."

Blaise takes a step back, trying to shield Echo.

"Let them go!" I yell at the men. "Take me. I'm the one you want. Let them go. Hurry. Someone will have heard Echo's scream. Take me now and let them go." Through the haze of both fear and adrenaline coursing through my veins, what I'm thinking is that this ambush is meant for me, not them. I'm used to being hunted. I'll fight these men every step of the way but *I don't want Echo and Blaise to be hurt by these men.* This was never supposed to happen to them. It's me they're after. It's me Dash wants.

It's not a train of thought I might have expected but I'm feeling it. Hard.

"Run!" I scream at them. "*Run.*"

I can see it in Blaise's eyes: surprise. And respect. My knee-jerk reaction to protect them has forged some kind of bond between us that's hard to describe. She wasn't expecting it and she won't forget this.

Blaise and Echo *do* run. I know they'll get help for me, if they can reach the men in time. I know they'll try to save me.

If I can be saved.

And it's enough.

Even so, it's then that the sickly weight of my terror settles in.

I'm slung over Dash's shoulder. I scream and kick and punch at him but someone holds my wrists and ties them together. A gag is tied over my mouth. I'm heaved up as Dash tries to climb the ladder but it breaks and the impact of his fall winds me.

I'm lifted up a rope. They struggle to hoist me as I fight them with everything I have. They're hurting me. They're bruising me with their rough hands and their desperation. I can smell their sweat and it makes my stomach roll.

Through the flurry of stars across my vision I can see that we're at the top of the wall now.

"*Hurry*, man," one them growls.

There are sounds but I can't tell what they are. Commotion down below us. We're at the top of the wall now.

Someone's yanking at us. There are shouts.

I see a knife slicing into Dash's leg. The red of the blood looks surreal, almost theatrical. There's so *much* of it.

I'm falling.

The hard, jolting collision with the ground is incredibly painful. I land on my tied-together arms. I can't breathe and my hair is in my face. I'm sandwiched between two men, one of them limp and the other one absolutely wild with fury. I can smell blood. Or maybe I can taste it.

The whole sky tilts and I'm going to pass out.

There's the sound of pain. And rage. And a thudding sound. A rabid growling sound.

The commotion starts to slow.

I feel hands on me.

"Cassidy."

It's him. Knox.

His voice sounds so strange. So dark and so worried.

He takes the gag from around my mouth. He unties my hands and gently pushes my hair back from my face.

"Cassidy, can you hear me? Angel, you're okay now. I'm here. You're all right. I'm here with you."

It takes me a few seconds to focus on his face and *wow*, it's worth the effort. His eyes are almost completely black and there's blood on his face and his hands. His eyes burn with an agonized despair as he stares down at me. Despite all that, he's, like, *mind-numbingly* beautiful.

"Angel. Cassidy. Please. Answer me. You're okay now, baby. Everything's okay."

"Knox." It's hard to speak.

"That's my girl. You're okay. I'm here now."

He helps me sit up a little and I can see now that Wolf is there, standing behind him, looking equally ferocious. "There's got to be more to this than a cut with a kitchen knife," Wolf says. "He's asking for all-out war."

I notice someone lying on the ground.

It's Dash. He's very, very still.

There's a thin slice across his neck and blood all over his neck and his chest. It's staining the grass all around him.

"*Oh my God*. He's dead."

"Of course he's dead," Knox says gruffly.

Three more of the men are scattered, lifeless, nearby.

"Holy shit. They're *all* dead." I can't believe it.

"Two of the fuckers ran," Wolf comments. "We're hunting them."

"Where's Echo? And Blaise? Are they all right?"

"They're fine," says Knox. "They're just fine."

"Because of you." Wolf's low comment surprises me.

"It's because of me they came here in the first place. I'm so sorry I brought this to you."

"You're worth fighting for, angel." Knox lifts me into his arms so, so carefully. "You're worth killing for. You're worth dying for."

Wolf is watching Knox as Knox gazes down at me. Wolf seems sort of riveted by his brother's intensity and behavior.

There are other people around. Lots of them. They move aside as Knox carries me through the small, gathering crowd.

I hardly notice them. All I can do is stare up at him with a starstruck awe. The fierceness of him. The crazy love in his eyes. I put my hand on his chest so I can feel his heartbeat. "Knox."

"Right here, baby girl. I've got you."

He's with me. And I'm with him. And that's the only thing I want or need in this whole wide world.

49

Cassidy

If I had any doubts that Knox Ramsey loves me, the next two days lay those doubts to rest.

There are only a few bruises around my wrists, my neck and across my ribs, but I'm put on bedrest for twenty-four hours by Hana until the shock and the aftermath of the adrenaline rush turns to exhaustion, relief and something close to an existential realization.

I'm glad to be alive. Obviously. "What happened to them?"

"To who?"

"To Dash. And those other men."

"They were buried at sea."

"On a boat?"

He gives me a look. "Yes. That's usually how people are buried at sea. They were taken far out and disposed of. All evidence that they were ever here at all has been erased. The two that got away were chased. One was caught. The other escaped."

"Escaped?"

"Yes. He disappeared and we weren't able to locate him."

The Ramseys take break-ins and attempted kidnappings very seriously, so it seems.

My Knox is gruff. *And* capable of killing anyone who threatens his own. Which is sort of intense.

But this ferocity is spliced with a side of him that's so caring and careful with me, it enchants me. Knox feeds me and won't let me out of bed unless it's to run me a bath or to carry me to the chair outside on the balcony of his apartment where he sits me on his lap and wraps his burly arms around me, kissing me but refusing to give me more. Because I'm supposed to be resting. He waits on me hand and foot and he watches over me as I sleep, or he spoons me and keeps me in a bear hug as we sleep together.

Now, he's sitting next to me in bed with a laptop resting on his stomach. He's been showing me how he checks his investments, explaining to me what the numbers mean. It's interesting but there's so much to learn.

"How do you feel?" I ask him.

"How do I feel about what?"

"About killing those men."

"I feel like it was what they deserved."

"It's a heavy thing."

"It's not heavy when the love of my life is being assaulted and kidnapped, sweetheart. It's fucking justice. They deserved what they got for touching a single hair on your head. If anything, they got off too easily."

I think about that for a second. "I guess so."

"I know so. That's just the way it has to be."

"Have you ever killed anyone before?"

"No. But I'd do it again. If one of my own is threatened, I wouldn't hesitate."

Love of my life. One of my own. I've been wondering about something so I ask it point blank. "Why is your marriage being arranged?"

He stops what he's doing and glances over at me. I can see the wall go up behind his eyes. He hates this topic. I've tried to gently bring it up before and he always shuts it down. But we can both feel the deadline looming, even if we're trying to ignore it. "My family has alliances with two other families. They've been in place for generations."

"Why you? Why are you the one that has to do it? Why can't Wolf? Or Remy?"

He sighs heavily. "I'm not going to ruin our day by talking about this. You need to heal. Our priority is getting you back on your feet."

"I'm already healing. I'm fine, Knox. The bruises are already fading."

The mention of my bruises makes his eyes burn even more darkly. "Soon, we're both going to talk to Remy and clear up a few things."

"Remy decides?"

"Remy thinks he decides." Knox tries to distract me by pointing at a column of numbers on the screen. "This one here is the PE ratio. You use this to decide whether a stock is undervalued, overvalued or valued at a fair price. This one here is too high. Are you listening?"

"Yes." I don't push him, even though I want to. He's obviously defying his brother's wishes—or orders—and I can understand that I've thrown a monkey wrench into the Ramseys' plans. I've introduced a major problem for Remy, and for all the Ramseys, and I feel bad about doing that.

At the same time, my transformation is complete.

I'm not just in love with Knox Ramsey, I'm alarmingly ... *his*.

Our blood bonded us. Our week at the beach house locked into place our addiction. But my rescue from Arrow has forged our connection into something else altogether.

I can admit I might possibly die without him. Which sounds over the top but it feels absolutely true. I need him and I'm weirdly okay with that. There's a power to falling in love this deeply. You're fully aware that you've been given a gift and that nothing else will ever feel this good or this life-changing. It's worth any price, whatever happens.

We have a lot to talk about. And plans to make. I need to get my pin, and find out if he's right about the number etched onto it. He mentioned that he'll have my pin retrieved and we'll talk to Enzo about the number once

I've been given the all-clear. But anything to do with the Kings or the Fitzpatricks causes his mood to shift.

The alliance and all that goes with it is the topic he avoids and I get that.

I have one too.

We both have a secret from each other. The one thing about ourselves that could be enough to drive us apart. He keeps his close to his chest and so do I.

But I've made my decision.

I'm going to show Knox my tattoo. If he's going to defy some ancient family rule for me then he deserves to know.

I know for a fact it's going to cause ripples. I just don't know how big they'll be or in which direction they'll be rippling. Pulling us together or forcing us apart. I'm waiting for a moment that's *not* perfect between us. So far there haven't been many. Or any.

Even when he's grumpy like this he's still beguiling to me. *And hot.* With his big, suntanned muscles and his scowl. He's surly because of the outside forces that are the only things that could potentially separate us.

I figure if he's willing to kill for me, and to go against his older brother's orders for me, then maybe he'll forgive me for whatever bad blood I've been born into.

I have to be brave enough to take that chance.

50

Cassidy

I *WILL* BE BRAVE ENOUGH.

Now, with his anger at my question crackling between us, might be as good a time as any. My heart's beating fast, though.

"Knox?"

He closes his laptop and puts it on the floor beside the bed. Then he lays on his side, staring over at me sort of aggressively, like he's expecting more of my interrogation. "Ask me any question except that one. I promise you, I'm working on it."

I'm wrapped in a duvet, laid back against a mountain of pillows on his bed. I turn on my side so we're laying face to face.

I can't quite bring myself to blurt it out.

He's so damn gorgeous I can't stand it. I don't want lose him. I can't.

So I stall just a little longer. "What's your favorite

color?" It suddenly seems wrong that I don't know some of the simpler things about him, when I've just admitted to myself that I'm basically unwilling to live without him. Whatever that means.

"Blue. What's yours?"

"Red."

"Not surprising. Goddess of Fire and all that." His eyes lose some of their aggression and the wall comes down. He's got the look of a golden god but this serious, studious side of him is a new weakness.

I love him so much my heart literally aches. "What's your favorite book?"

"The Art of War."

This almost makes me smile. "I guess I don't need to ask why."

"It'll teach you everything you need to know about fighting." He taps lightly on my temple. "Up here. But it also applies to life. To business. Investing. Anything that requires gaining power over another person. But then, you know all about power, don't you, baby girl?"

"What do you mean? I don't have any power."

"Wrong. You have *all* the power."

"How?"

"I can't resist a single thing about you. I've never known anyone as beautiful as you are. I would—and have —killed for you. I'd die for you. All of the above means you own me, pure and simple. If that's not power I don't know what is."

And once again, Knox Ramsey slays me with his

words, his voice, his body, his mind. I want to crawl into his soul with him. I want him in every possible way. And he's taken this whole bedrest thing way too seriously. Since the incident at the wall, he's been practically bullyish about making sure I rest and don't do anything too strenuous.

Which means he hasn't made love to me in a day and a half. He won't let me come and he won't let *me* make *him* come either.

I'm getting restless. And hot. I want to show him how much I love him. "I guess maybe I'll have to test that theory."

His gold hair is messy, framing his face in a halo of waves. There's a light stubble on his square jaw that matches his hair. I can see the pulse of his heartbeat in the veins on his tanned, corded neck. And in the ones that run down his beefed-up biceps.

He's always beautiful to me but there are times, like now, when his beauty hits differently. It overwhelms me. It becomes emotional and also primal. I feel hungry to touch his magnificence, and *feel* it. To taste it and take it inside.

The sheet is covering him to the waist. I can see the clearly-defined muscles of his eight-pack and the gigantic ridge below the sheet. His cock is laying thickly across his thigh, hiding just under the thin layer of cotton. The big, meaty bulk of it is ridiculously tantalizing.

I start trying to pull the sheet slowly off of him.

He holds it, giving me a stern look. "No, angel. You're supposed to be resting."

"I am rested. Now I want to ... eat."

"You're hungry?"

"No, I'm not hungry. You've fed me so much I'm surprised I can even move."

"You needed food."

It's true I've put on some weight in the past month and I feel amazing. I feel sexier.

I shift a little in bed, letting my legs fall open under the covers. I'm naked and my pussy feels warm and wet.

I pull again lightly at the sheet, displacing it just enough. I can see the bead of pre-cum at the tip of his cock. He's fully hard now, even though he's trying to hold back because he thinks I'm not up to it. But he can't tell me no when it's right there and so clearly ... *ready*.

He's protective of me. He wants to be in control. He frowns at me, but it morphs into a gentle intensity. "My greedy girl."

I know that if I offer myself to him submissively he'll get sort of crazily turned on. So I let the comforter that's wrapped around me slide open, so he can see my parted legs and my soaked pussy. I can't help it. My body craves him in a way that gives me no choice. "I want to taste you."

"I want you rested—"

"I *am* rested. Please?" I bite gently my lip and he watches me do this. "I want to suck on you."

He exhales but I know I've won. "Only if you're sure you're up to it."

"It'll help me." He's my superpower. I can't analyze it. I crawl to him, seeking out that seep of his cum like I've spent days in the desert and he's my oasis. "I want you to fuck my mouth."

His head drops back and there it is: his low laughter. "Fuck. See? Little dirty angel girl has *all* the power." He lays onto his back, offering his thick, hard cock to me. "All right then. But it's only fair. Let me at that perfect pink pussy." As I crawl onto him, he lifts my leg carefully over his chest, then he rolls us a little further so he can get better access. "Easy, baby girl."

I'm laying half on top of him with my stomach against his.

He's holding my spread legs with his big, rough hands. "Oh how I'm missed this pretty pussy," he whispers darkly, kissing me with an open mouth, licking me in long, heady strokes. I sigh because he's so *ravenous* and he feels so damn good. His scratchy stubble burns my sensitive skin.

I touch my tongue to the slit of his cock, sipping the wetness, taking him deeper as he eats me with a lot of freaking gusto.

Knox Ramsey *loves* going down on me. He could do it all night. "*So ... fucking ... gorgeous,*" he murmurs against my saturated flesh, flicking my clit with his thick tongue.

I take his engorged cock deeper.

It's insanely intimate. Taking him into my mouth as

he feasts on me. His fingers swivel and glide inside me and I can *hear* how wet I am.

God, I'm so addicted to the way he feels.

I arch my back and we get into a rhythm. In, out, in. His moves are measured and he *enjoys* it so much, the sensation rises and fills me with waves of hot, liquid pleasure.

He's fucking me with his fingers as he sucks hard on my clit. When his teeth graze my over-sensitive nub, a freight train of feeling bursts inside me, milking his fingers, forcing shuddering waves of the world's most intense orgasm to spasm over and over as he licks me through it.

I moan but the sound is muffled by the mouthful of cum he's shooting into me. I drink the flooding gushes thirstily and I almost don't recognize myself because this is basically what I live for. The milky taste of his pleasure. I feel slightly depraved because I love it so much.

His cock is still gently pulsating, emptying the last throbs onto my tongue. I keep tenderly suckling on him and kissing him until I hear the deep, low rasp of his voice.

"Come here, angel."

He helps me climb up his body. He wraps me in his arms and holds me close. He kisses me with a tenderness that makes my eyes sting because he's my perfect lover and there *is* no such thing as perfect. Or at least there shouldn't be.

"*Damn*, baby girl. We need each other."

It's the truth.

"Don't worry about anything, okay, sweetheart? I'll figure out a way."

Of course I believe him. I believe he'll try. And he's as stubborn as a mule, which gives me hope.

After a few minutes, Knox's phone rings. For a second I think he might ignore it, but then he reaches over and I can see Echo's name on the screen. He answers. "Hey, E. You're on speaker."

"Hey, bro. Hi, Cassidy." I guess it's sort of obvious that I'd be close to him. "How are you feeling?"

"I feel great," I tell her. Knox's grin is slow and cocky, his face still wet with my juices.

"Listen, I'm coming up there in twenty to bring you some choices for the dress you want to wear tonight. I have some ideas but you can choose your favorite. You're going to want to pull out all the stops for this one."

"Why? What's happening tonight?"

"Tonight's the start of our weekend party. We've been planning it for a month now. Tonight's the full moon."

"Wow. What's the occasion?"

Knox's expression has turned dark and his smile is gone. He'd forgotten, maybe, or lost track of time. "It's a party for the three families of the alliance. The Kings will start arriving in around two hours. And, soon after that, the Fitzpatricks."

51

Cassidy

THE DRESSES ECHO brings to me are the most beautiful I have ever, ever seen. She makes me try on all seven of them.

"Knox, what do you think of this one?" Echo asks him.

He's taken a shower and his hair is still damp. He's dressed in jeans and a white shirt that shows off the dark tan of his cinnamon skin. He looks insanely gorgeous. And I feel just a little bit nervous. *This is it. This is when everything will come to a head.*

Knox's mood has not improved since Echo's phone call. "She looks gorgeous no matter how you dress her." His phone rings and he answers it, taking the call outside. By the agitated tone of his voice and the way he's pacing along the wide balcony, my guess is he's talking to Remy.

The last dress Echo gives me to try on is short, sleeveless cream-colored silk with small sections cut out of it showing off my skin and soft, delicate fur detailing around the low neckline. It's tight but just a little bit stretchy. It fits me like a dream.

"This is it," says Echo. Her outfit is a to-die-for iridescent sequined halter top with a matching short skirt that has feathers attached to the hem. It shows off her slender figure and her long legs. "You totally *have* to wear this one."

I check myself out in the full-length mirror on the back of the bathroom door and, *wow*, it really does look amazing. The skirt is very short, the neckline deeply cut. It shows off more skin than anything I've ever worn before.

"You can't wear anything under it. It'll ruin the line." She adjusts the fur. "Knox is going to have a conniption when he sees you in this."

"He's having all kinds of conniptions," I admit.

"We're going to say you're my guest," Echo says lightly. "People will ask and it's just best to ... keep them guessing. Are you okay with that?"

"Sure. Of course. I'll tell them I'm a friend of yours, here for a visit, if anyone asks."

"Oh, they'll ask." She smiles at me and it's so genuine, I almost feel like we're friends. Like she's rooting for me. I remember listening to her and Blaise's conversation on the plane and wishing I could know her. I want to earn her friendship.

"Thank you so much, Echo."

"Sit down here in front of the mirror and I'll do your hair."

I'm relieved that the back of the neck of my dress is securely covering my ink. I've spent my whole life feeling sure that it's a mark of darkness that can only cause me trouble. I'm always aware of it, and whether or not it might be visible.

Echo starts doing my hair. She glances out to where Knox is still talking on the phone. "He's changed, we can all see it. He's never been like this before. You should know that. He's very, very into you."

"I'm very, very into him too." I don't know if I should say it or not, but for some reason I want her to know. "I love him."

She smiles again but, like Knox so often does, she artfully changes the subject. "I could braid it and wrap it, like a crown."

"That would be cool." I'm wondering if she's been put up to this. If they want to do whatever they can to have people *not* mistake me for ... something I'm not.

As Echo does my hair, Knox comes in. He stands there for a few seconds, all 6'3" inches of built, hot volatility and barely-held rage. Our eyes meet in the mirror. "I'm going to have to meet you two downstairs. Echo, keep her with you, will you?"

"Of course, Knox."

He stares at me and his energy swirls around me like wildfire. He heats up the room. "You okay, angel?"

"I'm fine. Don't worry about me. I'll see you downstairs."

With that, he leaves, and it's a strange feeling. We haven't been apart for almost an entire month. I feel like he's taken a piece of me with him. The biggest piece, where all my emotions and my heart and my happiness live.

Echo finishes doing my hair. She sends me into the bathroom to take off my panties, so the dress sits seamlessly. Then she does my make-up. I choose from a bag of shoes she's brought. Luckily we're the exact same size. I decide on a pair of gold high heeled sandals that are the highest I've ever worn. They're delicate-looking but also surprisingly comfortable.

"Perfect," she says as we both stare at me in the mirror. I hardly look like myself at all. I look like some kind of movie star or model.

And it's time.

52

Cassidy

ECHO and I take the elevator down to the roomy, glass foyer of the castle. There's one of those grandfather clocks with a pendulum swinging from side to side. The time is eight fifteen. I notice there's a transparent glass case mounted on the wall of the foyer, next to the face of the clock. Inside, there's an old-fashioned style pistol held by two hooks. "What's that?"

"Oh, that's the Remington my great great grandfather —I've lost count of how many greats—brought with him from California over a century ago."

"Does it still work?"

"Yes. My brothers keep it in perfect working order. Don't tell anyone, but we always keep it loaded. For good luck."

"Wow."

"Yeah. My family has some crazy superstitions that go way back."

We go out the main doors to the enormous lanai, where the Kings are just arriving. The scene is wildly glamorous—like the party Maggie and I went to, as servers, all those weeks ago. It's a much, much different experience here and now.

I'm almost surprised that I don't feel intimidated or out of place.

He loves me. Knowing this fortifies me.

I can still feel the nourishment of his seed, empowering me. Crazy, maybe, but as real to me as my own heartbeat.

It's evening. There are lanterns and fire pits that reflect off the water of the pools. There's an outdoor bar, and waitstaff are gliding around unobtrusively, offering drinks. Modern music wafts through the tropical air at the perfect volume. The moon is full and hangs over the scene like it's been placed there specifically for the occasion.

"Let me introduce you," Echo says, leading me toward the small crowd of people. Blaise is here. I recognize Jagger, Stone and Aurora.

Jagger is standing with a dark-haired, stunning-looking man with bright blue eyes. He's tall, and big. His black hair just touches the collar of his black shirt and his whole look has a definite gangster vibe.

"Cassidy," says Echo, "this is Enzo King. Enzo, this is my friend Cassidy. She's visiting for the weekend. And this is his brother Jagger."

Enzo kisses the back of my hand. "It's a pleasure." There's a dark edge to him but also a relaxed, perceptive intelligence. He might be a villain but he's exceptionally comfortable in his own skin.

"Nice to meet you, Enzo." Not quite the time and place, but maybe later I can ask him about the number etched onto my pin.

"This isn't a line," says Jagger, "but I feel like we've met before."

"I'm not sure. I don't think so." Not technically. But there's that same eerie feeling again. That something about him is vaguely familiar. He's watching me like he's thinking the same thing.

I'm introduced to Stone, who's taller than I remember him but still has that slightly-sinister glint in his green eyes.

And Aurora. She's dressed in a hot pink catsuit that clashes with the dark-copper red of her hair. It's a look that takes balls, money and an innate sense of glamour to pull off. She clearly has all three in spades.

Raven has dark brown hair with lighter highlights, wild, silver eyes and a look that screams hot mess. Her kohl eyeliner is already lightly smudged. She takes a glass of champagne from a passing waiter and uses it to wash down two pink pills. "Where are you from, Cassidy?"

"Honolulu."

"Oh, me too. Why haven't we seen you before?"

"I've been traveling," I hear myself say. It's sort of true.

"You're *so* lucky. I can't wait to get back to my apartment in New York. My dad won't let me use the private jets until my therapist clears it. Yawn. I'm *dying* of island fever. I love that dress, by the way."

"Thanks." We're interrupted then by the arrival of more people.

Who could only be the Fitzpatricks.

I brace myself.

And I'm wondering where Knox is.

The music is louder now, the drinks flowing.

I'm introduced to Silas Fitzpatrick, who's big and cocky, with longish brown hair. Malachi is fun and charming. He's hot and he knows it. I remember when Maggie first showed me a picture of him, my first impression was that he looked like the kind of guy who's the life of the party. And it's true. He tells jokes and has everyone laughing.

Tatum is wearing a white jumpsuit. She has a smooth, dyed-blond pixie hairdo. She's channeling old-Hollywood bombshell but with a modern, slightly-androgynous spin to it. She's talkative and bubbly.

Vivi is as shy and gorgeous as I remember her. Her dark hair has been cornrowed. Her dress is green and shows off her lithe, perfect body. There's an element of vulnerability to her that makes me wonder what's happening in the background of her life. She seems nice, but overpowered by something that holds her back. I have the urge to ask her if she's okay, but I hold it. I'm hardly the person who could help with whatever her problems are, if my hunch is right.

And then there's Perri.

The first thought that comes to mind as I meet her is that *she's so totally wrong for him*. It could never work.

She's wearing full, sort of severe-looking makeup and a black, see-through floor-length dress with what looks like a black bikini underneath it.

"We haven't met," she says, sizing me up with laser-focused attention. Her eyes are devoid of friendliness. Maybe she already senses that I'm a threat.

"I'm Cassidy. I'm a friend of Echo's."

"Are you staying the whole weekend?"

"I'm not sure yet." I'm just making this up as I go, but there's a light bite to my reply. I'm hardly going to roll over and let her take him without a fight. "Probably."

A passing waiter offers us glasses of champagne from a tray and we both take one. Perri looks around, for Knox, maybe, and she wanders over to where Silas and Enzo are standing, talking.

I drink maybe a little more quickly than I should be but it's a beautiful night. I'm here, for now, and I can't help enjoying the idyllic scene.

Jagger comes over to me. "You're freaking me out a little." His grin is impish and endearing. "I know we've met. Where?"

"I was at Vivi's birthday party." It's true, after all.

"Yeah?" He's still confused, trying to place me.

Malachi joins us. "How come *we* haven't met?" He grins at me, revealing his very-white teeth. "Where's Echo been hiding you?"

At that moment, Remy, Knox and Wolf join the party

and my heart beats faster. The three of them together are a spectacle, for their size and masculinity alone. They look like a force to be reckoned with, with their stunning looks and their flashing eyes. Their presence gets everyone's attention.

Knox's gaze immediately finds me. His eyes rake over my dress—and all it reveals—bringing a rush of heat to my skin. My dress is fitted and soft. And I'm wearing nothing underneath. He can't know this but his eyes are burning me in intimate places. I get wet just at the sight of him.

Hell.

He's sexual napalm and I can feel his flames from here.

Knox, Remy and Wolf shake hands with the men and kiss the women's cheeks, like the gentlemen they're supposed to be.

Including Perri's.

My blood gets hot at the sight of her touching him as she says hello to him. Her hand rests briefly on his arm. But then he moves it.

He's watching me as this happens and the fury we're both feeling clashes. *Don't let her touch you,* is what I'm thinking, and I can read in his eyes, *Your fucking dress is leaving almost nothing to the imagination.*

We know each other very well, already. A month of getting as close to each other as physically and emotionally possible is long enough.

I know what his hot cum tastes like. I know intimately the sound of his grunting growl as he comes hard.

Does she?

Is she one of the women who came before me?

I can't stand this.

And I know for a fact: I could never share him. Becoming his "mistress" after he marries Perri would never, ever work. We'd kill each other.

It suddenly occurs to me what this party is all about. It's to make the match. Knox has told me almost nothing about the alliance they've occasionally mentioned, but I know enough. The purpose of this weekend is to make the final arrangements for the happy couple, or maybe all three of them.

This should have occurred to me before, of course. But the reality settles heavily now. Too heavily.

This is a matchmaking party.

For my beautiful, fiery soulmate who I can no longer live without and the girl his family has chosen for him to marry.

53

Cassidy

Knox is momentarily distracted by the people gathered around him.

And I can't tell what he's thinking. Is he weighing up his choices—every one of them rich, gorgeous heiresses that ... I mean, who are we kidding? It's not like a marriage to any one of them would be all *that* hard to bear.

Perri Fitzpatrick says something to him and he leans in just slightly to hear her. As he does this, she catches my eye in a challenging glare, like she already knows about us. Or has somehow guessed.

I think about storming over there.

I also think about leaving.

I shouldn't be here.

I feel like the lost waif again, dressed up and pretending to be something I'm not.

Malachi Fitzpatrick blocks the sight of Knox and

Perri. "I don't feel like we've been properly introduced," he says. "Tell me more about the mysterious Cassidy. How do you know Echo?"

He grabs a bottle of champagne from a passing waiter and tops up my glass.

It's dark now, but the moon is bright. The music is loud and the waitstaff are starting to set up the buffet dinner. "We have a mutual friend."

A drop of the champagne from my filled-to-the-rim flute spills, wetting the skin of my exposed cleavage.

Malachi, noticing this, touches his finger very gently to the drop, swiping it. I take a step back from him, shocked that he would be so brazen about it, but he's watching my eyes as he licks his finger.

Malachi's hand is grabbed by a larger hand, surprising him.

A forceful presence is next to me and I can smell his scent, of sea salt and pure, uncut masculinity.

My lover and my love.

"Keep your fucking hands off her," Knox growls. He looks big and half-crazed in the moonlight.

Knox unclenches his fist from Malachi's wrist, which Malachi then rubs with his other hand, like it's sore. "Shit, man. I didn't know she was spoken for." But then, still rubbing his wrist, a grin of realization lights up Malachi's face. His contemplation shifts from Knox, to me, and back to Knox. "This is going to complicate things, now, isn't it?"

If looks could kill, Malachi would be a bloody pulp on

the ground right now. Knox is very on edge. "Looks like they're setting up the buffet, Malachi. Why don't you go and help yourself."

"Don't mind if I do." Malachi laughs, then walks off.

Knox's eyes follow Malachi as he walks away. "I can't take this."

A river of emotions are coursing through me and I don't know how to feel. I'm relieved Knox is here with me. I'm pissed off that Perri thinks of him as hers. I'm scared because ... well, what if he *is* hers? My question comes out as a petulant jibe. "Can't take what?" *That you're actually engaged to someone else?*

"Do you want me to kill him?"

"Of course I don't."

Remy joins us. "Silas wants to have a word with you, Knox." It's an order. Remy gives me an almost-sympathetic order of my own. "He won't be long."

I'm being gently told not to follow him.

It doesn't take a mind reader to figure out what Silas wants to talk to Knox about.

Why isn't Knox telling Remy that he and I are together? That he wants to marry me, like he told me he did?

I'm working on it, he'd said.

Why isn't he working on it now?

"Where do you want to wait for me?" Knox asks me. "With Echo?"

"I might go upstairs for a few minutes."

"Are you all right?"

"I'm fine. Just a little tired." I've drunk a glass of

champagne and I'm still slightly off-kilter after the whole getting-manhandled-by-several-thugs incident. The bruises on my ribs feel sore. The smell of food is making me feel weirdly nauseous.

Remy's relieved by this. "He'll see you a little later," he says.

I try to smile and I make my way toward the door.

I hate this. I hate the fact that, out here, he's theirs, not mine.

I go inside to try to find a bathroom.

I'm turning a corner down a hallway when I hear someone following me.

It's Perri.

She corners me.

"Are you *trying* to curse all of us, is *that* what you're trying to do?" Perri seethes.

I'm shocked by the venom in her. *She absolutely loathes me.* "What do you mean?"

She seems surprised by my question. "Hasn't he told you anything?"

I almost push past her but then I change my mind. I want to hear what she's about to say. "I don't know what you're talking about."

She glares at me intently, like she can't believe how uninformed I am. "Of course he didn't tell you. He thinks you're a fictional character come to life. He doesn't want you to vanish into thin air by getting too real with you. But you're not *actually* an angel, are you? You're just a girl. Just like all the rest of us." She pauses defiantly, like she's waiting for me to argue with her. When I don't, she asks me, "Did you know it was the curse that killed his parents? Did you know it killed Remy's wife and baby? Is *that* what you want for him? To be struck down by the doom his family is trying to save him from?"

"He didn't mention anything about ... a curse."

"Didn't he?" She lets out a short, sharp laugh. "Maybe he doesn't love you as much as you think he does if he's not willing to share his deepest, darkest secrets with you. Let me enlighten you. The rule—the curse—whatever you want to call it, was put in place by our forefathers over a hundred years ago. We *have* to keep the alliance going. He *has* to marry me. Terrible things will happen to all of us if he doesn't. Especially him. It *always* ends badly for the people who break it. And I know what that probably sounds like to you. You probably think I'm making it up. You think I'm crazy and melodramatic. But I'm not. *Everyone* who's ever broken it dies or loses someone they love in a horrible, tragic kind of a way. Remy's wife and baby prove that the curse hasn't gone away over time. If anything, it's only getting stronger."

A lot of puzzle pieces are falling into place. Now I understand why Remy is so solemn and serious all the time. He's grieving an unimaginable loss. He's gruff because he's in pain.

And I understand Knox's angst. He loves me. *I'll take any risk for you.* He's been in denial, maybe. Wishing he could avoid his fate by loving me even harder. All this time, he's been trying to protect me from the curse, maybe, by pretending it wasn't there. But he can't pretend tonight.

"You need to let him go," Perri says. "For his sake. And for yours. You don't want to end up like Remy's wife, do you?"

Of course I don't.

"You don't want *him*—and you—to end up like his parents either, do you? The curse could kill you both. Did you know his parents died when he was only three? His parents laughed off the curse, my grandfather told me. They thought it was stupid. They thought they were untouchable. Until their plane went down and they had to be identified by what was left of their charred teeth."

God. "I'm ... I'm so sorry to hear that."

"Then do something about it. Let him go."

Knox is willing to forsake his duty to his family. For *me*.

My heart hurts at the thought. It also hurts because if Knox Ramsey loves me enough to risk breaking the rule ... then I need to love *him* enough to not allow him to.

This is crazy. I don't want to be reason bad things happen to him. I don't want him to die because he loves me too much.

Perri's eyes are shiny with tears. "Cassidy? Is that your name?"

"Yes."

"Cassidy, I *love* him. I know you love him. I can tell by the way you look at him. *I* love him too. So much. We haven't spent all that much time together but I've loved him from afar for a long time and I ... well, he's all I think about. I'll treat him *so* well. And I'll give him a life that's not *cursed*. Which you can't do! Please. Let him do what he needs to do to keep his family safe. I'll take care of him, I promise I will. I'll make a good wife for him. Please don't make him fight his destiny. Please don't bring more pain to his family than they've already endured."

What a way to put it.

How can I argue with that?

"Leave now," she urges me. "Leave him a note and tell him not to follow you. Tell him you've changed your mind. Make it convincing so he doesn't chase after you and risk his life to do it. For his sake, *please.*"

I mean, it all sort of makes sense now. I stabbed him with my knife and almost killed him. If the knife had sliced just a little bit to the left, maybe, it would have a been a fatal wound.

And then I brought the Arrow recruits to Paradise, which meant he had to kill two men.

I've *already* cursed him. More than once.

If I stay, maybe it'll only get worse for him. Maybe the curse will make sure of that.

As though reading my thoughts and finding some-thing she can cling to, Perri urges me, "It *can't* be a happily ever after for you and Knox, Cassidy. It just can't. It'll never happen that way. It'll always be a life that's plagued by catastrophes that only get worse over time. *Please.* Please let him go."

I glance across the room, to the open doors onto the

lanai, where Knox is talking to some of the others. His beauty and his energy practically glows. He outshines everyone.

"Remy would be so relieved," Perri says. "He's been trying to get Knox to agree to this for ages. He's worried that more tragedy will strike. After everything he's already been through, it'll be such a relief to him if you just quietly disappeared."

She's not wrong. I've brought him only an endless stream of trouble.

And as I look around the grand space with its chandeliers and its priceless artworks, the stonework and the walls of glass, the views out over the gazillion-dollar property that goes on and on, I remember where I came from. It hits me again that this isn't me. This kind of luxury is reserved for people like Perri and Echo and Raven. I'm a lost soul with no family history and no ties.

"Please, Cassidy. Please save him from a life of sadness, like Remy's."

For Knox, I make my decision.

I can cut my hair. Dye it. Make sure I'm not mistaken again for something I'm clearly not. I'll go get my pin and my knife, then I'll disappear. I'm good at disappearing.

I make a move to walk away because if I don't do it now I won't be able to. Perri grabs my arm and her hands are ice cold even on this warm night. "Cassidy?" Her eyes are pleading.

"I'm leaving."

There's disbelief in her glittering eyes. And happiness.

So much of it. I hope she makes a good mother to his children. "Don't come back," she says.

And with that, she turns and walks away.

I take the elevator up to Knox's apartment. I pull on my old shoes but I don't bother changing my dress.

I write Knox a note, leaving it on the table.

I can't find any of his weapons, and I'll need one.

So I take the elevator back down to the foyer, which is empty.

Then I help myself to the Remington that hangs over the doorway.

We always keep it loaded.

Where I'm going, there will be danger, no doubt about. I'm going to need protection.

I walk down the hall to the door at the far end, where it's dark and quiet.

And I let myself out.

KNOX

THIS WHOLE THING IS A CLUSTERFUCK.

The lights, the music, the fucking disco ball. All of it is turning my world into a crashing, devastating nightmare.

I'm being horrifically rude, avoiding Perri, dodging her constant attempts to make eye contact, keeping my distance. Silas wants a date for the wedding so Perri can start planning it. I told him I'd let him know by the end of the weekend, to buy myself some time.

I know what Cassidy was thinking when she left the party, that I'm not fighting for us.

She's wrong.

I've let it simmer for a while, and it's late now. People are dancing and getting loose. All part of the plan to lubricate potential connections. It might be as late as 2 a.m. I've given it a few hours to see if there's anyone else is hitting it off. Aurora is sitting on Malachi's lap, so there's that. The third marriage will have to align the

Fitzpatricks and the Kings. And they're heating up, making out on one of the loungers at the far end of the outdoor area. The two of them have probably slept with everyone in Honolulu except each other so it could be a good match. But that doesn't help me.

Either way, I'm about to make an announcement that's going to ruin the rest of everyone's night.

I'm glad Cassidy decided to go upstairs. I don't want them staring at her or blaming her in any way for what I'm about to do.

I turn down the music. Then I stand on the low stone wall that runs the length of the pool. "I've got something to tell you all."

I've immediately got their undivided attention. This isn't like me. I'm the least talkative person in my family. More of a strong, silent type, maybe. Brooding and unapproachable. They're riveted.

Remy's got thunder in his eyes. I can read his thoughts from here. *Don't do it.*

She's worth the risks and the fights this will cause. I don't want to live without her. And if it means I get burned, then so be it. "I've made a decision and—"

Wolf steps up suddenly next to me and grabs the front of my shirt in his fist. "Brother, we need to talk. Now."

I try to push him off but the fucker's insistent. "Whatever it is, it can wait—"

"*Knox.* It can't wait."

His eyes are wild. There's a rabid urgency in him that sways me. "What can't wait?"

"False alarm, everyone," Wolf yells to the crowd, laughing off my behavior. "Someone crank the music back up."

They do, as Wolf pulls me down off the low wall, out of earshot of the others. Remy walks over to us.

"What the fuck are you doing, Wolf?" I seethe. "What's so urgent?"

"I'll marry Vivi."

I stare at him for a long moment, wondering if I've heard him correctly. "What?"

"I said I'll marry Vivi. So you can marry Cassidy."

I'm literally stunned. "You would do that?"

"I wanted to meet her again before I decided. It's been a few years. She won't want to, I know that. She looks at me like she's terrified I'm going to eat her for breakfast. Which I probably will at some point. But that'll get you off the hook, man. I want you to marry Cassidy. I know you love her."

"I do love her."

Remy's as shocked as I am. "Are you sure about this, Wolf? Once we tell the others, there's no going back."

"I'm sure," Wolf says. "She's fucking *beautiful*. Maybe she'll warm up to me once she gets to know me better."

I can't believe he's willing to do this for me. "You'd have to move to Seven Mile Beach, Wolf."

He shrugs, like it's no big deal. "We can divide our time between the two. I'll figure it out."

"Are you sure?"

"I wouldn't offer if I wasn't sure, bro."

I hug him. The relief is overwhelming. I don't know I've ever hugged my brother in my life but I do it now, then I slap him on the back. "Thank you, Wolf. I mean it."

Remy seems almost as relieved as I am. He actually smiles. "Okay, then. One down, one to go. I'll tell Silas."

So I hug him too. "Time for you to get back on the horse, by the way, Rem. It's been long enough."

And then I head for the door. I can't wait to tell her. It's been a few hours since she left the party and I miss her like an addict. I miss her soft hair and her expressive little angel's face. I miss her body. Her touch. I miss everything. I'm going through a fierce withdrawal and at the same time I feel *light*. The world is suddenly wide open. The big storm cloud of an unwanted future hanging over my head is gone. I'm *free*. I'm the luckiest man in the world. *I can marry my angel.*

I get to the apartment. I walk into the bedroom. "Angel?"

She's not in bed.

I knock on the bathroom door. "Cassidy?" I open it but she's not here.

She's not in any of the other rooms. Or on the balcony.

Where is she?

Something's wrong.

I see a note on the table and grab it.

To my Knox,

I love you more than I've ever loved or ever will love anyone in my life. You're my soulmate, my beautiful devil, my whole heart. Please listen to what I'm saying: it's because I love you so much that I have to leave you. I refuse to curse you or your family. I found out about the reasons you have to marry Perri. I want you to marry her. I want you to live, Knox. Find your happiness with her. Live a long and beautiful life without a black cloud hanging over your head. I don't want to be your black cloud, so please don't ask me to be. I want your days to be long, filled with sun and laughter. I'm asking you not to follow me or search for me. I don't want you to. Nothing good can come of that, we both know it. Be strong, let me go, and try to understand why I can't stay. You are and always will be the most beautiful part of my life and the very best of me.

Your angel,
Cassidy

55

KNOX

MY VISION BLURS, like my sanity has started to crack.

She fucking left me?

She can't have left me.

I need her.

Fuck. Perri must have told her about the curse and convinced her to leave me.

Where the fuck would she have gone?

I know exactly where she's gone. She's gone to get her pin and her knife.

My blood turns cold.

What if they're up there? What if Axel and his thugs are at the caves? They know she's here. They'll be prowling and trawling for clues.

The adrenaline surges through my veins. I grab my weapons belt from the top shelf of the closet where I left it, strapping it on. My hunting knife. My Glock. A taser and the newest addition, a Widowmaker.

She could have left hours ago. She could already be up there.

I take the back staircase and bolt through the back door, running through the orchards. Each tower along the wall has a stone ladder built into the interior side.

I climb one of these and jump to the ground, running up the steep slope.

Please be safe. Please be okay, angel girl. I'm coming.

It doesn't take me long to get there. My lungs are on fire but I can't feel anything. I increase my pace, wild with fear for her safety. Before long, I'm nearing the pools.

The moon is low and bright. It might be four or five in the morning. There's the faintest hint of dawn along the horizon.

I get to the pools and—*thank you thank you thank you*—there she is, looking exactly like the angel that always used to visit me in my dreams.

She's sitting in one of the pools, letting the waterfall rinse her hair. Her bag is packed, leaning against a tree nearby. The Remington pistol is sitting on top of it. Her dress is draped over a rock close to the edge.

"I told you not to follow me," she says.

"Hi to you too, baby girl." I check the area. "This was a bad idea. Is anyone else here?"

"No. I was careful. I checked first. There's no one here."

Once I've made sure we're alone, I approach the pool in ground-eating strides. I strip down and I climb in, splashing water everywhere.

"*Knox*. I mean it! I didn't want you to follow me. You have to go back."

"Not a chance in hell, sweetheart." I grab her, pulling her to me, wrapping my arms and legs around her. Already, I'd forgotten how small she was. How soft and stunning.

I am feverishly, desperately in love with her. I bury my face into her neck. She's wet and clean but I can still smell her scent. I hold her face. My palm gently, firmly, grips her neck. "Don't you ever leave me again. Do you hear me?" I sound crazed, and I am.

Her eyes are red, her long, dark eyelashes spiked with water. She's crying. "I told you not to follow me."

"Of course I was going to follow you. You left too soon. You should have trusted me to handle it, like I told you I would."

"I know about the curse, Knox."

"I don't care about the curse! I choose *you*. I always would have, no matter what it cost us, it was always going to be worth it. I *love* you, Cassidy. Nothing the curse could do to me would be worse than losing you. Nothing." I turn her face toward me, so she's staring into my eyes. "Wolf is going to marry Vivi."

She's breathing hard and so am I. "He is?"

"Yes."

"What does that mean?"

"It means I can marry you. Will you marry me, angel? Will you marry me?"

She blinks her eyes. "But what about the—"

"It's resolved. The rule will be followed, the curse appeased. Wolf stepped up. He's going to secure the alliance so I don't have to."

"He is?"

"Yes. He is."

She's quiet for a long second. "So you don't have to marry Perri?"

"No. I'm going to marry you."

"Knox," she whispers. "I can't believe it."

I'm hard as fuck and she's sitting on my lap. I can feel the insane softness of her pussy cradling my raging hard-on. "Even if Wolf didn't step up, honey, it wouldn't have mattered to me. I told you that. Life can be cursed even if you *do* follow the rules. Bad things sometimes happen. But so do good things. I would have been willing to endure all the hard stuff just to have one more day with you, angel. One more hour. I don't care about dying, as long as I can be with you."

"I didn't want to bring pain into your life, Knox."

"There's nothing more painful than losing you. I need you. Let's get married soon. Today. Now."

She kisses me and the head of my cock barely gains entry. *Ah hell*, there's nothing on this earth that feels as good as she feels. "Okay," she whispers. "Yes."

"Say it again." I lean her forward so I can fuck her from behind as the water cascades over us. My cock slides deeper into nirvana.

"Of course I'll marry you, Knox Ramsey. You know it's all I want to do. I love you."

We're kissing as she arches back against me and I slide deep inside her, all the way to the hilt. I'm fucking her hard, aggressively, desperately, as I grip her and plunge my tongue into her mouth. I can't get enough. I can't get deep enough, or close enough. "I love you so much, angel. I love you."

The tight, slippery friction tips us both over a crazy edge. She cries out. Her pussy clenches around my bursting cock. I grunt like a rutting animal, flooding her in hot throbs, pushing my seed deep as I ride her pleasure all the way in.

Once we start to come down, I pull her hair to the side, kissing her neck, her back. The first light of dawn turns her hair golden.

It's then that I notice it.

A small, circular tattoo between her shoulder blades.

I run my thumb over it and she tenses. "What is this?"

"I was ... going to show it to you."

I study it more closely. "I recognize this. But ... it can't be."

"You recognize it?" she whispers. There's a deep angst to her question.

"Why didn't you show me this? How did I not notice this before? Why have I never *seen* this?"

"I wanted to show you, Knox." She's crying again. "I was about to."

It's an intricately outlined circle. The interior of it is divided into three equal sections. One contains a sun, one a honu—a sea turtle that's the Hawaiian symbol for good luck and endurance—and one a fish hook, which symbolizes good fortune and strength. "This is the seal of Jethro King."

"W-what?"

"It's on the letters and formal invitations he sends. He seals them with wax with this symbol melted into it. We always used to say how old school it was."

"But why would the seal of Jethro King—"

"This can only mean one thing."

She stares at me with wide eyes as the realization sinks in.

"Your mother must have inked you and hidden you for your own protection. She was on the run. She was the one who they all suspected was killed by Jethro's wife. Jagger's mother is *your* mother, Cassidy. Jethro King is your father."

56

Cassidy

CRAZILY, it all makes sense. Somewhere inside myself, I can *feel* that it's true. *That's* why Jagger King seems so familiar to me, because aspects of him are like looking into a mirror. His hair. The shape of his eyes.

If it's true, then Jagger King is my full brother. And all the other Kings are my half siblings.

Knox pulls himself from my body. "We're getting the fuck out of here. We need to show this to Remy. And to Jethro." He holds my jaw and kisses me, staring into my eyes and smiling at me with manic zeal. "I can't believe you're the other *match*, angel. I *knew* you were my soulmate. I could feel it in my bones, from that very first time I saw you. I *love* you, baby. Now get dressed. We're leaving."

I climb out of the pool and pull my dress on, not worrying about getting it wet.

As I do this, I hear a sharp, loud, metallic clicking sound.

And Knox's dark growl, "*Run, Cassidy. RUN.*"

I turn, and I'm staggered to see five men standing in the clearing. Knox is standing there too, his jeans on but unbuttoned. One of the men is holding a gun to Knox's head.

Axel Archer.

Oh my God.

We've been ambushed.

Three of the men have black hoods over their faces. And one of them is ... a priest? He's wearing one of those white collars.

"Bad advice," Axel sneers. "Don't even *think* about running, sweetheart." One of the men has already blindsided me, blocking my escape.

Knox reacts, knocking the gun from Axel's hand.

The gun goes off and the sound is deafening. And terrifying.

Is he hit?

But Knox already has Axel to the ground.

It's a strange thing to think about at a time like this but *he's so freaking magnificent.* He's a born fighter. He easily overpowers Axel.

But as Knox is distracted by Axel, one of the hooded men confiscates Knox's weapons belt. The other hooded man cocks his gun and aims it at Knox.

"*No!* " I scream. But I'm grabbed by the man who blindsided me. He painfully grips my wrists behind my back and binds them with a sharp cord. He takes the Remington from where it's sitting on my pack and holds the barrel against my temple.

"Let him go, Ramsey," he yells. "I'll fucking kill her."

Knox has Axel in a vice grip and he's punching him relentlessly. Axel's face is bloody and covered in dirt. Damage is accumulating with each one of Knox's punches.

But when Knox looks up and sees the gun pointed at my head, he stops.

The barrel of the pistol at my temple digs in deeper, and the man holding it grips my arms painfully. "I've got a very itchy trigger finger, Ramsey. Don't fucking test me."

"Let her go." Knox's voice is low and menacing. "Take me. Let the girl go."

The sight of the gun at my head does something to him. He's not willing to take the risk. He allows the other two men to haul him and Axel to their feet.

"I'm going to make sure each and every one of you dies a slow and very painful death if anything happens to her," Knox says. "Do whatever you want with me but let the girl go."

Axel binds Knox's hands with a cable tie. Then he pulls Knox over to a palm tree and secures his hands to it. "The girl is no longer your concern," Axel tells him. "She's mine now."

"Over my dead body," Knox seethes.

"That can be arranged," Axel tells him. "You see, *I*

know about the tattoo too. I saw it the night she stabbed me and ran." To me, "You didn't really think you'd get away with that, did you, Cassidy?"

Axel walks over to me. He grabs me by the arm and pulls me over to the where the priest is standing. The priest looks absolutely terrified.

Fuck.

He's stolen the priest.

"It's perfect, isn't it?" Axel swipes his bloody nose with the sleeve of his leather jacket. "I'm doing what my father and grandfathers failed to do. Marrying back into the alliance. I'll be invited to live with the Kings alongside my gorgeous new bride. 'To be treated as royalty, with power and command equal to the decision-makers.' It's poetic justice, don't you think, Ramsey?" Then, to one of his henchmen, "Use the taser to begin with."

The henchman takes the taser from Knox's belt.

Axel aims his question at me. "Did you know that being tasered is described by some as the most excruciating pain of their lives? And that the maximum effect areas for a taser are the neck—directly to the jugular—and just below the rib cage? You choose."

I'm horrified at the thought. "*No. Please.* Please don't do it! Don't hurt him. Please!"

"You're going to obey me, then?"

I glare into his black eyes.

"Let us go and your life with be spared, Axel," Knox says. "I'll make sure you're rewarded. In land, money, whatever you want. You'll get a very rich reward for me."

Axel laughs. "What I *want* is to marry this hot little King. I'll have all the money and property I need once she's my wife. Among other things. Penthouse condos. Jethro and Enzo at my mercy. Not to mention *this* little minx in my bed, to do whatever I please with, day and night. Isn't that right, babe?" To the priest, he says, "Get started."

Knox is losing his mind with rage. "I'll fucking tear you limb from limb, Archer. *She's not yours.* You can't force her. You'll never get away with this. *I'll fucking kill you.*"

Axel grins at me. "Let's see if you're right about any of the above." Harshly, to the priest, "Do it."

57

Cassidy

THE PRIEST LOOKS like he's about to pass out. But he takes a Bible out of his pocket and opens it. "Our Holy Father, we ask—"

"Cassidy," Knox growls with fury. "Don't you say the vows. Not a word of them. *Not a single word.*"

Axel turns to the henchman who's holding the taser, nodding. "Now."

"*No!*" I plead, but the man holds the taser to Knox's neck. I scream as Knox falls to his knees. "*Stop! Please! Please stop! I'll do it.*" I turn to Axel, "I'll do anything. *Please.*"

"Good." Axel holds his palm toward the henchman and he stops. "Because we've got a whole arsenal here to try out on him until I get what I want from you."

Knox is on his knees with his arms bound behind him. His body is rigid, his eyes are closed. After five or ten seconds, he opens them. He's breathing hard and he's covered in sweat. "Don't do it, angel. No matter what. *Don't say the words.*"

"Keep going, Father," orders Axel. "Go straight to the vows. Do it now."

The wide-eyed priest clears his throat. He begins again. "Do you, Axel Archer, take—what's the young lady's name?"

"Cassidy King," Axel says.

It's sort of shocking to hear it said like that. *Cassidy King.*

"Of the *King* Kings?" asks the priest. "The banking family?" Like he's wary of crossing them.

"That's none of your concern, Father," Axel replies curtly. "Just get the fuck on with it."

The priest is shaking. "D-do you, Axel Archer, take Cassidy King to be your lawfully wedded wife—"

"I do," Axel says.

The minister turns to me and his eyes are apologetic. "Do you, Cassidy King, take Axel Archer to be your lawfully wedded husba—"

"*NO.*" Knox's voice is so dark, so rasped. "*Don't say it, angel. Do. Not. Say it.*"

"Again!" Axel snaps at the henchman.

He tasers Knox again and I scream and fall to my knees. "*Stop hurting him. Please. Please stop.*" I'm sobbing. I can't bear it.

"*Say it,*" Axel hisses at me. To the priest, "Announce us man and wife."

"Give me your consent, miss," the priest urges me. "The marriage is sealed only with your consent."

Knox's groan is wrought with pain. *"No, Cassidy. Don't give it. I can take a hundred more."*

Axel yanks me to my feet. "Give it! Give your consent."

I find my balance somehow. And I stare into Axel's eyes defiantly. "I'll never give you my consent."

A ripple of disbelief flits across his expression, quickly followed by all-out rage. "Bitch!" He slaps me hard across the face. Little stars swirl across my vision.

The priest is murmuring frantic, quiet prayers.

For a brief moment, my eyes meet Knox's and I know I'll remember the color of them and the sureness of their love as long as I live.

I'm shocked when one of the henchman, who's holding the Remington and standing on the opposite side of Knox from the one with the taser, takes off his hood.

He has dirty blond dreadlocks and bright green eyes.

Holy shit.

"Crew?"

With the knife from Knox's weapons belt, Crew cuts the cable ties binding Knox's wrists. "My allegiance has fucking flipped, Axel. I'm so sorry, Cassidy. He recruited me just after you disappeared. I had no idea *this* was going to be my assignment." Crew hands the Remington to Knox.

Knox doesn't hesitate. He aims it.

And fires.

The bullet hits Axel Archer squarely in the chest. It's a direct hit to the heart.

Axel falls to the ground in a heavy heap and goes still.

Holy fuck.

Knox is still on his knees. He grabs the guy with the taser by the neck and slams him to the ground. The man cries out at the impact. Knox holds the Remington to his head and I squeeze my eyes closed as the shot rings out.

Oh my God.

I open them a few seconds later to see Crew and the other hooded man aiming guns at each other at close range.

They shoot at the same time. The hooded man falls to the ground. He's been hit right between the eyes.

Crew's been hit too, but in the leg. He sits heavily on the ground. His leg is bleeding badly. But it doesn't look like it'll be a fatal wound. I can only hope.

The priest is praying, a low, steady litany.

Axel and the two hooded men are dead.

Knox.

My Knox.

Is he hurt?

He jumps to his feet and comes to me. He's unsteady but he's not damaged. He's in one piece and I'm so relieved I can hardly breathe.

Knox is checking me for injuries, wild-eyed with worry. "*Angel.* Did they hurt you? Are you all right? Talk to me. Tell me what hurts."

I can't seem to say anything. The terror, the fight, the

gunshots, the blood, the terrible things that happened and the *almost* terrible things that *almost* happened ... I'm in shock. And something else. It's impossible to know such a thing but I swear I can feel it. Something taking hold inside me. *Life.* Some cosmic, otherworldly, shifting beginning that tilts my entire world on its axis.

Knox cuts the cable tie that's binding my wrists.

There's the distinctive sound of a helicopter approaching. It lands in the clearing and a swarm of people jump out of it before the propellors even start to slow.

Remy. Wolf. Blaise. Malachi and Stone. Jagger.

As relieved as I am to see them, my equilibrium fails me. My stomach flutters at the same time my vision erupts with swirling stars.

I look at the men lying dead on the ground.

And the people around me, who are, and will be, *my family.*

Knox feels me swoon and he catches me, scooping me into his strong arms as the world goes black.

58

Cassidy

It's four days later.

The elevator pings and slides open. Knox and I step out into the foyer area of Jethro King's office, which is on the top floor of one of the highest of the city's skyscrapers. The floor-to-ceiling windows offer panoramic views out over Honolulu.

It feels strange to be back in the city, seeing it now from an entirely new vantage point.

We flew from Kauai with the Kings on their private jet, which is like an in-flight party lounge.

They were surprisingly accepting of me, once my tattoo was revealed to them. They were stunned, amazed ... and then excited. They all recognized it. And studied it, which felt so strange to me, their fascination over something I've been self-conscious about and have tried so hard to keep hidden my entire life.

They were all, and especially the Ramseys, wildly

relieved that the King-Ramsey alliance is now taken care of.

Jethro was promptly contacted. He agreed to take a paternity test once he heard all the details and it's one of the things we're here to discuss.

Aurora hugged me and seems genuinely excited to have me as a sister. Raven reminded us all that it's not confirmed yet, but fawned over me anyway. Stone was more stand-offish, but winked at me.

And Jagger was more elated than I could ever have imagined. He seems thrilled to have found me. He never knew his mother. She disappeared on his second birthday. He has no memory of her. She was banished by Jethro's wife, who'd threatened to have her killed if she was ever seen again—and especially if Jethro saw her again. Which he obviously did.

Jagger and I have spent time over the past few days talking, and comparing ourselves. The color of our eyes and our hair. Our personalities and interests.

These conversations felt deep and important. He's fun, quick to laugh and he has a playful, mischievous sense of humor.

These are the first people I've ever met who are related to me by blood and I can not only *see* the resemblance, I can *feel* it, as a connective, visceral link.

Enzo has already taken on the role of my advisor. He wears a ring with the same symbol that's inked onto my skin. Knox told him about the number etched onto my pin, which I'm wearing now, pinned near the high neck of my dress. Enzo confirmed it's a safety deposit box in one of the King-owned banks. He called ahead and it's also one of the things we'll be discussing with Jethro today in our meeting.

Here, in the Kings' building, we're safe. But Knox isn't taking any chances. In case some of the Arrow second-in-commands want retribution, he won't let me out of his sight and a team of bodyguards are traveling with us.

Now, the city skyline, the ocean and the mountains are all on display like a picture postcard. Two leather couches face each other with a low coffee table between them. There are tall, leafy tropical plants in giant pots. To the right is a large, ornately carved wooden door. We were asked by the receptionist on the ground floor to wait here until Jethro is ready to see us.

I'm wearing a dress designed by Echo. Knox took me to her studio, where she has sewing machines and more fabrics than I've ever seen in one place. She wants me to start designing some of my own clothes with her and she said I can use any of the materials I want. It's basically a dream come true. I can't wait to get started.

My hair has been trimmed—just a little, Knox loves my hair and for the first time in my life I don't have to hide it—and styled. It feels soft and swishy whenever I move.

Knox pulls me carefully into a nook by the window and leans me up against the wall, kissing me lightly. He can't stop staring at me, touching me, kissing me. Keeping me close.

My true love showed up when I least expected him, a gorgeous devil who almost killed me. Our hearts knew, even then. Every minute we spend together only compounds the profound addiction we have for each other. I'm his and he's mine, that's the way our stars were written and we both feel this like it's been branded onto our souls. Our blood runs through each other's veins. Our essences have mixed and entwined.

And I have some news to share with him.

He tucks a strand of my hair behind one ear. "Whatever happens in this office today doesn't matter. I adore you. I'm obsessed with you. I can't breathe without you. You're the best thing that's ever happened to me in this life. Whether or not you're the daughter of Jethro King doesn't matter to me. I hope you are, but either way, as soon as we get out of this meeting, I've already booked out all of Tiffany and Co so we can have a private viewing of the biggest and best diamond rings they have on offer. I'm going to get down on one knee and ask you to marry me. And then we're going to live happily ever after, either in this life or—if you're not Jethro's daughter and the curse takes us—the next one."

I feel like we've already been through enough. "I hope it's this one. And ... well, if you do ask me to marry you, I might have to say yes. Especially after the news Hana gave me this morning."

Knox and I haven't been alone since then, but Hana

made sure we were thoroughly checked over after we returned to the castle, in every possible way. Since I fainted and I've been feeling nauseous, there was one final test she wanted to do first thing this morning.

"Turns out a few weeks of good food is all it takes," I tell him.

"For what?"

"Oh, and a virile beefcake who can't get enough of ..." I lower my voice "... *pumping his seed inside me* whenever he gets the opportunity. That also might have something to do with it."

The little furrow appears between his eyebrows but he's beginning to get my meaning. "Are you saying—?"

"It's very early, but Hana confirmed it."

I don't think he could look any more shocked. "A *baby?*" Really, he shouldn't be *that* shocked.

"Yes, Mr. I Don't Want Any Barriers Between Us. A baby." *I'm pregnant with Knox Ramsey's baby.* I didn't in a million years plan on having children this young. I obviously took more than a few chances. And I feel like the luckiest person on earth.

I'm not alone anymore.

I have him. I might even have brothers and sisters. Brothers-in-law and sisters-in-law. A father. And now this. "Are you happy?" I ask, in a whisper because I think he is but I want to make sure he is.

"My angel is having *my baby. Nothing* could make me happier than that. Not a single thing."

I smile through my tears and Knox kisses me. The kiss is slow and tender.

"I love you," he murmurs against my lips. "You're my soulmate. My one true love. I love you so fucking much, baby girl."

We both jump a little when a woman appears around the corner. "Excuse me. You must be Cassidy. And Knox. Mr. King is ready to see you now."

"Oh." *This is it. It's time.* "Thank you."

She smiles and leads us to the open door of the office, motioning for us to enter. Then she closes the door behind us and leaves us alone.

Knox is holding my hand. The warm, rough clasp of it anchors me. I need him so much. I have never, ever seen such a luxurious place and the possibilities that are on the table here are hard to even comprehend.

The office is palatial—the entire top story of a high rise owned by the Kings—with those same panoramic views of the city and the water. The sky is just beginning to purple with hazy, golden dusk.

And there he is.

Jethro King.

My father.

59

Cassidy

JETHRO KING STANDS from behind his gigantic, shiny desk.

He's tall, and solidly built, with wide shoulders. I can see Enzo in him. And Stone. And Jagger.

I can see myself.

His black hair has touches of silver at the temples. His eyes are very blue. He's regal-looking, maybe in his late fifties. His business suit is expensive but there are details of it that hint at an eccentric, artistic edge. A silver bracelet. A tattoo on the back of his hand. Hair that's a fraction longer than your usual banker. It's these details that I'm drawn to most of all. He writes his own rules, it's easy to see that in the way he carries himself. There's a calm confidence to him that ... I almost recognize.

He's studying me intently. His expression is ... dazzled. There's no other way to describe it. "You look so much like her." His voice is edged with emotion. "It's remarkable."

"What was she like?" I hear myself ask him. We're not even sure yet, officially, if Jethro King *is* my father and if the woman he's remembering is my mother. We want it to be true, I know *I* do and I can see in his eyes that he does too. Desperately.

"Her name was Camille. You look just like she did when I first met her. She had dark eyes, like yours, and her hair was the same bright white-gold. She was working as a waitress. She was French."

"French?"

"Yes. From Paris. She was gorgeous inside and out. As feisty as they come." He smiles at his own memories. "She was the love of my life," he says simply.

"I wish I could have met her."

"I do too, child. Can I hug you?"

"S-sure."

Jethro King gives me a genuine, heartfelt bear hug. His hug feels strangely restorative and I feel myself sigh, breathing in the fatherly scent of him and along with it a sense of well-being, of security and most of all, of resolution. I'm crying again. My emotions are on overdrive.

He releases me and holds me gently by the shoulders, drinking in the sight of me like he can't get enough of it. Then he turns to Knox. He shakes Knox's hand. "Knox Ramsey. You were a schoolboy the last time I saw you. It's been far too long."

"Good to see you again, Mr. King."

"Jethro," Jethro insists. He studies my pin for a few seconds, running his fingers over the grooves. "I gave her this pin, with her initials engraved into it. Camille Madison and K for King, although she was never a King, of course. I made sure she was very well provided for. And my wife was a very jealous woman. But I could never have let your mother go." I get the feeling there's much more to this story than Jethro might be willing to share at this stage. "I never expected my wife to do what she did. She did it to get revenge. On me." He pauses there and I don't push him, even though I'm dying to know the story. In time, I'll ask him the questions I've wondered about all my life. "May I see your tattoo, Cassidy?"

"Of course."

Knox unzips the top of my dress at the back. Jethro touches his fingers to my ink. "She was clever to do this when she had the chance. You might think it would be easy for anyone to draw a copy of this seal, but it's actually very difficult to duplicate precisely, because of the pattern here." He draws around the outline of the circle. "There's a binary code inked into the outside ring that, when translated, spells out the names of my children. I changed it after each one was born. I'll now have to have the seal redrawn." After a few more seconds of rapt silence, Jethro zips my dress up and pats me lightly. "Which brings us to the first matter at hand."

He picks up an envelope that's sitting on his desk.

"Are you ready?"

I take a deep breath. *Am I?* "I'm ready when you're ready."

Knox squeezes my hand as Jethro opens and reads from the paper. "'Based on the analysis of the DNA loci profiles of Jethro Luther King and Cassidy Meadow Kelley, the probability of paternity is 99.98%.'"

Oh my.

Jethro gives me another one of those heartfelt hugs. "I'm so very happy to have found you," he says to me.

"I'm very happy to be found."

It's a heavy moment and we're both sort of starstruck at this news.

Knox looks so relieved it makes me smile. He kisses me and weaves his fingers through mine.

Then he says to Jethro, "Sir, with your permission, I'm going to ask Cassidy to marry me. Today. Right after this meeting. Even without your permission, I'm afraid. Because I can't live without her. I love her. I'll protect her with my life and I'll make sure she has everything she wants and needs, and then some. We'll move here to Honolulu if you'd like us to, and I can offer my services to whatever business ventures you could use another family member to help you with. She's also carrying my baby— your grandchild. We'd like to get married as soon as possible."

I can see how Jethro might be intimidating to strangers or business colleagues or clients. But his eyes light up now with unfiltered joy and he shakes Knox's hand again. "You have more than my permission, son.

You have my blessing. I insist on paying for the wedding. And the building you'll live in when you're here in Honolulu. My view is that the forefathers didn't have access to private jets and helicopters, which we do. So there's no reason you can't divide your time between Paradise and your home here in Honolulu. There will be nothing but the best for my daughter and my very first grandchild. I don't know what's taking the others so long."

Wow.

His tone turns more serious as he says to Knox, "Enzo mentioned you had some trouble with Arrow."

"It's been taken care of," Knox tells him.

"If you need extra security or help with ... taking care of anything else, consider it done." The way Jethro offers this is sincere, and almost chilling.

"Likewise, Mr.—"

"Jethro."

Knox almost smiles. "Jethro. We have good intelligence, we're trained and we're fortified as f— ... we're very fortified. I appreciate the offer, and it goes both ways."

I can almost understand why they need the alliance now, and why their grandfathers insisted on the arranged marriages. For better or worse, it makes sense.

"Cassidy, there's one other business matter to attend to," Jethro says. "Enzo passed on the information you gave him about your safety deposit box. He gave me the number, which I see is here on your pin. Your mother must have had it engraved there. I have one of our senior bankers waiting to talk to you by video call."

"Now?"

"Yes. Would you like to speak to him?"

"Um ... okay. Yes."

Jethro takes his phone out of his pocket and makes the call, which is answered immediately. "Greg, this is my daughter, Cassidy," he says to the man on the screen. Wow. It's emotional to hear him say it like that. *My daughter.* "I have confirmed her identity and you may read her the letter."

"Hi, Cassidy," the man says. "I'm Greg Booth."

"Hi."

"First, I'll read you the unsealed letter your mother left in the safety deposit box."

He begins to read:

My Dear Cassidy,

Your name is Cassidy Madison King. You are the daughter of Jethro Luther King. My name is Camille Antoinette Madison. I was born in Paris and I met your father when I was twenty-two and waitressing in Waikiki. I had come to Hawaii for a holiday and fell in love with it. And with him. He was married, of course, but we shared a very special bond. You are very loved. And you were very wanted. I'm so very sorry I had to leave you. I wanted you to live and it was the only way I could make sure you would.

In this safety deposit box, there is a sealed letter that tells the full story of why I left you. Take your time reading it. It's a story that I fear will have an unhappy ending. I know you'll have many questions and I hope it will answer some of them.

I will spend the rest of my days hoping and praying that you're safe and that you will one day find your way to this letter, and to your family.

I love you so much.

All my love,

Your mother,

Camille

I'm vaguely aware that my face is wet with tears.

"There's also," continues Greg, "cash in the amount of just over three million dollars, which I've taken the liberty of putting into a bank account with your name on it. Bank cards have been couriered to Mr. King and should arrive within the next ten minutes. Do you have any other questions, Ms. King?"

"Um ... yes. Yes, I do. Did you just say ... *three million dollars?*"

"Three million, fifty seven thousand, four hundred and twelve dollars and thirty-two cents, to be exact."

Holy shit.

"Have a nice evening, Cassidy."

I can't believe this. "Thank you."

60

Cassidy

A WEEK LATER, my four bridesmaids, Echo, Blaise, Raven and Aurora, are gathered around me in Knox's—our—apartment in the castle, making sure my dress is perfect and my veil is in place. Echo designed my wedding dress and it's beyond anything I could have imagined. It has a fitted lace bodice with tiny capped sleeves and a low, lacy neckline. It tapers into a full-length feather-embroidered skirt with a long train. The veil is also edged with silky white feathers, carrying through with the angel vibe she was going for. It almost looks like wings.

"Knox is going to lose it when he sees you in this," Blaise smiles. All four of them are dressed in blue. Knox's favorite color.

Tatum sent her apologies because she left for Europe to shoot another film.

Perri, not surprisingly, wasn't invited. Knox was adamant about that.

I was tempted to write her a letter, telling her I hope she finds her own happily ever after and that I hope there aren't any hard feelings. But there was no way to frame it in a way that seemed kind enough. *He's mine, I hope you find your own* was never going to be helpful.

As for Vivi, I can only imagine how she's feeling. Wolf is rough, buff, huge, armed to the teeth and lethal as all hell. He's also now her husband. There have been moments during the few times I've spent with Wolf that I've seen through his fierceness, which is always the most pronounced thing about him. When he smiles and the deeper layers of his personality are allowed to shine through, it's like a cloud has moved away from the sun. He's funny, honest and intensely loyal to his family. I think Vivi could do a lot worse.

I don't, though, know what it would be like to be alone with him every night. I'm glad I never have to find out.

But I do hope that Vivi and I can get to know each other at some point. The glimpses of a soft and beautiful charisma that I've seen in her and also a bruised vulnerability make me want to be a friend to her.

Aurora and Malachi's wedding will take place at one of the Kings' residences in Honolulu within the next few weeks.

Vivi and Wolf married the day after we had our run-in with Axel Archer. I don't know why it was so rushed, but it seemed like Remy, Silas—and Wolf—wanted the marriage signed and sealed as quickly as possible.

Aside from the Tatum and Perri, everyone else from all three families is here at the castle, including Jethro, who's walking me down the aisle.

They're all waiting for us.

Waiting for *me*.

I only need one of them.

But it feels more than a little emotional to have a *family*. It's a foreign and very addictive feeling to *belong*.

I can hear music coming from outside and down below the open doors of the balcony. I haven't seen Knox since yesterday. Echo and Blaise insisted on keeping the tradition of not allowing the groom to see the bride on the wedding day until I'm walking down the aisle. "We're nothing if not superstitious romantics," Echo explained.

The beach house has been decorated and stocked for our wedding night. It's where we both decided we want to spend our honeymoon. We might take a trip somewhere in a month or two, and I'd like to one day see Paris, where my mother came from. But for now all we want to do is be together and be able to savor our bond, without curses or threats or deadlines hanging over our heads.

It's amazing how quickly you can put together a very extravagant wedding when you have the kind of resources on hand that they—*we*, I have to keep reminding myself—do.

"You look so beautiful," Aurora tells me, hugging me. All four of my new sisters have accepted me as one of their own. They all have very different, complicated personalities, and beginning to get to know each of them feels like a gift that I will never take for granted.

"That ring is insane." Raven is already on her third glass of champagne and her silver eyes are as wild as usual. She's slightly unhinged but also surprisingly thoughtful and generous. She gave me a gold charm bracelet to wear on my wedding day, with a charm of an angel on it, one of a star, for good luck, and one of a tiny gold triangle, to symbolize three sisters, forever linked. I teared up when she gave it me. She told me she's always here for me if I ever need someone to talk to.

Now, her phone chirps with an incoming message. "Jethro's ready when you are."

I'm handed a bouquet of white roses and we take the elevator down to the foyer, where Jethro is waiting there to give me away. The old Remington, I can't help notice, is back in its glass box next to the grandfather clock.

Jethro looks handsome in an aging gangster kind of way, and he holds out his arm to me. He kisses my cheek and the music starts.

Beside the pool, an altar has been set up and decorated with billowing white silk awnings. Archways of white roses and plumeria scent the air. The many rows of seats are full. I can see Malachi and Stone. Hana and her husband Leo. All of Knox's cousins and extended family, who I've met most of by now. Even Crew. After saving our lives, he was invited to stay in Paradise. Once his leg is healed, he's going to start working with the builders, on a house he's designing. He smiles at me and gives me a thumbs up. His bandaged leg is propped up on a chair and I notice he's sitting next to one of Knox's cousins, whose name is Willow.

And there he is.

My Knox.

I catch my breath when I see him.

My beautiful devil, dressed in a tux and looking tall and golden and so gorgeous I still sometimes wonder if I'm going to wake up from this beautiful dream. My soulmate, who crossed my path when I least expected him. What a journey it has been.

He watches me walk down the aisle and I can feel his love and the pull of his soul on my own. Twin hearts that beat as one.

Echo, Blaise, Aurora and Raven have taken their places on one side of Silas, who's officiating the wedding. Remy, Wolf, Jagger and Nero stand on the other side of Knox, all in their tuxes, looking like a bunch of fallen Greek gods.

Jethro kisses my cheek and shakes Knox's hand.

Then Knox takes both my hands in his.

"Angel," he grins down at me, his ocean-blue eyes full of emotion. "Promise me something."

"I promise."

Smiling, he tips my chin gently with his finger until I'm gazing up at him. "No more secrets."

"No more secrets." I can definitely agree to that.

"Any other tattoos I need to know about?"

I laugh lightly. "No, that's the only one."

"I love you, baby," he whispers.

"We're gathered here today ..." begins Silas.

As we listen to his words, I can only see Knox. He's framed by the colorful early evening sky and the first of the evening stars. Shining their encouragement. Lighting our way.

"Do you, Knox Alexander Ramsey take Cassidy Madison King to be your lawfully wedded wife?"

"I do." His smile basically lights up my life.

"And do you, Cassidy Madison King take Knox Alexander Ramsey to be your lawfully wedded husband?"

This time, I say it with my whole heart. "I do."

EPILOGUE

Cassidy

Seven months later ...

THE PENTHOUSE APARTMENT Jethro gave us as a wedding present—along with the entire building—is ridiculously amazing. It has two stories, five bedrooms, an outdoor area with a pool and jacuzzi, views of the ocean and an army of staff. I told Jethro—he told me I could call him Dad but all his other children call him Jethro, so I'm sticking to it—we didn't need staff. But he said it's non-negotiable. Especially since he insists I spend all my time concentrating exclusively on growing him a healthy grandchild—his first—and nothing else.

We spend a week out of every month at the penthouse in Honolulu. The rest of the time we spend in Kauai, in Paradise, mostly at the beach house, which Knox had two more bedrooms added to, or in our apartment in the castle.

Remy, now that the alliance marriages are in place, is more relaxed than I've yet seen him. I guess the pressure of making sure the curse didn't strike again, especially after he married and lost his own true love and their baby, has been a huge weight on his shoulders. He told me he's very happy I showed up, and he and I have struck up a friendship I wasn't quite expecting. He's mellower now that the marriages are sealed, and Blaise and Echo have even started gently hinting that maybe he's ready to be set up on a few blind dates.

Knox and I spend time with Wolf and Vivi and I have to say their marriage and the way the two of them both seem much happier isn't something I expected. When I first met them, they seemed as different as two people could be. Him, so wild and rugged; her, so sweet and shy. But under his influence, Vivi has really come out of her shell. She seems a lot less spooked and much more comfortable in her own skin. I guess lashings of hot sex with a Ramsey beefcake is good for the soul. Actually, I don't have to guess. I know first-hand that it's a powerful remedy to all of life's problems.

Malachi and Aurora's wedding was held at a rooftop of one of the Kings' penthouses and was completely over the top. No expense was spared. Before their wedding, I got in touch with Maggie—she's assistant manager of Perfection Catering now and was going to be working the event. Instead, she came as a (very excited) guest. We had a fun time catching up. She couldn't believe the story of how I met Knox and she visits me often when we're in Honolulu.

Blaise feels to me now like a true older sister. She calls me every few days to check on me, to make sure I'm taking my vitamins and eating well. To ask me if I'm okay and getting everything I need. Even though I never considered myself someone who cries easily, for the first week she called regularly, I cried every time we hung up. It's just so comforting to have someone like Blaise, so strong and capable and empathetic, who genuinely cares. After a lifetime of craving it, I'm grateful for it in a way that digs deep. I don't know if Blaise feels indebted to me or just relieved that we can all have our happily ever afters, now that the alliance marriages are in place. She's in love with an artist named Tristan and recently got engaged.

And Echo has become my best friend. We hang out in her design studio and it has become one of my favorite places. She said she's come up with all her best designs since we started bouncing ideas off each other. I have so many creative visions rolling around in my head I can hardly draw them fast enough.

Echo and I have decided to start our own fashion label. With her social media following—a crazy three hundred *million*—she thinks we should do it. As for my own social media following, which was obviously nonexistent only a few months ago, it has exploded. Knox bought me one of those newest iPhones and Echo is helping me use it. The day I posted my first post, of Echo and me in her studio, I got ten million followers. Knox refuses to be photographed but one of my posts accidentally included part of his tattooed, muscular arm and it went viral. The day after that, I was up to fifty million. I don't care all that much about the numbers, but the idea of creating and maybe even selling my own designs is exciting.

Jagger and I have become close. We have so much in common and we hang out often, either at our place in the city or at his. He even came to the beach house in Paradise for a few days and spent the whole time surfing, spearfishing and making us laugh with his terrible jokes.

The sealed letter my mother wrote to me was devastating in many ways. She'd written a letter to Jagger too and we've shared them with each other. Our mother left Jagger with our father on Jagger's second birthday and never came back for him. By then she was heavily pregnant with me. When Jethro's wife Eva—Raven and Stone's mother—found out that our father was still being unfaithful, she basically put a hit out on Camille and her baby. Jagger was spared because Stone and Raven adored him. But our mother wouldn't have been spared. And neither would I.

Eva never forgave Jethro for loving his mistress more than he loved her.

By all accounts, Eva was drop-dead gorgeous—and as mad as they come. She was Jethro's second wife and before they married had also been his mistress. Jethro's first wife, Clara, who's Enzo's mother, found out about Eva—*from* Eva, and very dramatically, according to

Jethro. I've asked him a lot of careful questions and he answers most of them, but not all. Clara divorced him once Eva came along, and soon after, she married an Italian billionaire. They're still together and they live in Tuscany. She and Jethro still keep in touch. And Aurora's mother, Lucienne, was Jethro's third wife but the two of them divorced around five years ago. He's currently not married but has several "companions" he spends time with.

It's a crazy, convoluted family history.

We'll never really know for sure if Camille was murdered by Eva. In her letters, Camille wrote that she believed she was going to be killed. It's why she left me. It's why she was on the run.

According to Camille's death certificate, which Jagger searched for and found, she died by arsenic poisoning very soon after she left me. I've gone through as many dates as I know and I figured she might have died just *days* after she left me. Eva took her own life soon after that. She was found floating in the pool with enough alcohol and pharmaceuticals in her system to medicate a small town.

I'm grateful I was hidden and saved, of course. All the years of struggling and feeling lost now seem like they were footsteps along a path I needed to take. Because it would lead me to Knox, and back to my family.

I have my one true north star, my best friend of all. My insatiable husband and the love of my life. We knew it in that cave. We know it every second we spend together.

As we make love and in the smaller moments. Every night he asks me low, husky questions. *What do you wish you had today that you didn't have? What was your favorite part? Are you happy? Do you know how much your besotted husband adores you?* Our connection deepens every day. It feels to me like our souls have weaved themselves together. If he's worried about something, I can feel it. When he needs me, I can sense it. I give him everything he wants.

Knox has been working with Enzo on their investments. Just recently, Knox finished his MBA. Because of that and also because he's Enzo's new brother-in-law and the two of them have hit it off in a way I don't think either of them was expecting, Enzo has put Knox in charge of one of their major investment accounts. Enzo will guide him and work alongside him to begin with, but Knox has a knack, Enzo said. Knox has been managing his own investments for years and has created the kind of wealth, just through his smallest portfolio alone, that boggles my mind. I asked him what he's going to spend it on. He said me. And our baby, which he's convinced is a girl.

"Why do you think it's a girl?" We decided not to find out because we both want a surprise.

"I just know," he says lazily, sliding two fingers gently into me as he takes my erect nipple lightly between his teeth. We're in the castle, since my due date was two days ago. There's a team of doctors and midwives checking on me around the clock. Knox insisted. Remy is also making sure I'm getting all the medical care a person can possibly get. They're both determined to the point of obsession, that *this* baby will live.

"What should we name her, then?" I gasp a little and close my eyes because what he's doing feels *so good*. We've talked about names but we haven't agreed on one yet.

"How about Havyn? With a Y."

It's the first time he's mentioned this name and I instantly love it. I remember all those months ago when I'd fantasized about finding a haven. And now I have one. Him. "It's perfect. Havyn." And the Y gives it a uniqueness, like Ramsey names tend to have.

He's suckling on my nipple playfully, and I remember the very first time he did this to me, in the cave, when we didn't know if we'd live. "Havyn it is, then."

There's a stillness to him that gets my attention, and I open my eyes to the glittering blue of his eyes. He's aghast at something and I glance down to see what.

My breasts are leaking. Clear milk forms beads on the tips of my nipples.

I'm shocked by this—although I shouldn't be, of course. The sight of the pale liquid is simultaneously lusty and life-giving. I'm filled with heavy awe, that it could come from my own body.

Knox, holding my gaze, leans close. Instead of covering me or wiping me clean, like I might have expected, he seems mesmerized. He teases me with his tongue, circling, licking the moisture, fastening his lips around the taut, wet bud. Sucking tenderly.

"*Knox.*" I push at his head but he only moves to my other breast. I can't believe what he's doing. "You *can't.*"

"I *can*, baby girl. More than that, I *need* to," he murmurs against my breast. "I love my wife. Everything, everything. Your face. Your hair. Your lips. Your belly, all round and beautiful with my baby inside you. Your perfect breasts. Your juicy pink nipples. And *this*, most of all. Do you know how much I worship you, angel girl?" He's holding me down with his iron-strong hands, sucking me, pulling deeply with his mouth. The sensation is indescribable. So outrageously intimate. "I'd die without you, sweet Cassidy. You're so fucking sexy I can't handle it."

One thing I know for a fact is that Knox Ramsey loves me. He tells me this many times a day. I might have thought pregnancy would change his desire for me but if anything he's even more turned on by my lush, curvy body. My fertility is like a drug to him. And I *feel* sexy. More than sexy. *I'm a freaking vessel for his seed.* I'm growing his baby inside me and it's a wildly intense and powerful thing.

He's kissing me and nuzzling me, sort of mindless with love and lust. His hand slides over the roundness of my belly. And lower. He opens my legs wide and glides his fingers over my pussy. I can feel the slipperiness of my own creamy arousal. "You're so *wet* for me, baby. You *love* how hot I am for you. Do you know how precious you are to me? Do you feel me, angel?"

As he's murmuring low, soft words to me, he slowly swirls the moisture over my swollen flesh, teasing my clit with all of his fingers, sliding inside me as he sucks the leaking moisture from my nipples. I'm so wet I can hear the sounds as he very gently fucks me with three fingers.

"*I feel you.*" Nothing feels as good as Knox Ramsey. "*I need you, Knox.*"

"You want my big cock inside you, sweet angel? You're so ready for me. Look how beautiful you are." He continues his loving caresses until the pleasure almost peaks. "Can you take me? I don't want to hurt you."

"The midwife said it's perfectly safe. She said it can be a good way to ... get things moving." It's not like we don't make love several times a day and have all the way through my pregnancy.

Knox climbs up my body, holding his weight with his burly, muscular arms. He kisses me, sliding his tongue into my mouth. I take the offering eagerly, sucking him gently as one of my hands rests on his bicep, savoring the feel of his flexed, sculpted hardness. My other hand finds his huge, hard shaft, oozing a slick of pre-cum. I stroke him with my careful fist, using his moisture to coat the engorged, slippery head.

"I'm going to fuck you nice and slow now. You just tell me if it's too much."

"*Please.*"

"All right, baby. Shh. I'll give you everything. Hold still. I'll be so careful with you."

He guides the head of his cock to my saturated pussy, slowly nudging just inside me with his thick length. He holds his weight above me so his warm, quilted abs barely brush against my swollen belly. His kiss is passionate as he slides his big cock out, then deeper inside.

"*Oh, that feels so good,*" I moan.

"You're perfect, you know that? My angel is the most beautiful girl in the world. That's it, take a little more. Relax ... that's it. You're heaven on earth. *Oh, fuck, yes.* That's my good girl."

He's all the way inside me now and I feel *so full.* Full of him and full of us. Overflowing with emotion and drunk with love. I'm losing my mind, I love him so much. My orgasm was waiting for the thick, gliding nudge of his ridged, veined cock deep inside me. His slow, measured thrusts tip me easily over a cascading waterfall of pleasure. The luscious, clenching tugs of my pussy pull the release from him and I can feel the hot throb flooding me with warm, rhythmic beauty. The sensation lengthens my own climax, which glides and ripples lushly, endlessly.

Still holding his weight, he rests his forehead against mine. "My love," he whispers.

I hold his face and kiss his lips. "My Knox. You're my whole heart."

He pulls out of me and the milky gush spills to coat my thighs. Knox gets up and goes into the bathroom to get a towel, wetting it with warm water. He carefully washes and dries me, kissing my pussy. Then he tosses the towel aside and pulls the sheet over me, wrapping his body around me. "You okay, angel? You want to sleep a little? Are you hungry?"

Just then, without warning, I feel a rolling ache deep inside me. "*Oh.*"

Knox lifts his head, watching my eyes. "Oh?"

I have the urge to move. I sit up and slide to the side of the bed. "*Knox.*"

He's instantly by my side, his strong arm around me as he helps me stand. A low bloom of pain swells in a rising wave. There's a momentous shift inside me and a torrent of clear fluid streams down my legs, wetting the floor. We both stare at it for a second.

"Holy fuck, honey. Your water just broke."

"Knox. *Shit.* This is it. It's happening." My voice sounds panicked. No wonder.

Knox grabs his phone from the bedside table. "You're going to be just fine. I'm calling Hana." I've been assigned a team of doctors and midwives but Hana is the one Knox trusts the most. He's steady, not panicking, taking full control.

An agonizing ache rolls through my body with a force that stuns me. I can't hold back the moan but I don't fight the pain. An instinct tells me to go with it, to ride the wave. I place my hands on my belly as the pain wracks through me. *My baby is about to be born.*

"We're coming in," Knox's big body is crouched in front of me, holding my hand as he talks to Hana, who I can vaguely recognize is on speaker phone.

"We're ready for her," Hana says. "Bring her down to the clinic now. Usually labor for first babies lasts eight to twelve hours, so we've got time. But it's safest if she's here."

Another contraction hits and it's so fucking painful I moan again.

There's a slightly more urgent note in Hana's voice when she says, "It sounds like the contractions are already close together."

"We'll see you in five," Knox says gruffly, ending the call. "Come on, sweet girl. Time to go." He wraps a plush white cotton bathrobe around me, ties it loosely and he carefully lifts me into his arms like I'm made of glass. He starts carrying me to the door.

"Knox?"

"Yeah?"

"You're not wearing any clothes." Even through the pain this almost makes me laugh.

"Oh. Fuck." So he gently seats me on the bed and pulls on a pair of jeans, stuffing his phone into his back pocket. He lifts me again and takes me to the elevator.

It's only a short walk down to the main street of the town and the medical clinic where Hana and the other doctors are already waiting for us. They've been on stand-by for this moment for more than a week.

By the time we get there, the contractions are so close together they feel like they're crashing through my body in a blinding, searing rhythm, wave after wave. My awareness shifts, as though veiling me in a protective trance. Time becomes pain-soaked and dreamlike.

I'm laid onto a bed but I grip Knox's hand like I'm holding on for dear life.

He's right next to me, his head close to mine. "I'm right here and I'm not going anywhere. Hold on to me. I've got you. That's it, my Cassidy girl. Squeeze my hand. Harder. I'm right here. Feel me. You're so strong and so beautiful. You can do this. Squeeze harder."

I can feel someone touching me. Hana. "It's good you came so quickly, Knox. This baby is in a serious rush. Something must have triggered full-on labor. She's fully dilated and the baby's head is already starting to crown. Cassidy, with the next contraction I want you to push."

"You're the Goddess of Fire," Knox is murmuring in my ear, gripping my hand. "You're stronger than you know. Our beautiful baby is ready to be born. You're strong and so is she." I listen to his words and I let them soothe me like a cool stream through a river of lava. "Squeeze my hand and push our baby out, angel girl."

The next contraction hits and I do it. I focus on the anchoring squeeze of his hand and I push. I have never known pain like this. It's extreme and all-encompassing, but I let it come.

And again.

After what feels like a long time, finally, I feel the beautiful, slithery relief as my baby slides from my body.

"It's a girl," Hana gasps. She almost sounds like she's crying.

Knox is kissing my face, smoothing my damp hair

back from my face. "You did it, angel. You're so beautiful. *You did it.*"

The baby is cleaned and weighed. Hana hands the tiny wrapped bundle to Knox. "Congratulations, you two. She's a healthy seven pounds, two ounces. Do you have a name?"

The baby looks so tiny in Knox's big, suntanned hands. It's something I'll never forget as long as I live. My gorgeous, rough, wild, huge, muscular, tattooed, shirtless husband, gazing down at his brand new baby daughter like he's absolutely starstruck. "Her name is Havyn Cassidy Camille Madison King Ramsey."

Knox brings her to me and I can only stare at her in wonder. Her little perfect scrunched up face. Her dark, soulful eyes. Her tiny hands. Knox and Hana help her latch onto my nipple. It takes her a few tries but she settles in, suckling in lusty pulls and *I'm so in love with her.*

Knox kisses me and we both have tears in our eyes. "We're going to raise her on the beach and live a beautiful life," he says.

And that's exactly what we do.

Thank you for reading! If you enjoyed Knox and Cassidy's story, please consider leaving a quick review or rating on Amazon for **Devil's Angel**.

Below I'm including a sneak peek at **Wild Hearts**, the second book in the Paradise series, Wolf and Vivi's book!

xoxo,
Julie

Please come join my Facebook reader group, Julie Capulet's Romantics, where I share cover reveals, insider info and we discuss all things romance!

Sign up for my newsletter to receive my free bonus content and get access to sneak peeks and exclusive giveaways!

Visit my website @ www.juliecapulet.com

The first time I saw Wolf Ramsey was at his family's estate in Kauai. He was huge and imposing. Armed to the teeth. When he looked right at me, fascination wasn't my first reaction. It was fear.

His outrageous good looks were shadowed only by his wild intensity. You could tell he would be reckless and brutal. Even from a distance, his dark, dangerous energy made my heart beat faster in a way I wasn't expecting. I knew he would take me places I've never been and ruin me, body and soul, if he ever got the chance. I was relieved when it was time to leave.

But before I could escape him, one single announcement changed my entire life. Because it's not going to be my sister who secures the family alliance between the Ramseys and the Fitzpatricks.

It's going to be me. And my new husband-to-be, Wolf Ramsey.

WILD HEARTS is the explosive second book in the epic Paradise Series. It's a steamy standalone arranged marriage romance, set in paradise, complete with an HEA and no cliffhangers.

Paradise Series

CHAPTER ONE

"Give her more of that kohl eyeliner. Really lay it on. She needs a smokier eye. And for god's sake, get rid of that insipid pink lip gloss. Are you serious with that bullshit? We want a siren, fuck-me red. For lips *this* naturally perfect, it would be a crime not to pimp them out to every hot bachelor with a heartbeat. Think sultry, people. *Sexy.* It's time to get this girl some goddamn action."

Okay, wow.

My head stylist, whose name is Lana Lee, is at it again. Micromanaging me to within an inch of my life, meanwhile endlessly pointing out how nonexistent my love life is. Which isn't entirely my fault, but it's true enough. She's obsessed with shining a high-beam spotlight onto the obvious at every available opportunity.

I have limits. Sure, I've never *acted* on my limits but they're there. I'm not sure exactly where my line is but I know I'm getting dangerously close to it.

They call me sweet. Shy. Quiet. I'm the good girl, the one who always does what she's told. But simmering just under the surface of my obedience is a wild heart. Some little spark in me is biding its time, craving … something. Freedom. Rebellion. Danger. I can feel it coming. Which is both daunting and sort of thrilling, to be honest.

I *know* I'm going to do something reckless that no one sees coming. I just don't know when.

I guess Lana has reason to be full of herself. Every A-list actor, model and influencer wants to work with her, from here to L.A., Aspen, the Hamptons, Manhattan, London, Paris, Milan, you name it. Even so, she spends most of her time here at Seven Mile Beach, my family's compound in Waikiki.

This is because my sisters pay her astronomical amounts of money to dress us and basically manage our lives—or at least the part of our lives that involves fashion, which is most of it. She also lives in one of our guesthouses as part of her employment package. Which has a cute, Juliet-style balcony that overlooks its own secluded sugar-sand beach.

Lana is in such white-hot demand, she sometimes gets caught up in her own hype. Like now, for example. And I'm tired of her non-stop commentary about my so-called "innocence." It's her favorite topic.

For a brief moment I think about getting up and

walking out. Just standing up without saying a word to anyone and walking through our huge, busy fashion studio—with its racks of garments, walls of mirrors, expansive windows that overlook the ocean, teams of stylists and tables strewn with designs and patterns and sewing machines, where ten or more dressmakers are finalizing tonight's looks for us, along with all the outfits we'll need for the rest of our weekend. Not to mention all the other upcoming photoshoots and events on our jam-packed schedules.

I picture myself silently making my way down the grand staircase of my family's estate, under the giant crystal chandelier, right out the front door, down the driveway and out the gate. Just walking away into the big, wide-open world where no one knows me and I can do whatever I want.

I won't, of course.

I'd probably be kidnapped within minutes. For ... reasons.

We're famous. We own the most expensive piece of real estate in Waikiki, along with many others.

I understand why I'm guarded. I know why it's necessary and I'm used to it.

Mostly.

I'm watched like a hawk. My team of bodyguards protects my every move. My phone calls, posts and texts are monitored and filtered. My schedule is lorded over and controlled. Some days I don't even feel like a real person. Like I'm more of a carefully-curated brand who lives in a gilded cage than an actual human being.

They mean well, of course they do.

But my cage's bars feel extra thick today. More and more, it occurs to me that there's a reason they keep me on such a tight rein.

I wonder what Ash is doing. It's his day off. I told him I'd go see him before we leave for our weekend away.

My brothers and my cousins would kill me if they found out I've been sneaking down to the pool house to see him. Even more, they'd kill Ash.

They get to choose who I hang out with, in their own minds at least.

Usually I just go with the flow. Because that's what's expected of me and also because they enforce it.

But right now, I feel restless in a way that's new. Some hidden corner of my psyche wants to break free of them all.

"Weave a few more of those jade beads into her hair," Lana orders her underlings. "And make sure the emerald gemstones are at the front." My hair is braided into an elaborate up-do with jewels woven into it that makes me look like an Egyptian princess, maybe. Or a beach bum who won the lottery. I like the effect, but I had no idea it would take so long to create. If I'd known, I could have worn my hair loose, and spent the last two hours with Ash.

Then why didn't you?

Because I don't have the freedom to make choices like that.

Which suddenly feels very wrong. Thinking about it now, I'm not sure I've ever made a single decision about *my own life*. It's crazy. I'm so used to being told what to do, I hardly even notice. But something about the whole scenario is hitting differently today.

Stand up to them. You're giving them too much.

CHAPTER TWO

More mascara is brushed onto my eyelashes. Someone else tugs at my hair, pinning it into place.

"Ow," I grumble.

"More eyeliner," Lana snaps from where she's swiping manically through several of the garment racks. "Her look needs to scream horny-as-hell untouched heiress on the prowl."

It does?

For better or worse—worse, usually—I hate offending people or causing any kind of conflict. It's one of my weaknesses, so I've been told. Ironically, it's the same people telling me it's a weakness who are the ones who make sure I walk their line.

"The shy virgin needs to get her halo dirty," Lana says. "It'll add value to her brand. This pure-as-the-driven-snow schtick has a shelf life."

I've really had just about enough of this. Even worse, I *agree* with her. I *want* to get my halo dirty. Problem is, they never let me near anyone who might do me the honors.

It's part of the reason why I've been sneaking down to visit Ash almost every day. Not that we're anything more than friends at this point but I feel like that might change.

"She's only twenty, Lana," Perri says. My sister is standing in front of the mirrors as five people pin and adjust the black dress she's wearing to the party we're going to tonight. The dress is entirely sheer, revealing what looks like a minuscule black bikini underneath, leaving almost nothing to the imagination. She's curvy and the bikini doesn't cover much. It's sexy to the extreme, and I know why she's chosen it. She's hoping to get a marriage proposal tonight. From Knox Ramsey, the buff, reclusive middle son of the Ramsey family. "Vivi's holding out for the real thing."

Am I?

Sure, true love would be the ideal. It's what everyone dreams of. But my status as an inexperienced hermit isn't exactly the one I've chosen. I'm holding out because my family doesn't allow me to go anywhere without a chaperone. For my safety, according to them.

Lana has the confident, take-control personality of an army general. And when she decides my entire wardrobe is going to revolve around whether or not I'm getting laid —which everyone knows I never have—it's more than a little humiliating.

My brothers and sisters control who I see and where I go. Lana controls what I wear. My brigade of assistants, stylists, social media curators, personal trainers, nutritionists, yoga instructors, make-up artists, beauty experts, designers, event planners and publicists control every aspect of my days and nights, down to the minute.

The only person who *doesn't* have any control over my life is me.

I'm the youngest of five and all my siblings have always been overprotective of me. My mother died when I was a baby and when I was ten, my father began his downward spiral into the kind of dementia that doesn't just take a person's memory and personality but twists it into something unrecognizable. He died around two years ago and it was a mercy.

Because I was the youngest and had no mother, from the very beginning, I became everyone else's pet project.

Silas is the oldest and he's mostly done a decent job of running our family's affairs, I guess. The one exception is his heavy-handed supervision of me. Our cousin Jett is Silas's advisor and his bodyguard. Jett is also my bodyguard, or at least when he or Silas thinks I need extra protection, which happens to be most of the time. My other brother Malachi is Silas's wingman. And Tatum too, although from a young age she always loved to travel, so she's the one who has spent the most time away from Seven Mile Beach. She got cast in her first movie when she was seventeen, became a huge hit and has spent most of the past eight years on film locations. She's now one of the most bankable stars in Hollywood.

Malachi is also a major movie star but he's only interested in blockbusters and he comes home when he's not filming. He's the king of the Waikiki party scene and he has a harem of women who give him anything he wants.

As for Perri, it was always her dream to become a model. She works to achieve this goal night and day. But to her unending despair, she's never been offered a modeling contract. Not once, even though she has a massive following and gets a huge amount of publicity for being an heiress and a socialite.

After years of no offers, partly through sheer spite, she created a bunch of her own global brands purely so she can model her products herself. She doesn't need to rely on her beauty to get herself seen. She can be the face of her lines of cosmetics, fragrance, clothing, hair products and so on because she runs the company. She even has a lifestyle blog. My sister has more followers on Instagram than anyone else in the world.

I admire her ambition. I just sometimes wish she wasn't so cut-throat about everything she does. She's competitive to the extreme. That kind of obsession can't be great for a person's mental health, I figure. She's always stressed out and irritable. She can be prickly and hard to be around, especially when she's in one of her moods.

It's always bothered her that I *do* get offered modeling contracts. She's never said so but I can tell. She works out non-stop with her team of personal trainers and she's already had a lot of fillers. Tatum keeps telling her not to overdo it, but Perri already looks a little bit … plastic. Even when money is no object, there's only so much Botox you can pump into your face before it starts to look weird.

Perri is known for her savvy and her style. *But never for my beauty*, she cries to me all the time. It breaks her heart. *They've never called me beautiful. Not once.*

I tell her *I* think she's beautiful. And she is. She's my guide and she's my closest sister, even though there's the tiniest edge behind her love, which I can feel simmering there. A jealousy and a resentment she does her best to control. We both try to ignore it.

"I said sexy, not street-corner whore," Lana barks at several of the make-up artists. Cody, Lana's senior assistant, who has the patience of a saint, blinks his long eyelashes at me in solidarity as he smooths the kohl around my eyes with a tiny sponge.

"I don't know why they're bothering," I mutter, looking out the wall of windows to the white sand of our private beach with its loungers and blue umbrellas, to the turquoise ocean waves beyond. "This is all a waste of time."

"Girl, you're outshining all of them, like you always

do," Cody whispers. "Ignore her. You're going to rock someone's *world*, you gorgeous thing. You just wait, you'll find your person. And once you do, you'll be glad you waited."

I wonder if I'll ever find my person.

Sometimes I wish Ash was my person. But there are gray areas with Ash that make me wonder if Ash could ever be my person. Mainly: I don't think *Ash* thinks he's my person. The way I see it, your person should *want* to be your person.

I sigh without meaning to.

"Better," Lana says approvingly, walking over to another rack of dresses.

Lana is good at her job and most of the outfits she picks out for me are custom made and to-die-for. She has a knack for putting pieces together in a way that's original and cutting edge. The looks she creates for me and my sisters get noticed. Which, according to Lana, is a key part of putting our brands on the map.

I don't bother mentioning it also puts *her* brand very much on the map and is the reason she's now the most sought-after stylist in the world.

My sisters and I get a lot of attention. Our social media platforms are like mini-corporations. Everything we wear gets scrutinized and copied. Every post has a business plan behind it.

Gabrielle, who's in charge of my Instagram team, comes over and holds one of my phones up to me. It's the one we use exclusively for Instagram. Her green eyes are bright with excitement. She glances over to where Perri is momentarily distracted and out of earshot.

"Check out your follower numbers," Gabrielle whispers. The screen shows my Instagram page. 775,659,308. "You've passed Perri! You're number one in the world, Vivi!"

"Wow." That's exciting, I guess. I smile, reacting the way I'm expected to react. But Perri will be seething when she finds out.

"Vivi, this is amazing!" Gabrielle gushes. "We did it!"

It *is* amazing. *Isn't it?*

But … what does it all *mean?* Why don't I *feel* anything?

At all?

Ever?

CHAPTER THREE

I mean, I haven't *done* anything to deserve this kind of attention.

It probably sounds like I'm ungrateful.

I'm not ungrateful. I know how lucky I am and I try

to share my luck. On my eighteenth birthday, I secretly set up a foundation that donates money to charities, medical research and scholarships. No one knows about it except my cousin Jericho, our family's senior accountant. He helped me set it up and promised it would be our secret.

Silas is more focused on growing our wealth than giving it away. I didn't want him to know about it. I wanted it to be mine.

It's the most rebellious thing I've ever done and the one thing I'm most proud of. I did it because the shallower side of this life sometimes gets to me. The staging, the likes, the followers—it always feels just a little bit empty.

I fully realize that most people would kill for the kind of attention I get, so I try to appreciate it. My sisters love it. My brothers revel in it. As for me, none of it ever feels like a perfect fit. Like I'm wearing a diamond-studded straitjacket that's just a little too heavy and a lot too tight.

I know what Ash would say. *Poor little rich girl. It's so hard. Poor Vivi.*

It's not hard. Nothing's hard. Nothing's easy and nothing's hard. I glide through my existence with a dull ache in my heart, like now, with swarms of people fussing over me, making sure my hair and makeup are photo-worthy, dressing me and undressing me like I'm a puppet on a string.

I've spent my life following orders. But I can feel it: somewhere inside me, something is shifting.

Maybe it's the full moon.

Right. What are you, a werewolf now?

It's why this date was chosen for the party we're going to. To see if two of us can make a love match.

"Put this on." Lana is holding the dress she's chosen for me to wear tonight.

We're taking our jet to Kauai in a few hours, to stay with the Ramsey family for the weekend. They're having a two-day party for the three families that are part of our so-called "alliance." It's an old, weird tradition I've never paid much attention to.

There's an archaic rule that's attached to it. We're all big, extended families, but once each generation, the three families are supposed to link through marriage. According to the rule, one of us Fitzpatricks has to marry a King and one of us has to marry a Ramsey.

Some generations follow the rule and some don't. People rebel against it, not surprisingly. Some people think bad things happen to those who refuse to obey its laws.

The way I see it, bad things happen anyway. All the time. To everyone. I don't really buy into all the mysticism that surrounds the rule.

But Silas and Malachi do. And so does Perri. She wants to be the one to marry a Ramsey. She's got her heart set on it and she's been badgering Silas to arrange it for months. My sister is totally obsessed with Knox, even though she's only met him a few times.

"God, I can't wait." Perri's standing close to me now,

checking her look in the mirror. "I might even be married by the end of the weekend, Vivi."

"It's so exciting," I say, trying hard to infuse my tone with something resembling enthusiasm.

I can't remember ever meeting Knox Ramsey. There aren't many photos of him online. Only one or two, which Perri has saved onto her phone. One of them is her screensaver and every time I see it I wonder if that's a good idea. It almost feels like she's jinxing it, getting ahead of herself. But I don't say anything. I just hope it works out for her.

Echo is the youngest Ramsey and she's a year older than me. Occasionally we see each other at parties. Whenever I see her, she's fun and nice. Blaise is too. She's a few years older than Echo. She's stunning and she comes across as wise beyond her years and sort of no-nonsense. Both of them have a sense of realness I always find compelling. They're the kind of people you wish you could spend more time with.

I don't know the Ramsey brothers at all. They all seem insanely intimidating. They train in martial arts or something and they're very outdoorsy. Probably because they have a sprawling hundred square acre ranch in Kauai, which is where we're going tonight. I've never been there, but Silas has and he said it lives up to its name. They call it Paradise.

Remington is the oldest Ramsey sibling. He's gruff and serious and built like a fighter, according to Silas. Silas meets with him occasionally because the alliance families co-own a bunch of companies and have for generations.

I don't know much about Knox or the other brother, whose name is Wolf. They're not on social media and they're not part of the see-and-be-seen crowd. They mainly keep to themselves.

Rumors are that they're rough and huge and sort of wild. They carry weapons and spend most of their time swimming, hunting, surfing and living off the land.

"How do I look?" Perri asks me. I can tell she's nervous about tonight. "Do you like this dress, Vivi?"

"You look sexy." Almost *too* sexy, but then again, what do I know? Maybe that's the key to getting your halo dirty.

She's checking her phone again. I hope she hasn't noticed my Instagram numbers.

"Any reply?" I ask her.

I know she's been texting and leaving messages for Knox for the past few weeks. So far, she hasn't heard back from him. "He might be out of range," she says. "Apparently there are areas on their ranch that don't get cell phone coverage. Echo said he spends a lot of time at his beach house, which is remote."

"You'll see him tonight, though."

She's eager, but there's an edge to it. "What if …"

Perri hesitates but I know what she's thinking. What if he doesn't want to marry her? What happens then? "I'm sure he does, Perri. Didn't Remington tell Silas it's a done deal and that Knox agreed to it?"

"He hasn't actually confirmed it but Silas said he's thinking about it."

"I'm sure all the arrangements will be made this weekend. Relax."

Perri smiles at me but Lana's tapping her foot, waiting for me to try on the dress she's still holding.

I stand, and Cody takes off my robe. All I'm wearing is a tiny white thong but I'm so used to being dressed and undressed I barely notice.

"We're juxtaposing the sultry siren lips and the smoky eyes with a more demure outfit," Lana tells me. "Tonight, you're a timid waif who's on the cusp of an awakening. A fallen angel who's about to be sullied."

What the hell?

I stare at myself in the wall of mirrors. I look like I've time-warped to an 90s music video, and not in a good way. "No."

Lana glares at me, half-shocked and half-dismissive. "What do you mean *no*?"

"I can't wear this. It's all wrong."

"Wrong? How can it possibly be *wrong*?"

The dress is white and flowing. It looks oversized and childish, with lacy embellishments. "It's bad enough that I *am* a shy virgin and everyone knows it—thank you for pointing out the obvious, Lana. But the last thing I want to do is to *look* like one. I'm not wearing this."

They're all speechless for a few seconds. It's not like me to have outbursts or make demands. Lana sputters. "But it's perfe—"

"Give me something darker. Edgier. Something … fierce-looking." It sounds weird and I wish I could take it back as soon as it's out there.

"Fierce-looking?" Lana regains her composure.

I walk over to one of the many racks of garments that fill the room.

"Vivi." Perri watches me, like she's concerned about my behavior. "You should wear the one you have on. It looks so pretty on you."

"I've had enough of pretty."

I pull out something that catches my eye. It's a green sequined tight-fitting mini-dress with a plunging neckline. "This."

Lana stares at the outfit. Then she gives a light shrug, like she half-approves of my choice. "It's Valentino. It just arrived yesterday."

I take off the white dress and toss it over a chair. Then I put on the sequined outfit and Cody zips it. It fits me perfectly, if maybe a little on the tight side. It makes my boobs look full and bouncy. My eyes are a deep shade of amber—the exact same shade as my mother's were. The jewel-bright jade of the sequins makes my irises look almost golden. I slide my feet into a pair of gold high-heeled sandals with gem-stone detailing, checking myself out in the mirror. "This is it."

She wants me to dirty my halo? In this outfit, I might just be able to do that.

It won't happen this weekend, since Perri and Knox

will end up getting engaged and so will one of my brothers.

But at least I don't *look* as insecure as I feel.

In this dress, I can feed those tiny sparks of fire that are taking hold inside me.

Timid, obedient virgin on the cusp of a fiery awakening?

Bring it on.

ALSO BY JULIE CAPULET

I Love You Series

The Obsession Begins (free)

XOXO I Love You

XOXX I Love You More

Love You the Most (free)

Sexy Standalones

Max

Cowboy

McCabe Brothers Series

Hopeless Romantic

My Hero

Arrogant Player

Music City Lovers Series

Nashville Days

Nashville Nights

Nashville Dreams

Nashville Lights

Hawthorne U Series

Lovestruck

Paradise Series

Devil's Angel

Wild Hearts

New York Billionaires Series

Billionaire Boss

Billionaire Grump

Billionaire Devil

Billionaire Romantic

Fun Standalone Rom-com

Beautiful Savages

Julie Capulet is an Amazon top 20 bestselling author of contemporary romance. She writes steamy he-falls-first romance with heart, heat and fairy tale HEAs. Her stories are inspired by true love and she's married to her own real life hero. When she's not writing, she's reading, traveling, walking on the beach and watching rom-coms.

www.juliecapulet.com